A Knight Two-in-One Special Edition

FIVE FALL INTO ADVENTURE
FIVE ON A HIKE TOGETHER

The Famous Five are Julian, Dick,
George (Georgina by rights), Anne and
Timmy the dog.

This book brings together their ninth
and tenth exciting adventures.

Join the Famous Five . . .

ENID BLYTON

FIVE FALL INTO ADVENTURE

Illustrated by Betty Maxey

KNIGHT BOOKS
Hodder and Stoughton

*This Famous Five Two-in-One Special Edition
was first published by Knight Books 1990*

FIVE FALL INTO ADVENTURE

CONTENTS

Chapter One

AT KIRRIN COTTAGE AGAIN

GEORGINA was at the station to meet her three cousins. Timmy her dog was with her, his long tail wagging eagerly. He knew quite well they had come to meet Julian, Dick and Anne, and he was glad. It was much more fun when the Five were all together.

'Here comes the train, Timmy!' said George. Nobody

called her Georgina, because she wouldn't answer if they did. She looked like a boy with her short curly hair and her shorts and open-necked shirt. Her face was covered with freckles, and her legs and arms were as brown as a gipsy's.

There was the far-off rumble of a train, and as it came nearer, a short warning hoot. Timmy whined and wagged his tail. He didn't like trains, but he wanted this one to come.

Nearer and nearer it came, slowing down as it reached Kirrin station. Long before it came to the little platform three heads appeared out of one of the windows, and three hands waved wildly. George waved back, her face one big smile.

The door swung open almost before the train stopped. Out came a big boy, and helped down a small girl. Then came another boy, not quite so tall as the first one, with a bag in each hand. He dragged a third bag out, and then George and Timmy were on him.

'Julian! Dick! Anne! Your train's late; we thought you were never coming!'

'Hallo, George! Here we are at last. Get down, Timmy, don't eat me.'

'Hallo, George! Oh, Timmy, you darling – you're just as licky as ever!'

'Woof,' said Timmy joyfully, and bounded all round like a mad thing, getting into everybody's way.

'Any trunk or anything?' asked George. 'Only those three bags?'

'Well, we haven't come for long this time, worse luck,'

said Dick. 'Only a fortnight! Still, it's better than nothing.'

'You shouldn't have gone off to France all those six weeks,' said George, half-jealously. 'I suppose you've gone all French now.'

Dick laughed, waved his hands in the air and went off into a stream of quick French that sounded just like gibberish to George. French was not one of her strong subjects.

'Shut up,' she said, giving him a friendly shove. 'You're just the same old idiot. Oh, I'm so glad you've come. It's been lonely and dull at Kirrin without you.'

A porter came up with a barrow. Dick turned to him waved his hands again, and addressed the astonished man in fluent French. But the porter knew Dick quite well.

'Go on with you,' he said. 'Argy-bargying in double-Dutch like that. Do you want me to wheel these up to Kirrin Cottage for you?'

'Yes, please,' said Anne. 'Stop it, Dick. It isn't funny when you go on so long.'

'Oh, let him go on,' said George, and she linked her arms in Anne's and Dick's. 'It's lovely to have you again. Mother's looking forward to seeing you all.'

'I bet Uncle Quentin isn't,' said Julian, as they went along the little platform, Timmy capering round them.

'Father's in quite a good temper,' said George. 'You know he's been to America with Mother, lecturing and hearing other scientists lecturing too. Mother says everyone made a great fuss of him, and he liked it.'

George's father was a brilliant scientist, well-known all

over the world. But he was rather a difficult man at home, impatient, hot-tempered and forgetful. The children were fond of him, but held him in great respect. They all heaved a sigh of relief when he went away for a few days, for then they could make as much noise as they liked, tear up and down the stairs, play silly jokes and generally be as mad as they pleased.

'Will Uncle Quentin be at home all the time we're staying with you?' asked Anne. She was really rather afraid of her hot-tempered uncle.

'No,' said George. 'Mother and Father are going away for a tour in Spain – so we'll be on our own.'

'Wizard!' said Dick. 'We can wear our bathing costumes all day long then if we want to.'

'And Timmy can come in at meal-times without being sent out whenever he moves,' said George. 'He's been sent out every single meal-time this week, just because he snapped at the flies that came near him. Father goes absolutely mad if Timmy suddenly snaps at a fly.

'Shame!' said Anne, and patted Timmy's rough-haired back. 'You can snap at every single fly you like, Timmy, when we're on our own.'

'Woof,' said Timmy, gratefully.

'There won't be time for any adventure these hols,' said Dick, regretfully, as they walked down the lane to Kirrin Cottage. Red poppies danced along the way, and in the distance the sea shone as blue as cornflowers. 'Only two weeks – and back we go to school! Well, let's hope the weather keeps fine. I want to bathe six times a day!'

Soon they were all sitting round the tea-table at Kirrin Cottage, and their Aunt Fanny was handing round plates of her nicest scones and tea-cake. She was very pleased to see her nephews and niece again.

'Now George will be happy,' she said, smiling at the hungry four. 'She's been going about like a bear with a sore head the last week or two. Have another scone, Dick? Take two while you're about it.'

'Good idea,' said Dick, and helped himself. 'Nobody makes scones and cakes like you do, Aunt Fanny. Where's Uncle Quentin?'

'In his study,' said his aunt. 'He knows it's tea-time, and he's heard the bell, but I expect he's buried in something or other. I'll have to fetch him in a minute. I honestly believe he'd go without food all day long if I didn't go and drag him into the dining-room!'

'Here he is,' said Julian, hearing the familiar impatient footsteps coming down the hall to the dining-room. The door was flung open. Uncle Quentin stood there, a news-paper in his hand, scowling. He didn't appear to see the children at all.

'Look here, Fanny!' he shouted. 'See what they've put in this paper – the very thing I gave orders was NOT to be put in! The dolts! The idiots! The . . .'

'Quentin! Whatever's the matter?' said his wife. 'Look – here are the children – they've just arrived.'

But Uncle Quentin simply didn't see any of the four children at all. He went on glaring at the paper. He rapped at it with his hand.

'*Now* we'll get the place full of reporters wanting to see

me, and wanting to know all about my new ideas!' he said, beginning to shout. 'See what they've said! "This eminent scientist conducts all his experiments and works out all his ideas at his home, Kirrin Cottage. Here are his stack of notebooks, to which are now added two more – fruits of his visit to America, and here at his cottage are his amazing diagrams," and so on and so on.

'I tell you, Fanny, we'll have hordes of reporters down.'

'No, we shan't, dear,' said his wife. 'And, anyway, we are soon off to Spain. Do sit down and have some tea. And look, can't you say a word to welcome Julian, Dick and Anne?'

Uncle Quentin grunted and sat down. 'I didn't know they were coming,' he said, and helped himself to a scone. 'You might have told me, Fanny.'

'I told you three times yesterday and twice today,' said his wife.

Anne suddenly squeezed her uncle's arm. She was sitting next to him. 'You're just the same as ever, Uncle Quentin,' she said. 'You never, never remember we're coming! Shall we go away again?'

Her uncle looked down at her and smiled. His temper never lasted very long. He grinned at Julian and Dick. 'Well, here you are again!' he said. 'Do you think you can hold the fort for me while I'm away with your aunt?'

'Rather!' said all three together.

'We'll keep everyone at bay!' said Julian. 'With Timmy's help. I'll put up a notice: "*Beware, very fierce dog*".'

'Woof,' said Timmy, sounding delighted. He thumped

his tail on the floor. A fly came by his nose and he snapped at it. Uncle Quentin frowned.

'Have another scone, Father?' said George hurriedly. 'When are you and Mother going to Spain?'

'Tomorrow,' said her mother firmly. 'Now don't look like that, Quentin. You know perfectly well it's been arranged for weeks, and you *need* a holiday, and if we don't go tomorrow all our arrangements will be upset.'

'Well, you might have *warned* me it was tomorrow,' said her husband, looking indignant. 'I mean – I've all my notebooks to check and put away, and . . .'

'Quentin, I've told you heaps of times that we leave on September the third,' said his wife, still more firmly. '*I* want a holiday, too. The four children will be quite all right here with Timmy – they'll love being on their own. Julian is almost grown-up now and he can cope with anything that turns up.'

Timmy snapped twice at a fly, and Uncle Quentin jumped. 'If that dog does that again,' he began, but his wife interrupted him at once.

'There, you see! You're as touchy and nervy as can be, Quentin, dear. It will do you good to get away – and the children will have a lovely two weeks on their own. Nothing can possibly happen, so make up your mind to leave tomorrow with an easy mind!'

Nothing can possibly happen? Aunt Fanny was wrong of course. *Anything* could happen when the Five were left on their own!

Chapter Two

A MEETING ON THE BEACH

IT really was very difficult to get Uncle Quentin off the next day. He was shut up in his study until the last possible moment, sorting out his precious notebooks. The taxi arrived and hooted outside the gate. Aunt Fanny, who had been ready for a long time, went and rapped at the study door.

'Quentin! Unlock the door! You really must come. We shall lose the plane if we don't go now.'

'Just one minute!' shouted back her husband. Aunt Fanny looked at the four children in despair.

'That's the fourth time he's called out "Just one minute",' said George. The telephone shrilled out just then, and she picked up the receiver.

'Yes,' she said. 'No, I'm afraid you can't see him. He's off to Spain, and nobody will know where he is for the next two weeks. What's that? Wait a minute – I'll ask my mother.'

'Who is it?' said her mother.

'It's the *Daily Clarion*,' said George. 'They want to send a reporter down to interview Daddy. I told them he was going to Spain – and they said could they publish that?'

'Of course,' said her mother, thankfully, 'Once that's in the papers nobody will ring up and worry you. Say, yes, George.'

George said yes, the taxi hooted more loudly than ever, and Timmy barked madly at the hooting. The study door was flung open and Uncle Quentin stood in the doorway, looking as black as thunder.

'Why can't I have a little peace and quiet when I'm doing important work?' he began. But his wife made a dart at him and dragged him down the hall. She put his hat in one hand, and would have put his stick into the other if he hadn't been carrying a heavy despatch case.

'You're not doing important work, you're off on a holiday,' she said. 'Oh, Quentin, you're worse than ever! What's that case in your hand? Surely you are not taking work away with you?'

The taxi hooted again, and Timmy woofed just behind Uncle Quentin. He jumped violently, and the telephone rang loudly.

'That's another reporter coming down to see you, Father,' said George. 'Better go quickly!'

Whether that bit of news really did make Uncle Quentin decide at last to go, nobody knew – but in two seconds he was sitting in the taxi, still clutching his despatch case, telling the taxi-driver exactly what he thought of people who kept hooting their horns.

'Good-bye, dears,' called Aunt Fanny, thankfully. 'Don't get into mischief. We're off at last.'

The taxi disappeared down the lane. 'Poor Mother!' said George. 'It's always like this when they go for a holiday. Well, there's one thing certain – I shall NEVER marry a scientist.'

Everyone heaved a sigh of relief at the thought that Uncle Quentin was gone. When he was over-worked he really was impossible.

'Still, you simply have to make excuses for anyone with a brain like his,' said Julian. 'Whenever our science master at school speaks of him, he almost holds his breath with awe. Worst of it is, he expects *me* to be brilliant because I've got a brilliant uncle.'

'Yes. It's difficult to live up to clever relations,' said Dick. 'Well – we're on our own, except for Joan. Good old Joan! I bet she'll give us some smashing meals.'

'Let's go and see if she's got anything we can have now,' said George. 'I'm hungry.'

'So am I,' said Dick. They marched down the hall into the kitchen, calling for Joan.

'Now, you don't need to tell me what you've come for,' said Joan, the smiling, good-tempered cook. 'And I don't need to tell you this – the larder's locked.'

'Oh Joan – what a mean thing to do!' said Dick.

'Mean or not, it's the only thing to do when all four of you are around, to say nothing of that great hungry dog,' said Joan, rolling out some pastry vigorously. 'Why, last holidays I left a meat pie and half a tongue and a cherry tart and trifle sitting on the shelves for the next day's meals – and when I came back from my half-day's outing there wasn't a thing to be seen.'

'Well, we thought you'd left them there for our supper,' said Julian, sounding quite hurt.

'All right – but you won't get the chance of thinking anything like that again,' said Joan, firmly. 'That larder door's going to be kept locked. Maybe I'll unlock it sometimes and hand you out a snack or two – but I'm the one that's going to unlock it, not you.'

The four drifted out of the kitchen again, disappointed. Timmy followed at their heels. 'Let's go down and have a bathe,' said Dick. 'If I'm going to have six bathes a day, I'd better hurry up and have my first one.'

'I'll get some ripe plums,' said Anne. 'We can take those down with us. And I expect the ice-cream man will come along to the beach too. We shan't starve! And we'd better wear our shirts and shorts over our bathing costumes, so we don't catch too much sun.'

Soon they were all down on the sand. They found a good place and scraped out comfortable holes to sit in. Timmy scraped his own.

'I can't imagine why Timmy bothers to scrape one,' said George. 'Because he always squeezes into mine sooner or later. Don't you, Timmy?'

Timmy wagged his tail, and scraped so violently that they were all covered with sand. 'Pooh!' said Anne, spitting sand out of her mouth. 'Stop it, Timmy. As fast as I scrape my hole, you fill it up!'

Timmy paused to give her a lick, and then scraped again, making a very deep hole indeed. He lay down in it, panting, his mouth looking as if he were smiling.

'He's smiling again,' said Anne. 'I never knew a dog that smiled like Timmy. Timmy, it's nice to have you again.'

'Woof,' said Timmy, politely, meaning that it was nice to have Anne and the others back again, too. He wagged his tail and sent a shower of sand over Dick.

They all wriggled down comfortably into their soft warm holes. 'We'll eat the plums first and then we'll have a bathe,' said Dick. 'Chuck me one, Anne.'

Two people came slowly along the beach. Dick looked at them out of half-closed eyes. A boy and a man – and what a ragamuffin the boy looked! He wore torn dirty shorts and a filthy jersey. No shoes at all.

The man looked even worse. He slouched as he came, and dragged one foot. He had a straggly moustache and mean, clever little eyes that raked the beach up and down. The two were walking at high-water mark and were obviously looking for anything that might have been cast up by the tide. The boy already had an old box, one wet shoe and some wood under his arm.

'What a pair!' said Dick to Julian. 'I hope they don't come near us. I feel as if I can smell them from here.'

The two walked along the beach and then back. Then, to the children's horror, they made a bee-line for where they were lying in their sandy holes, and sat down close beside them. Timmy growled.

An unpleasant, unwashed kind of smell at once came to the children's noses. Pooh! Timmy growled again. The boy took no notice of Timmy's growling. But the man looked uneasy.

'Come on – let's have a bathe,' said Julian, annoyed at the way the two had sat down so close to them. After all, there was practically the whole of the beach to choose from – why come and sit almost on top of somebody else?

When they came back from their bathe the man had gone, but the boy was still there – and he had actually sat himself down in George's hole.

'Get out,' said George, shortly, her temper rising at once. 'That's my hole, and you jolly well know it.'

'Findings keepings,' said the boy, in a curious singsong voice. 'It's my hole now.'

George bent down and pulled the boy roughly out of the hole. He was up in a trice, his fists clenched. George clenched hers, too.

Dick came up at a run. 'Now, George – if there's any fighting to be done, I'll do it,' he said. He turned to the scowling boy. 'Clear off! We don't want you here!'

The boy hit out with his right fist and caught Dick unexpectedly on the jawbone. Dick looked astounded. He hit out, too, and sent the tousle-headed boy flying.

'Yah, coward!' said the boy, holding his chin tenderly. 'Hitting someone smaller than yourself! I'll fight that first boy, but I won't fight *you*.'

'You can't fight him,' said Dick. 'He's a girl. You can't fight girls – and girls oughtn't to fight, anyway.'

'Ses you!' said the dirty little ragamuffin, standing up and doubling his fists again. 'Well, you look here – *I'm* a girl, too – so I can fight her all right, can't I?'

George and the ragamuffin stood scowling at one another, each with fists clenched. They looked so astonishingly alike, with their short, curly hair, brown freckled faces and fierce expressions that Julian suddenly roared with laughter. He pushed them firmly apart.

'Fighting forbidden!' he said. He turned to the raga-muffin. 'Clear off!' he ordered. 'Do you hear me? Go on – off with you!'

The gipsy-like girl stared at him. Then she suddenly burst into tears and ran off howling.

'*She's* a girl all right,' said Dick, grinning at the howls. 'She's got some spunk though, facing up to me like that. Well, that's the last we'll see of *her*!'

But he was wrong. It wasn't!

Chapter Three

FACE AT THE WINDOW

THE five curled up in their holes once more. Dick felt his
jaw-bone. 'That ragamuffin of a girl gave me a good
bang,' he said, half-admiringly. 'Little demon, isn't she!
A bit of live wire!'

'I can't see why Julian wouldn't let me have a go at
her,' said George sulkily. 'It was my hole she sat in – she
meant to be annoying! How dare she?'

'Girls can't go about fighting,' said Dick. 'Don't be an
ass, George. I know you make out you're as good as a boy,
and you dress like a boy and climb trees as well as I
can – but it's really time you gave up thinking you're as
good as a boy.'

This sort of speech didn't please George at all. 'Well,
anyway, I don't burst into howls if I'm beaten,' she said,
turning her back on Dick.

'No, you don't,' agreed Dick. 'You've got as much
spunk as any boy – much more than that other kid had.
I'm sorry I sent her flying now. It's the first time I've
ever hit a girl, and I hope it'll be the last.'

'I'm jolly glad you hit her,' said George. 'She's a nasty little beast. If I see her again I'll tell her what I think of her.'

'No, you won't,' said Dick. 'Not if I'm there, anyway. She had her punishment when I sent her flying.'

'Do shut up arguing, you two,' said Anne, and sent a shower of sand over them. 'George, don't go into one of your moods, for goodness' sake – we don't want to waste a single day of this two weeks.'

'Here's the ice-cream man,' said Julian, sitting up and feeling for the waterproof pocket in the belt of his bathing trunks. 'Let's have one each.'

'Woof,' said Timmy, and thumped his tail on the sand.

'Yes, all right – one for you, too,' said Dick. 'Though what sense there is in giving *you* one, I don't know. One lick, one swallow, and it's gone. It might be a fly for all you taste of it.'

Timmy gulped his ice-cream down at once and then went into George's hole, squeezing beside her, hoping for a lick of her ice, too. But she pushed him away.

'No, Timmy. Ice-cream's wasted on you! You can't even have a lick of mine. And do get back into your hole – you're making me frightfully hot.'

Timmy obligingly got out and went into Anne's hole. She gave him a little bit of her ice-cream. He sat panting beside her, looking longingly at the rest of the ice. 'You're melting it with your hot breath,' said Anne. 'Go into Julian's hole now!'

The five of them had a thoroughly lazy morning. As none of them had a watch they went in far too early for lunch, and were shooed out again by Joan.

'How you can come in at ten past twelve for a one o'clock lunch, I don't know!' she scolded. 'I haven't even finished the housework yet.'

'Well – it *felt* like one o'clock,' said Anne, disappointed to find there was so long to wait. Still, when lunch-time came, Joan really did them well.

'Cold ham and tongue – cold baked beans – beetroot – crisp lettuce straight from the garden – heaps of tomatoes – cucumber – hard-boiled egg!' recited Anne in glee.

'Just the kind of meal I like,' said Dick, sitting down. 'What's for pudding?'

'There it is on the sideboard,' said Anne. 'Wobbly blancmange, fresh fruit salad and jelly. I'm glad I'm hungry.'

'Now don't you give Timmy any of that ham and tongue,' Joan warned George. 'I've got a fine bone for him. Coming, Timmy?'

Timmy knew the word 'bone' very well indeed. He trotted after Joan at once, his feet sounding loudly in the hall. They heard Joan talking kindly to him in the kitchen as she found him his bone.

'Good old Joan,' said Dick. 'She's like Timmy – her bark is worse than her bite.'

'Timmy's got a good bite, though,' said George, helping herself to three tomatoes at once. 'And his bite came in useful heaps of times for us.'

They ate steadily, thinking of some of the hair-raising adventures they had had, when Timmy and his bite had

certainly come in very useful. Timmy came in after a
while, licking his lips.

'Nothing doing, old chap,' said Dick, looking at the
empty dishes on the table. 'Don't tell me you've chomped
up that bone already!'

Timmy had. He lay down under the table, and put his
nose on his paws. He was happy. He had had a good
meal, and he was with the people he loved best. He put
his head as near George's feet as he could.

'Your whiskers are tickling me,' she said, and screwed
up her bare toes. 'Pass the tomatoes, someone.'

'You *can't* manage any more tomatoes, surely!' said
Anne. 'You've had five already.'

'They're out of my own garden,' said George, 'so I can
eat as many as I like.'

After lunch they lazed on the beach till it was time for
a bathe again. It was a happy day for all of them – warm,
lazy, with plenty of fun and romping about.

George looked out for the ragamuffin girl, but she
didn't appear again. George was half sorry. She would
have liked a battle of words with her, even if she couldn't
have a fight!

They were all very tired when they went to bed that
night. Julian yawned so loudly when Joan came in with
a jug of hot cocoa and some biscuits that she offered to
lock up the house for him.

'Oh, no, thank you, Joan,' said Julian at once. 'That's
the man's job, you know, locking up the house. You can
trust me all right. I'll see to every window and every door.'

'Right, Master Julian,' said Joan, and bustled away

to wind up the kitchen clock, rake out the fire, and go up to bed. The children went up, too, Timmy, as usual, at George's heels. Julian was left downstairs to lock up.

He was a very responsible boy. Joan knew that he wouldn't leave a single window unfastened. She heard him trying to shut the little window in the pantry, and she called down:

'Master Julian! It's swollen or something, and won't shut properly. You needn't bother about it, it's too small for anyone to get into!'

'Right!' said Julian, thankfully, and went upstairs. He yawned a terrific yawn again, and set Dick off, too, as soon as he came into the bedroom they both shared. The girls, undressing in the next room, laughed to hear them.

'*You* wouldn't hear a burglar in the middle of the night, Julian and Dick!' called Anne. 'You'll sleep like logs!'

'Old Timmy can listen out for burglars,' said Julian, cleaning his teeth vigorously. 'That's his job, not mine. Isn't it, Timmy?'

'Woof,' said Timmy, clambering on to George's bed. He always slept curled up in the crook of her knees. Her mother had given up trying to insist that George didn't have Timmy on her bed at night. As George said, even if *she* agreed to that, Timmy wouldn't!

Nobody stayed awake for more than five seconds. Nobody even said anything in bed, except for a sleepy good night. Timmy gave a little grunt and settled down, too, his head on George's feet. It was heavy, but she liked it there. She put out a hand and stroked Timmy gently.

He licked one of her feet through the bed-clothes. He loved George more than anyone in the world.

It was dark outside that night. Thick clouds had come up and put out all the stars. There was no sound to be heard but the wind in the trees and the distant surge of the sea – and both sounded so much the same that it was hard to tell the difference.

Not another sound – not even an owl hooting to its mate, or the sound of a hedgehog pattering in the ditch.

Then why did Timmy wake up? Why did he open first one eye and then another? Why did he prick up his ears and lie there, listening? He didn't even lift his head at first. He simply lay listening in the darkness.

He lifted his head cautiously at last. He slid off the bed as quietly as a cat. He padded across the room and out of the door. Down the stairs he went, and into the hall, where his claws rattled on the tiled floor. But nobody heard him. Everyone in the house was fast asleep.

Timmy stood and listened in the hall. He knew he had heard something. Could it have been a rat somewhere? Timmy lifted his nose and sniffed.

And then he stiffened from head to tail, and stood as if turned into stone. Something was climbing up the wall of the house. Scrape, scrape, scrape – rustle, rustle! Would a rat dare to do that?

Upstairs, in her bed, Anne didn't know why she suddenly woke up just then, but she did. She was thirsty, and she thought she would get a drink of water. She felt for her torch, and switched it on.

The light fell on the window first, and Anne saw something that gave her a terrible shock. She screamed loudly, and dropped her torch in fright. George woke up at once. Timmy came bounding up the stairs.

'Julian! wailed Anne. 'Come quickly. I saw a face at the window, a horrible, dreadful face looking in at me!'

George rushed to the window, switching on her torch as she did so. There was nothing there. Timmy went with her. He sniffed at the open window and growled.

'Hark – I can hear someone running quickly down the path,' said Julian, who now appeared with Dick. 'Come on, Timmy – downstairs with you and after them!'

And down they all went – Anne too. They flung the front door wide and Timmy sped out, barking loudly. A face at the window? He'd soon find out who it belonged to!

Chapter Four

THE NEXT DAY

THE four children waited at the open front door, listening to Timmy's angry, excited barking. Anne was trembling, and Julian put his arm round her comfortingly.

'What was this dreadful face like?' he asked her. Anne shivered in his arm.

'I didn't see very much,' she said. 'You see, I just switched on my torch, and the beam was directed on the window nearby – and it lighted up the face for a second. It had nasty gleaming eyes, and it looked very dark – perhaps it was a black man's face! Oh, I *was* frightened!'

'Then did it disappear?' asked Julian.

'I don't know,' said Anne. 'I was so frightened that I dropped my torch and the light went out. Then George woke up and rushed to the window.'

'Where on earth was Timmy?' said Dick, feeling suddenly surprised that Timmy hadn't awakened them all by barking. Surely he must have heard the owner of the face climbing up to the window?

'I don't know. He came rushing into the bedroom when I screamed,' said Anne. 'Perhaps he *had* heard a noise and had gone down to see what it was.'

'That's about it,' said Julian. 'Never mind, Anne. It

was a tramp, I expect. He found all the doors and windows downstairs fastened – and shinned up the ivy to see if he could enter by way of a bedroom. Timmy will get him, that's certain.'

But Timmy didn't get him. He came back after a time, with his tail down, and a puzzled look in his eyes. 'Couldn't you find him, Timmy?' asked George, anxiously.

'Woof,' said Timmy, mournfully, his tail still down. George felt him. He was wet through.

'Goodness! Where have you been to get so wet?' she said, in surprise. 'Feel him, Dick.'

Dick felt him, and so did the others. 'He's been in the sea,' said Julian. 'That's why he's wet. I guess the burglar, or whatever he was, must have sprinted down to the beach, when he knew Timmy was after him – and jumped into a boat! It was his only chance of getting away.'

'And Timmy must have swum after him till he couldn't keep up any more,' said George. 'Poor old Tim. So you lost him, did you?'

Timmy wagged his tail a little. He looked very downhearted indeed. To think he had heard noises and thought it was a rat – and now, whoever it was had got away from him. Timmy felt ashamed.

Julian shut and bolted the front door. He put up the chain, too. 'I don't think the Face will come back again in a hurry,' he said. 'Now he knows there's a big dog here he'll keep away. I don't think we need worry any more.'

They all went back to bed again. Julian didn't go to

sleep for some time. Although he had told the others not
to worry, he felt worried himself. He was sorry that Anne
had been frightened, and somehow the boldness of the
burglar in climbing up to a bedroom worried him, too.
He must have been determined to get in somehow.

Joan, the cook, slept through all the disturbance.
Julian wouldn't wake her. 'No,' he said, 'don't tell her
anything about it. She'd want to send telegrams to Uncle
Quentin or something.'

So Joan knew nothing about the night's happenings,
and they heard her cheerfully humming in the kitchen
the next morning as she cooked bacon and eggs and
tomatoes for their breakfast.

Anne was rather ashamed of herself when she woke
up and remembered the fuss she had made. The Face
was rather dim in her memory now. She half wondered
if she had dreamed it all. She asked Julian if he thought
she might have had a bad dream.

'Quite likely,' said Julian, cheerfully, very glad that
Anne should think this. 'More than likely! I wouldn't
worry about it any more, if I were you.'

He didn't tell Anne that he had examined the thickly-
growing ivy outside the window, and had found clear
traces of the night-climber. Part of the sturdy clinging
ivy-stem had come away from the wall, and beneath the
window were strewn broken-off ivy leaves. Julian showed
them to Dick.

'There *was* somebody,' he said. 'What a nerve he had,
climbing right up to the window like that. A real cat-
burglar! '

There were no footprints to be seen anywhere in the garden. Julian didn't expect to find any, for the ground was dry and hard.

The day was very fine and warm again. 'I vote we do what we did yesterday – go off to the beach and bathe,' said Dick. 'We might take a picnic lunch if Joan will give us one.'

'I'll help her to make it up for us,' said Anne, and she and George went off to beg for sandwiches and buns. Soon they were busy wrapping up a colossal lunch.

'Do for twelve, I should think!' said Joan, with a laugh. 'Here's a bottle of home-made lemonade, too. You can take as many ripe plums as you like as well. I shan't prepare any supper for you tonight – you'll not need it after all this lunch.'

George and Anne looked at her in alarm. No *supper*! Then they caught the twinkle in her eye and laughed.

'We'll make all the beds and do our rooms before we go,' said Anne. 'And is there anything you want from the village?'

'No, not today. You hurry up with your jobs and get along to the beach,' said Joan. 'I'll be quite glad of a peaceful day to myself. I shall turn out the larder and the hall cupboards and the scullery, and enjoy myself in peace!'

Anne seemed quite to have forgotten her fright of the night before as they went down to the beach that day, chattering and laughing together. Even if she *had* thought about it, something soon happened that swept everything else from her mind.

The little ragamuffin girl was down on the beach again!
She was alone. Her dreadful old father, or whatever he
was, was not there.

George saw the girl first and scowled. Julian saw the
scowl and then the girl, and made up his mind at once.
He led the others firmly to where rocks jutted up from
the beach, surrounded by limpid rock-pools.

'We'll be here today,' he said. 'It's so hot we'll be glad
of the shade from the rocks. What about just here?'

'It's all right,' said George, half sulky and half amused
at Julian for being so firm about things. 'Don't worry.
I'm not having anything more to do with that smelly girl.'

'I'm glad to hear it,' said Julian. They had now turned
a corner, and were out of sight of the girl. Big rocks ran
in an upwards direction behind them, and jutted up all
around them. Julian sat down in a lovely little corner, with
rocks protecting them from the sun and the wind.

'Let's have a read before we bathe,' said Dick. 'I've
got a mystery story here. I simply MUST find out who
the thief is.'

He settled himself comfortably. Anne went to look for
sea anemones in the pool. She liked the petal-like
creatures that looked so like plants and weren't. She liked
feeding them with bits of biscuit, seeing their 'petals' close
over the fragment and draw them quickly inside.

George lay back and stroked Timmy. Julian began to
sketch the rocks around, and the little pools. It was all
very peaceful indeed.

Suddenly something landed on George's middle and
made her jump. She sat up, and so did Timmy.

'What was that?' said George indignantly. 'Did you throw something at me, Dick?'

'No,' said Dick, his eyes glued to his book.

Something else hit George on the back of the neck, and she put her hand up with an exclamation. 'What's happening? Who's throwing things?'

She looked to see what had hit her. Lying on the sand was a small roundish thing. George picked it up. 'Why – it's a damson stone,' she said. And 'Ping'! Another one hit her on the shoulder. She leapt up in a rage.

She could see nobody at all. She waited for another damson stone to appear, but none did.

'I just wish I could draw your face, George,' said Julian,

with a grin. 'I never saw such a frown in my life. Ooch!'

The 'ooch!' was nothing to do with George's frown;
it was caused by another damson stone that caught Julian
neatly behind the ear. He leapt to his feet too. A helpless
giggle came from behind a rock some way behind and
above them. George was up on the ledge in a second.

Behind one of the rocks sat the ragamuffin girl. Her
pockets were full of damsons, some of them spilling out
as she rolled on the rocks, laughing. She sat up when she
saw George, and grinned.

'What do you mean, throwing those stones at us?'
demanded George.

'I wasn't throwing them,' said the girl.

'Don't tell lies,' said George scornfully. 'You know you
were.'

'I wasn't. I was just spitting them,' said the awful girl.
'Watch!' She slipped a stone into her mouth, took a deep
breath and then spat out the stone. It flew straight at
George and hit her sharply and squarely on the nose.
George looked so extremely surprised that Dick and
Julian roared with laughter.

'Bet I can spit stones farther than any of you,' said the
ragamuffin. 'Have some of my damsons and see.'

'Right!' said Dick promptly. 'If you win I'll buy you
an ice-cream. If I do, you can clear off from here and
not bother us any more. See?'

'Yes,' said the girl, and her eyes gleamed and danced.
'But I shall win!'

Chapter Five

RAGAMUFFIN JO

GEORGE was most astonished at Dick. How very shocking to see who could spit damson stones out the farthest.

'It's all right,' said Julian to her in a low voice. 'You know how good Dick is at that sort of game. He'll win – and we'll send the girl scooting off, well and truly beaten.'

'I think you're horrible, Dick,' said George, in a loud voice. 'Horrible!'

'Who used to spit cherry-stones out and try and beat me last year?' said Dick at once. 'Don't be so high-and-mighty, George.'

Anne came slowly back from her pool, wondering why the others were up on the rocks. Damson stones began to rain round her. She stopped in astonishment. Surely – surely it couldn't be the others doing that? A stone hit her on her bare arm, and she squealed.

The ragamuffin girl won handsomely. She managed to get her stones at least three feet farther than Dick. She lay back, laughing, her teeth gleaming very white indeed.

'You owe me an ice-cream,' she said, in her sing-song voice. Julian wondered if she was Welsh. Dick looked at her, marvelling that she managed to get her stones so far.

'I'll buy you the ice-cream, don't worry,' he said. 'Nobody's ever beaten me before like that, not even Stevens, a boy at school with a most enormous mouth.'

'I do think you really are dreadful,' said Anne. 'Go and buy her the ice-cream and tell her to go home.'

'I'm going to eat it here,' said the girl, and she suddenly looked exactly as mulish and obstinate as George did when she wanted something she didn't think she would get.

'You look like George now!' said Dick, and immediately wished he hadn't. George glared at him, furious.

'What! That nasty, rude tangly-haired girl like *me*!' stormed George. 'Pooh! I can't bear to go near her.'

'Shut up,' said Dick, shortly. The girl looked surprised. 'What does she mean?' she asked Dick. 'Am I nasty? You're as *rude* as I am, anyway.'

'There's an ice-cream man,' said Julian, afraid that the hot-tempered George would fly at the girl and slap her. He whistled to the man, who came to the edge of the rocks and handed out six ice-creams.

'Here you are,' said Julian, handing one to the girl. 'You eat that up and go.'

They all sat and ate ice-creams, George still scowling. Timmy gulped his at once as usual. 'Look – he's had all his,' marvelled the girl. 'I call that a waste. Here, boy – have a bit of mine!'

To George's annoyance, Timmy licked up the bit of ice-cream thrown to him by the girl. How *could* Timmy accept anything from her?

Dick couldn't help being amused by this queer, bold

little girl, with her tangled short hair and sharp darting eyes. He suddenly saw something that made him feel uncomfortable.

On her chin the girl had a big black bruise. 'I say,' said Dick, '*I* didn't give you that bruise yesterday, did I?'

'What bruise? Oh, this one on my chin?' said the girl, touching it. 'Yes, that's where you hit me when you sent me flying. *I* don't mind. I've had plenty worse ones from my Dad.'

'I'm sorry I hit you,' said Dick, awkwardly. 'I honestly thought you were a boy. What's your name?'

'Jo,' said the girl.

'But that's a *boy's* name,' said Dick.

'So's George. But you said she was a girl,' said Jo, licking the last bits of ice-cream from her fingers.

'Yes, but George is short for Georgina,' said Anne. 'What's Jo short for?'

'Don't know,' said Jo. 'I never heard. All I know is I'm a girl and my name is Jo.'

'It's probably short for Josephine,' said Julian. They all stared at the possible Josephine. The short name of Jo certainly suited her – but not the long and pretty name of Josephine.

'It's really queer,' said Anne, at last, 'but Jo *is* awfully like you, George – same short curly hair – only Jo's is terribly messy and tangly – same freckles, dozens of them – same turned-up nose . . .'

'Same way of sticking her chin up in the air, same scowl, same glare!' said Dick. George put on her fiercest glare at these remarks, which she didn't like at all.

'Well, all I can say I hope I haven't her layers of dirt and her sm –' she began, angrily. But Dick stopped her.

'She's probably not got any soap or hair-brush or anything. She'd be all right cleaned up. Don't be unkind, George.'

George turned her back. How *could* Dick stick up for that awful girl? 'Isn't she ever going?' she said. 'Or is she going to park herself on us all day long?'

'I'll go when I want to,' said Jo, and put on a scowl, so exactly like George's that Julian and Dick laughed in surprise. Jo laughed, too, but George clenched her fists furiously. Anne looked on in distress. She wished Jo would go, then everything would be all right again.

'I like that dog,' said Jo, suddenly, and she leaned over to where Timmy lay beside George. She patted him with a hand that was like a little brown paw. George swung round.

'Don't touch my dog!' she said. '*He* doesn't like you, either!'

'Oh, but he does,' said Jo, surprisingly. 'All dogs like *me*. So do cats. I can make your dog come to me as easy as anything.'

'Try!' said George, scornfully. 'He won't go to *you*! Will you, Tim?'

Jo didn't move. She began to make a queer little whining noise down in her throat, like a forlorn puppy. Timmy pricked up his ears at once. He looked inquiringly at Jo. Jo stopped making the noise and held out her hand.

Timmy looked at it and turned away – but when he heard the whining again he got up, listening. He stared intently at Jo. Was this a kind of dog-girl, that she could so well speak his language?

Jo flung herself on her face and went on with the small, whining noises that sounded as if she were a small dog in pain or sorrow. Timmy walked over to her and sat down, his head on one side, puzzled. Then he suddenly bent down and licked the girl's half-hidden face. She sat up at once and put her arms round Timmy's neck.

'Come here, Timmy,' said George, jealously. Timmy shook off the brown arms that held him and walked over to George at once.

Jo laughed.

'See? I made him come to me and give me one of his best licks! I can do that to any dog.'

'How can you?' asked Dick, in wonder. He had never seen Timmy make friends before with anyone who was disliked by George.

'I don't know, really,' said Jo, pushing back her hair again, as she sat up. 'I reckon it's in the family. My mother was in a circus, and she trained dogs for the ring. We had dozens – lovely they were. I loved them all.'

'Where is your mother?' asked Julian. 'Is she still in the circus?'

'No. She died,' said Jo. 'And I left the circus with my Dad. We've got a caravan. Dad was an acrobat till he hurt his foot.'

The four children remembered how the man had dragged his foot as he walked. They looked silently at dirty little Jo. What a strange life she must have led!

'She's dirty, she's probably very good at telling lies and

thieving, but she's got pluck,' thought Julian. 'Still, I'll be glad when she goes.'

'I wish I hadn't given her that awful bruise,' thought Dick. 'I wonder what she'd be like cleaned up and brushed? She looks as if a little kindness would do her good.'

'I'm sorry for her, but I don't much like her,' thought Anne.

'I don't believe a word she says!' thought George angrily. 'Not one word! She's a humbug. And I'm *ashamed* of Timmy for going to her. I feel very cross with him.'

'Where's your father?' asked Julian at last.

'Gone off somewhere to meet somebody,' said Jo vaguely. 'I'm glad. He was in one of his tempers this morning. I went and hid under the caravan.'

There was a silence. 'Can I stay with you today till

my Dad comes back?' said Jo suddenly, in her sing-song voice. 'I'll wash myself if you like. I'm all alone today.'

'No. We don't want you,' said George, feeling as if she really couldn't bear Jo any longer. 'Do we, Anne?'

Anne didn't like hurting anyone. She hesitated. 'Well,' she said at last, 'perhaps Jo *had* better go.'

'Yes,' said Julian. 'It's time you scooted off now, Jo. You've had a long time with us.'

Jo looked at Dick with mournful eyes, and touched the bruise on her chin as if it hurt her. Dick felt most uncomfortable again. He looked round at the others.

'Don't you think she could stay and share our picnic?' he said. 'After all – she can't *help* being dirty and – and ...'

'It's all right,' said Jo, suddenly scrambling up. 'I'm going! There's my Dad!'

They saw the man in the distance, dragging his foot as he walked. He caught sight of Jo and gave a shrill and piercing whistle. Jo made a face at them all, an impudent, ugly, insolent face.

'I don't like you!' she said. Then she pointed at Dick. 'I only like *him* – he's nice. Yah to the rest of you!'

And off she went like a hare over the sand, her bare feet hardly touching the ground.

'What an extraordinary girl!' said Julian. 'I don't feel we've seen the last of her yet!'

Chapter Six

WHAT HAPPENED IN THE NIGHT?

THAT night Anne began to look rather scared as darkness fell. She was remembering the Face at the Window!

'It won't come again, Ju, will it?' she said to her big brother half a dozen times.

'No, Anne. But if you like I'll come and lie down on George's bed instead of George tonight, and stay with you all night long,' said Julian.

Anne considered this and then shook her head. 'No. I think I'd almost rather have George and Timmy. I mean – George and I – and even you – might be scared of Faces, but Timmy wouldn't. He'd simply leap at them.'

'You're quite right,' said Julian. 'He would. All right then, I won't keep you company – but you'll see, nothing whatever will happen tonight. Anyway, if you like, we'll all close our bedroom windows and fasten them, even if we are too hot for anything – then we'll know nobody can possibily get in.'

So that night Julian not only closed all the doors and windows downstairs as he had done the night before (except the tiny pantry window that wouldn't shut), but he also shut and fastened all the ones upstairs.

'What about Joan's window?' asked Anne.

'She *always* sleeps with it shut, summer and winter,' said Julian, with a grin. 'Country folk often do. They think the night air's dangerous. Now you've nothing at all to worry about, silly.'

So Anne went to bed with her mind at rest. George drew the curtains across their window so that even if the Face came again they wouldn't be able to see it!

'Let Timmy out for me, Julian, will you?' called George. 'Anne doesn't want me to leave her, even to take old Timmy out for his last walk. Just open the door and let him out. He'll come in when he's ready.'

'Right!' called Julian, and opened the front door Timmy trotted out, tail wagging. He loved his last sniff round. He liked to smell the trail of the hedgehog who was out on his night-rounds; he liked to put his nose down a rabbit-hole and listen to stirrings down below; and he loved to follow the meanderings of rats and mice round by the thick hedges.

'Isn't Timmy in yet?' called George from the top of the stairs. 'Do call him, Ju. I want to get into bed. Anne's half-asleep already.'

'He'll be in in a moment,' said Julian, who wanted to finish his book. 'Don't fuss.'

But no Timmy had appeared even when he had finished his book. Julian went to the door and whistled. He listened for Timmy to come. Then, hearing nothing, he whistled once more.

This time he heard the sound of pattering footsteps coming up the path to the door. 'Oh there you are, Tim,' said Julian. 'What have you been up to? Chasing rabbits or something?'

Timothy wagged his tail feebly. He didn't jump up at Julian as he usually did. 'You look as if you've been up to some mischief, Tim,' said Julian. 'Go on – up to bed with you – and mind you bark if you hear the smallest sound in the night.'

'Woof,' said Timmy, in rather a subdued voice, and went upstairs. He climbed on to George's bed and sighed heavily.

'What a sigh!' said George. 'And what have you been eating, Timmy? Pooh – you've dug up some frightful old bone, I know you have. I've a good mind to push you off my bed. I suppose you suddenly remembered one you buried months ago. Pooh!'

Timmy wouldn't be pushed off the bed. He settled down to sleep, his nose on George's feet as usual. He snored a little, and woke George in about half an hour.

'Shut up, Timmy,' she said, pushing him with her feet. Anne woke up, alarmed.

'What is it, George?' she whispered, her heart thumping.

'Nothing. Only Timmy snoring. Hark at him. He won't stop,' said George, irritated. 'Wake up, Timmy, and stop snoring.'

Timmy moved sleepily and settled down again. He stopped snoring and George and Anne fell sound asleep. Julian woke once, thinking he heard something fall – but hearing Timmy gently snoring again through the open doors of the two rooms, he lay down, his mind at rest.

If the noise had *really* been a noise Timmy would have heard it, no doubt about that. George always said that Timmy slept with one ear open.

Julian heard nothing more till Joan went downstairs at seven o'clock. He heard her go into the kitchen and do something to the kitchen grate. He turned over and fell asleep again.

He was wakened suddenly twenty minutes later by loud screams from downstairs. He sat up and then leapt out of bed at once. He rushed downstairs. Dick followed him.

'Look at this! The master's study – turned upside down – those drawers ransacked! The safe's open, too. Mercy me, who's been here in the night – with all the doors locked and bolted, too!' Joan wailed loudly and wrung her hands as she gazed at the untidy room.

'I say!' said Dick, horrified. 'Someone's been searching for something pretty thoroughly! Even got the safe open – and wrenched the drawers out.'

'How did he get in?' said Julian, feeling bewildered. He went round the house, looking at doors and windows. Except for the kitchen door, which Joan said she had unlocked and unbolted herself as soon as she came down, not a window or door had been touched. All were fastened securely.

Anne came down, looking scared. 'What's the matter?' she said. But Julian brushed her aside. How did that burglar get in? That was what he wanted to know. Through one of the *upstairs* windows, he supposed – one

that somebody had opened last night after he had fastened
it. Perhaps in the girls' room?

But no – not one window was open. All were fastened
securely, including Joan's. Then a thought struck him
as he looked into George's room. Why hadn't Timmy
barked? After all, there must have been quite a bit of
noise, however quiet the thief had been. He had himself
heard something and had awakened. Why hadn't Timmy,
then?

George was trying to pull Timmy off the bed. 'Ju, Ju!
There's something wrong with Timmy. He won't wake
up!' she cried. 'He's breathing so heavily, too – just listen
to him! And what's the matter downstairs? What's
happened?'

Julian told her shortly while he examined Timmy.
'Somebody got in last night – your father's study's in
the most awful mess – absolutely ransacked from top to
bottom, safe and all. Goodness knows how the fellow got
in to do it.'

'How awful!' said George, looking very pale. 'And
now something's wrong with Tim. He didn't wake up
last night when the burglar came – he's ill, Julian!'

'No, he's not. He's been doped,' said Julian, pulling
back Timmy's eyelids. 'So *that's* why he was so long outside last night! Somebody gave him some meat or something with dope in – some kind of drug. And he ate it,
and slept so soundly that he never heard a thing – and
isn't even awake yet.'

'Oh, Julian – will he be all right?' asked George
anxiously, stroking Timmy's motionless body. 'But how

could he take any food from a stranger in the night?'

'Maybe he picked it up – the burglar may have flung it down hoping that Timmy would eat it,' said Julian. 'Now I understand why he looked so sheepish when he came in. He didn't even jump up and lick me.'

'Oh, dear – Timmy, do, do wake up,' begged poor George, and she shook the big dog gently. He groaned a little and snuggled down again.

'Leave him,' said Julian. 'He'll be all right. He's not poisoned, only drugged. Come down and see the damage!'

George was horrified at the state of her father's study. 'They were after his two special books of American notes, I'm sure they were,' she said. 'Father said that any other country in the world would be glad to have those. Whatever are we to do?'

'Better get in the police,' said Julian, gravely. 'We can't manage this sort of thing ourselves. And do you know your father's address in Spain?'

'No,' wailed George. 'He and Mother said they were going to have a *real* holiday this time – no letters to be forwarded, and no address left till they had been settled somewhere for a few days. Then they'd telegraph it.'

'Well, we'll certainly have to get the police in, then,' said Julian, looking rather white and stern. George glanced at him. He seemed suddenly very grown-up indeed. She watched him go out of the room. He went into the hall and rang up the police station. Joan was very relieved.

'Yes, get in the police, that's what we ought to do,' she said. 'There's that nice Constable Wilkins, and that other one with the red face, what's he called – Mr. Donaldson. I'll be making some coffee for them when they come.'

She cheered up considerably at the thought of handing out cups of her good hot coffee to two interested policemen, who would ask her plenty of questions that she would be only too delighted to answer. She bustled off to the kitchen.

The four children stared silently at the ruins of the study. What a mess! Could it ever be cleared up? Nobody would know what was gone till Uncle Quentin came back. How furious he would be.

'I hope nothing very important has been taken,' said Dick. 'It looks as if somebody knew there was something valuable here, and meant to get it!'

'And has probably got it,' said Julian. 'Hallo – that must be the police! Come on – I can see it will be a long time before we get our breakfast this morning!'

Chapter Seven

POLICEMEN IN THE HOUSE

THE police were very, very thorough. The children got tired of them long before lunch-time. Joan didn't. She made them cups of coffee and put some of her home-made buns on a plate and sent Anne to pick up ripe plums. She felt proud to think that it was she who had discovered the ransacked study.

There were two policemen. One was a sergeant, rather solemn and very correct. He interviewed each of the children and asked them exactly the same questions. The other man went over the study bit by bit, very thoroughly indeed.

'Looking for finger-prints, I suppose,' said Anne. 'Oh dear – when can we go and bathe?'

The thing that puzzled everyone, the police included, was – how did the thief or thieves get in? Both policemen went round the house, slowly and deliberately trying every door and window still locked or fastened. They stood and looked at the pantry window for some time.

'Got in there, I suppose,' said one of them.

'Must have been as small as a monkey then,' said the other. He turned to Anne, who was the smallest of the

52

four children. 'Could you squeeze through there, Missy, do you think?'

'No,' said Anne. 'But I'll try if you like.' So she tried – but she stuck fast before she got even half-way through, and Julian had to pull hard to get her down again.

'Have you any idea what has been stolen, sir?' the sergeant asked Julian, who seemed extraordinarily grown-up that morning.

'No, sergeant – none of us has,' said Julian. 'Not even George here, who knows her father's work better than any of us. The only thing we know is that my uncle went to America to lecture a short time ago – and he brought back two notebooks, full of valuable diagrams and notes. He did say that other countries might be very glad to get hold of those. I expect they were in that safe.'

'Well – they'll certainly be gone then,' said the sergeant, shutting his own fat notebook with a snap. 'Pity when people leave such things in an ordinary safe – and then go off without leaving an address. Can't we possibly get in touch with him? This may be terribly important.'

'I know,' said Julian, looking worried. 'We shall have an address in a day or two – but I honestly don't see how we can get in touch before then.'

'Right,' said the sergeant. 'Well – we'll go now – but we'll bring back a photographer with us after lunch to photograph the room – then your cook can tidy it up. I know she's longing to.'

'Coming back *again*!' said Anne, when the two men had solemnly walked down the path, mounted very solid-looking bicycles, and gone sailing down the lane. 'Good gracious! Have we got to answer questions all over again?'

'Well, we'll go down to the beach and take a boat and go rowing,' said Julian, with a laugh. 'We'll be out of reach then. I don't see that we can give them any more help. I must say it's all very peculiar – I wish to goodness I knew how the thief got in.'

George had been very quiet and subdued all the morning. She had worried about Timmy, fearing that he had been poisoned, and not merely drugged, as Julian had said. But Timmy was now quite recovered, except that he seemed a bit sleepy still, and not inclined to gambol round in his usual ridiculous way. He looked extremely sheepish, too.

'I can't think why Timmy looks like that,' said George, puzzled. 'He usually only puts that look on when he's done something he's ashamed of – or got into mischief. He couldn't possibly know, could he, that whatever he picked up and ate last night was something he shouldn't eat?'

'No,' said Dick. 'He's sensible though, I think, not to touch poisoned meat – but he couldn't know if some harmless sleeping powder had been put into anything. It might have no smell and no taste. Perhaps he's just ashamed of being so sleepy!'

'If only he'd been awake!' groaned George. 'He would have heard any noise downstairs at once – and he'd have barked and waked us all, and flown downstairs himself to attack whoever was there! Why, oh why didn't

I take him out myself last night as I usually do?'

'It was a chapter of accidents,' said Julian. 'You didn't take him out, so he was alone – and it happened that someone was waiting there with drugged food – which he either found or took from the thief. . . .'

'*No,*' said George. 'Timmy would never, never take anything from someone he didn't know. I've always taught him that.'

'Well, he got it somehow – and slept through the very night he should have been awake,' said Julian. 'What I'm so afraid of, George, is that the thieves have got your father's two American notebooks. They seem to have left most of the stuff – piles and piles of books of all kinds, filled with your father's tiny handwriting.'

Joan came in to say lunch was ready. She told the children that the policemen had eaten every one of her home-made buns. She still felt important and excited, and was longing to get out to the village and tell everyone the news.

'You'd better stay in and give the policemen a good tea,' said Julian. 'They're coming back with a photographer.'

'Then I'd better do another baking,' said Joan, pleased.

'Yes. Make one of your chocolate cakes,' said Anne.

'Oh, do you think they'd like one?' said Joan.

'Not for *them*, Joan – for us, of course!' said George. 'Don't waste one of your marvellous chocolate cakes on policemen. Can you make us up a picnic tea? We're fed up with being indoors – we're going out in a boat.'

Joan packed them a good tea after they had had their

lunch and they all set off before the police came back.
Timmy was much less sleepy now and did a little caper
round them as they walked to the beach. George brightened up at once.

'He's getting better,' she said. 'Timmy, I simply shan't
let you out of my sight now! If anyone's going to dope
you again they'll have to do it under my very nose.'

They had a lovely time out in George's boat. They
went half-way to Kirrin Island and bathed from the boat,
diving in and having swimming races till they were tired
out. Timmy joined them, though he couldn't swim nearly
as fast as they could.

'He doesn't really *swim*,' said Anne. 'He just tries to
run through the water. I wish he'd let me ride on his
back like a sea-dog – but he always slips away under me
when I try.'

They got back about six o'clock to find that the policemen had eaten the whole of the chocolate cake that Joan
had made, besides an extraordinary amount of scones and
buns.

Also the study was now tidied up, and a man had come
to mend the safe. Everything was safely back there, though
the police had told Joan that if there was anything of
real value it should be handed to them till George's father
came back.

'But we don't know which of all those papers are valuable!' said Julian. 'Well – we'll have to wait till Uncle
Quentin cables us – and that may not be for days.
Anyway, I don't expect we'll be worried by the thief
again – he's got what he wanted.'

The exciting happenings of the day had made them all tired except Julian. 'I'm off to bed,' said Dick, about nine o'clock. 'Anne, why don't you go? You look fagged out.'

'Yes, I will,' said Anne. 'Coming, George?'

'I'm going to take Timmy out for his last walk,' said George. 'I shall never let him go out alone at night again. Come on, Timmy. If you want to go to bed I'll lock up the front door, Ju.'

'Right,' said Julian. 'I'll go up in a minute. I don't fancy staying down here by myself tonight. I'll fasten everything and lock up, except the front door. Don't forget to put up the chain, too, George – though I'm pretty certain we don't need to expect any more burglaries!'

'Or faces at the window,' said Anne, at once.

'No,' said Julian. 'There won't be any more of those either. Good night, Anne – sleep well!'

Anne and Dick went upstairs. Julian finished the paper he was reading, and then got up to go round the house and lock up. Joan was already upstairs, dreaming of policemen eating her chocolate cakes.

George went out with Timmy. He ran eagerly to the gate and then set off down the lane for his usual night walk with George. At a gate in the lane he suddenly stood still and growled as if he saw something unusual.

'Silly, Timmy!' said George, coming up. 'It's only somebody camping in a caravan! Haven't you seen a caravan before! Stop growling!'

They went on, Timmy sniffing into every rathole and rabbit-hole, enjoying himself thoroughly. George was enjoying the walk, too. She didn't hurry – Julian could always go up to bed if he didn't want to wait.

Julian did go up to bed. He left the front door ajar, and went yawning upstairs, suddenly feeling sleepy. He got into bed quietly and quickly seeing that Dick was already asleep. He lay awake listening for George. When he was half asleep, he heard the front door shut.

'There she is,' he thought, and turned over to go to sleep.

But it wasn't George. Her bed was empty all that night, and nobody knew, not even Anne. George and Timmy didn't come back!

Chapter Eight

WHERE CAN GEORGE BE?

ANNE woke up in the night, feeling thirsty. She whispered across the room:

'George! Are you awake?'

There was no answer, so, very cautiously and quietly Anne got herself a drink from the decanter on the washstand. George was sometimes cross if she was awakened in the middle of the night. Anne got back into bed, not guessing that George hadn't answered because she wasn't there!

She fell asleep and didn't wake till she heard Dick's voice. 'Hey, you two – get up; it's a quarter to eight. We're going for a bathe!'

Anne sat up, yawning. Her eyes went to George's bed. It was empty. More than that, it was all neat and tidy, as if it had just been made!

'Well!' said Anne in astonishment. 'George is up already, and has even made her bed. She *might* have waked me, and I could have gone out with her. It's such a lovely day. I suppose she's taken Timmy for an early morning walk, like she sometimes does.'

Anne slipped into her bathing costume and ran to join the boys. They went downstairs together, their bare feet padding on the carpet.

'George has gone out already,' said Anne. 'I expect she woke early and took Timmy; I never even heard her!'

Julian was now at the front door. 'Yes,' he said. 'The door isn't locked or bolted – George must have slipped down, undone it and then just pulled the door softly to. How very considerate of her! Last time she went out early she banged the door so hard that she woke everyone in the house!'

'She may have gone fishing in her boat,' said Dick. 'She said yesterday she'd like to some early morning when the tide was right. She'll probably arrive complete with stacks of fish for Joan to cook.'

They looked out to sea when they got to the beach. There was a boat far out on the water with what looked like two people in it, fishing.

'I bet that's George and Timmy,' said Dick. He yelled and waved his hands, but the boat was too far away, and nobody waved back. The three of them plunged into the cold waves. Brrrr-rrr-rrr!

'Lovely!' said Anne, when they came out again, the drops of sea-water running down their bodies and glistening in the early morning sun. 'Let's have a run now.'

They chased one another up and down the beach, and then, glowing and very hungry, went back to breakfast.

'Where's George?' asked Joan, as she brought in their breakfast. 'I see her bed's made and all – what's come over her?'

'I think she's out fishing with Timmy,' said Dick. 'She was up and about long before we were.'

'I never heard her go,' said Joan. 'She must have been very quiet. There you are now – there's a fine breakfast for you – sausages and tomatoes and fried eggs!'

'O-o-o-o-h, lovely,' said Anne. 'And you've done the sausages just how I like them, Joan – all bursting their skins. Do you think we'd better eat George's too? She's still out in the boat. She may not be back for ages.'

'Well, then you'd better eat her share,' said Joan. 'I've no doubt she took something out of the larder before she went. Pity I didn't lock it last night, as usual!'

They finished George's share between them and then started on toast and marmalade. After that Anne went to help Joan make the beds and dust and mop. Julian and Dick went off to the village to do the morning's shopping at the grocer's.

Nobody worried about George at all. Julian and Dick came back from their shopping and saw the little boat still out on the sea.

'George will be absolutely starving by the time she comes back,' said Julian. 'Perhaps she's got one of her moods on and wants to be alone. She was awfully upset about Timmy being drugged.'

They met the ragamuffin Jo. She was walking along the beach, collecting wood, and she looked sullen and dirtier than ever.

'Hallo, Jo!' called Dick. She looked up and came towards them without a smile. She looked as if she had been crying. Her small brown face was streaked where the tears had run through the dirt.

'Hallo!' she said, looking at Dick. She looked so miserable that Dick felt touched.

'What's the matter, kid?' he said, kindly.

Tears trickled down Jo's face as she heard the kindness in his voice. She rubbed them away and smudged her face more than ever.

'Nothing,' she said. 'Where's Anne?'

'Anne's at home, and George is out in that boat with Timmy fishing,' said Dick, pointing out to sea.

'Oh!' said Jo, and turned away to go on with her collecting of wood. Dick went after her.

'Hey!' he said. 'Don't go off like that. You just tell me what's wrong with you this morning.'

He caught hold of Jo and swung her round to face him.

He looked closely at her and saw that she now had two bruises on her face – one going yellow, that he had given her when he had sent her flying two or three days before – and a new one, dark purple.

'Where did you get *that* bruise?' he said, touching it lightly.

'That was my dad,' said Jo. 'He's gone off and left me – taken the caravan and all! I wanted to go, too; but he wouldn't let me into the caravan. And when I hammered at the door, he came out and pushed me down the steps. That's when I got this bruise – and I've got another on my leg, too.'

Dick and Julian listened in horror. What kind of a life was this that Jo had to live? The boys sat down on the beach, and Dick pulled Jo down between them.

'But surely your father is coming back?' said Julian. 'Is the caravan your only home?'

'Yes,' said Jo. 'I've never had another home. We've always lived in a caravan. Mum did, too, when she was alive. Things were better then. But this is the first time Dad's gone off without me.'

'But – how are you going to live?' asked Dick.

'Dad said Jake would give me money to buy food,' said Jo. 'But only if I do what he tells me. I don't like Jake. He's mean.'

'Who's Jake?' asked Julian, most astonished at all this.

'Jake's a gipsy fellow. He knows my father,' said Jo. 'He's always turning up for a day or two, and going away again. If I wait about here, he'll come and give me five pence or so, I expect.'

'What will he tell you to do?' said Dick, puzzled. 'It all seems very queer and horrible to me. You're only a kid.'

'Oh, he may tell me to go poaching with him or – or – well, there's things we do that folks like you don't,' said Jo, suddenly realizing that Dick and Julian would not at all approve of some of the things she did. 'I hope he gives me some money today, though. I haven't got any at all, and I'm hungry.'

Dick and Julian looked at one another. To think that in these days there should be a forlorn waif like Jo, going in fear of others, and often hungry and lonely.

Dick put his hand in the shopping basket and pulled out a packet of chocolate and some biscuits. 'Here you are,' he said. 'Tuck into these – and if you'd like to go to the kitchen door some time today and ask Joan, our cook, for a meal, she'll give you one. I'll tell her about you.'

'Folks don't like me at kitchen doors,' said Jo, cramming biscuits into her mouth. 'They're afraid I'll steal something.' She glanced up at Dick. 'And I do,' she said.

'You shouldn't do that,' said Dick.

'Well, wouldn't you, if you were so hungry you couldn't even bear to look at a baker's cart?' said Jo.

'No – I don't think so. At least, I hope not,' said Dick, wondering what he really would feel like if he were starving. 'Where's this Jake fellow?'

'I don't know. Somewhere about,' said Jo. 'He'll find me when he wants me. I've got to stay on the beach, Dad said. So I couldn't come to your house, anyway. I dursent leave here.'

The boys got up to go, worried about this little ragamuffin. But what could they do? Nothing, except feed her and give her money. Dick had slipped five pence into her hand, and she had pocketed it without a word, her eyes gleaming.

George was still not home by lunch-time; and now Julian for the first time began to feel anxious. He slipped out to the beach to see if the boat was still at sea. It was just pulling in – and with a sinking heart Julian saw that it was not George and Timmy who were in it, but two boys.

He went to look for George's boat – and there it was, high up on the boat-beach with many others. George had not been out in it at all!

He ran back to Kirrin Cottage and told the others. They were at once as anxious as he was. What *could* have become of George?

'We'll wait till tea-time,' said Julian. 'Then if she's not back we'll really have to do something about it – tell the police, I should think. But she *has* sometimes gone off for the day before, so we'll just wait a bit longer.'

Tea-time came – but no George, and no Timmy. Then they heard someone pattering up the garden path – was it Timmy? They leaned out of the window to see.

'It's Jo,' said Dick, in disappointment, 'She's got a note or something. Whatever does *she* want?'

Chapter Nine

AN EXTRAORDINARY MESSAGE –
AND A PLAN

JULIAN opened the front door. Jo silently gave him a plain
envelope. Julian tore it open, not knowing what in the
least to expect. Jo turned to go – but Julian put out his
hand and caught hold of her firmly, whilst he read the
note in complete amazement.

'Dick!' he called. 'Hold on to Jo. Don't let her go.
Better take her indoors. This is serious.'

66

Jo wasn't going to be taken indoors. She squealed, and wriggled like an eel. Then she began to kick Dick viciously with her bare feet.

'Let me go! I'm not doing any harm. I only brought you that note!'

'Stop squealing and being silly,' said Dick. 'I don't want to hurt you, you know that. But you must come indoors.'

But Jo wouldn't stop wriggling and pulling and kicking. She looked scared out of her life. It was as much as Dick and Julian could do to get the little wriggler into the dining-room and shut the door. Anne followed, looking very frightened. Whatever was happening?

'Listen to this,' said Julian, when the door was shut. 'It's unbelievable!' He held out the typewritten note for the others to see as he read it out loud.

'We want the second notebook, the one with figures in, and we mean to have it. Find it and put it under the last stone on the crazy paving path at the bottom of the garden. Put it there tonight.

'We have got the girl and the dog. We will set them free when we have what we want from you. If you tell the police, neither the girl nor the dog will come back. The house will be watched to see that nobody leaves it to warn the police. The telephone wires are cut.

'When it is dark, put the lights on in the front room and all three of you sit there with the maid Joan, so that we can keep a watch on you. Let the big boy leave the house at eleven o'clock, shining a torch and put the note-book where we said. He must then go back to the lighted

*room. You will hear a hoot like an owl when we have
collected it. The girl and the dog will then be returned.'*

This amazing and terrifying note made Anne burst
into tears and cling to Julian's arm.

'Julian! Julian! George can't have come back from
her walk with Timmy last night! She must have been
caught then – and Timmy, too. Oh, why didn't we start
hunting for her then?'

Julian looked very grim and white. He was thinking
hard. 'Yes – someone was lying in wait, I've no doubt –
and she and Timmy were kidnapped. Then the kid-
napper – or one of them – came back to the house and
shut the front door to make it seem as if George was back.
And someone has probably been hanging round all day
to find out whether we're worried about George, or just
think she's gone off for the day!'

'Who gave you the note?' said Dick, sharply, to the
scared Jo.

She trembled.

'A man,' she said.

'What sort of a man?' asked Julian.

'I don't know,' said Jo.

'Yes, you do,' said Dick. 'You *must* tell, Jo.'

Jo looked sullen. Dick shook her, and she tried to get
away. But he held her far too tightly. 'Go on – tell us
what the fellow was like,' he said.

'He was tall and had a long beard and a long nose and
brown eyes,' rattled off Jo suddenly. 'And he was dressed
in fisherman's clothes, and – he spoke foreign.'

The two boys looked sternly at her. 'I believe you're making all that up, Jo,' said Julian.

'I'm not,' said Jo sulkily. 'I'd never seen him before, so there.'

'Jo,' said Anne, taking Jo's brown little paw in hers, 'tell us truly anything you know. We're so very worried about George.' Tears sprang out of her eyes as she spoke, and she gave a little wail.

'Serve that George-girl right if she's got taken away,' said Jo fiercely. 'She was rude to me – she's crool and unkind. Serve her right, I say. I wouldn't tell you anything – not even if I knew something to tell.'

'You *do* know something,' said Dick. 'You're a bad little girl, Jo. I shan't have anything more to do with you. I felt sorry and unhappy about you, but now I don't.'

Jo looked sullen again, but her eyes were bright with tears. She turned away. 'Let me go,' she said. 'I tell you, that fellow gave me fifteen pence to bring this note to you, and that's all I know. And I'm *glad* George is in trouble. People like her deserve it, see!'

'Let her go,' said Julian wearily. 'She's like a savage little cat – all claws and spite. I thought there might be some good in her, but there isn't.'

'I thought so, too,' said Dick, letting go Jo's arm. 'I quite liked her. Well, go, Jo. We don't want you any more.'

Jo rushed to the door, wrenched it open, and fled down the hall and out of the house. There was a silence after she had gone.

'Julian,' whispered Anne. 'What are we going to do?'

Julian said nothing. He got up and went into the hall. He picked up the telephone receiver and put his ear to it, listening for the faint crackling that would tell him he was connected to the exchange. After a moment he put it back again.

'No connection,' he said. 'The wires have been cut, as the note said. And no doubt there's somebody on watch to see we don't slip out to give warning. This is all crazy. It can't be true.'

'But it is,' said Dick. 'Horribly true. Julian, do you know what notebook they want? I've no idea!'

'Nor have I,' said Julian. 'And it's impossible to go and hunt for it, because the safe has been mended and locked – and the police have the key.'

'Well, that's that, then,' said Dick. 'What are we going to do? Shall I slip out and warn the police?'

Julian considered. 'No,' he said at last. 'I think these people mean business. It would be terrible if anything happened to George. Also, you might be caught and spirited away yourself. There are people watching the house, don't forget.'

'But Julian – we can't just sit here and do nothing!' said Dick.

'I know. This will have to be thought about carefully.' said Julian. 'If only we knew where George had been taken to! We could rescue her then. But I can't see how we can find out.'

'If one of us went and hid down the bottom of the garden and waited to see whoever came to take up the notebook – we could follow the fellow and maybe he'd lead us to where George is hidden,' suggested Dick.

'You forget that we've all got to sit in the lighted front room, so it would easily be spotted if one of us were missing,' said Julian. 'Even Joan has to sit there. This is all very stupid and melodramatic.'

'Does anyone come to the house this evening? Any of the tradesmen, for instance?' asked Anne, again in a whisper. She felt as if people must be all round the house, listening and watching!

'No. Else we could give them a note,' said Julian. Then he gave the table a rap that made the others jump. 'Wait a bit! Yes, of course – the paper-boy comes! Ours is almost the last house he delivers at. But perhaps it would be risky to give him a note. Can't we think of something better?'

'Listen,' said Dick, his eyes shining. 'I've got it! I know the paper-boy. He's all right. We'll have the front door open and yank him in as soon as he appears. And I'll go out immediately, with his cap on, and his satchel of papers, whistling – jump on his bike and ride away. And none of the watchers will know I'm not the boy! I'll come back when it's dark, sneak round the garden at the bottom and hide to watch who comes for the hidden notebook – and I'll follow him!'

'Good idea, Dick!' said Julian, turning it quickly over in his mind. 'Yes – it's possible. It would be better to watch and see who comes rather than tell the police – because if these kidnappers mean business, George would certainly be in trouble once they knew we'd been able to get in touch with the police.'

'Won't the newspaper boy think it's queer?' asked Anne.

'Not very. He's a bit simple,' said Dick. 'He believes anything he's told. We'll make up something to satisfy him and give him such a good time that he'll want to keep visiting us!'

'About this notebook,' said Julian. 'We'd better get some kind of book out of one of the drawers and wrap it up with a note inside to say we hope it's the one. The fellow who comes to collect it will have to have some kind of parcel to take off with him to give to the kidnappers. It isn't likely he'd undo it and look at it – or even know if it was the right one or not.'

'Go and hunt out a book, Anne,' said Dick. 'I'll be looking out for the newspaper boy. He's not due till half-past seven, but I don't dare to risk missing him – and he may be early, you never know.'

Anne shot off to the study, thankful to have something to do. Her hands were trembling as she pulled out drawer after drawer to look for a big notebook that would do to wrap up in a parcel.

Julian went with Dick to the front door, to help him to deal with the unsuspecting newspaper boy. They stood there, patiently waiting, hearing the clock strike six o'clock, then half-past, then seven.

'Here he comes!' said Dick, suddenly. 'Now – get ready to yank him in! Hallo, Sid!'

Chapter Ten

SID'S WONDERFUL EVENING

S<small>ID</small>, the paper-boy, was most amazed to find himself yanked quickly through the front door by Julian. He was even more amazed to find his very lurid check cap snatched off his head, and his bag of papers torn from his shoulder.

' 'Ere!' he said feebly. 'What you doing?'

'It's all right, Sid,' said Julian, holding him firmly. 'Just a joke. We've got a little treat in store for you.'

Sid didn't like jokes of this sort. He struggled, but soon gave it up. Julian was big and strong and very determined. Sid turned and watched Dick stride out with his bright check cap sideways on his head, and his paper-bag over his shoulder. He gasped when he saw Dick leap on the bicycle that he, Sid, had left by the gate, and go sailing off up the lane on it.

'What's he doing?' he asked Julian, amazed. 'Funny sort of joke this.'

'I know. Hope you don't mind,' said Julian, leading him firmly into the sitting-room.

'Somebody betted him he wouldn't deliver the papers, maybe?' said Sid. 'So he's taken the bet on?'

'You're clever, you are, Sid,' said Julian, and Sid

beamed all over his round, simple face.

'Well, I hope he'll deliver them all right,' he said. 'Anyway, there's only two more, up at the farm. Yours is the last house but one that I go to. When's he coming back?'

'Soon,' said Julian. 'Will you stay and have supper with us, Sid?'

Sid's eyes nearly fell out of his head. 'Supper with you folks?' he said. 'Coo! That'd be a rare treat!'

'All right. You sit and look at these books,' said Julian, giving him two or three story books belonging to Anne. 'I'll just go and tell our cook to make a specially nice supper for you.'

Sid was all at sea about this unexpected treat, but quite willing to accept a free meal and sit down. He sat beaming on the couch, turning over the pages of a fairy-story book. Coo! What would his mother say when she heard he'd had supper at Kirrin Cottage? She wouldn't half be surprised, thought Sid.

And now Julian had to tackle Joan, and get her to join in their little plot. He went into the kitchen and shut the door. He looked so grave that Joan was startled.

'What's the matter?' she said.

Julian told her. He told her about the kidnapping of George, and the strange note. He gave it to her to read. She sat down, her knees beginning to shake.

'It's the kind of thing you read in the papers, Master Julian,' she said, in rather a shaky voice. 'But it's queer when it happens to *you*! I don't like it – that's flat, I don't.'

'Nor do we,' said Julian, and went on to tell Joan all they had arranged to do. She smiled a watery smile when he told her how Dick had gone off as the paper-boy in order to watch who took the notebook that night, and described how surprised Sid was.

'That Sid!' she said. 'We'll never hear the last of it, down in the village – him being invited here to supper. He's simple, that boy, but there's no harm in him.

'I'll get him a fine supper, don't you worry. And I'll come and sit with you tonight in the lighted room – we'll play a card game, see? One that Sid knows – he's never got much beyond Snap and Happy Families.'

'That's a very good idea,' said Julian, who had been wondering how in the world they could amuse Sid all the evening. 'We'll play Snap – and let him win!'

Sid was quite overcome at his wonderful evening. First there was what he called a 'smasher of a supper,' with ham and eggs and chip potatoes followed by jam tarts and a big chocolate mould, of which Sid ate about three-quarters.

'I'm partial to chocolate mould,' he explained to Anne. 'Joan knows that – she knows I'm partial to anything in the chocolate line. She's friendly with my Mum, so she knows. The things I'm partial to I like very much, see?'

Anne giggled and agreed. She was enjoying Sid, although she was very worried and anxious. But Sid was so comical. He didn't mean to be. He was just enjoying himself hugely, and he said so every other minute.

In fact, he was really a very nice guest to have. It wasn't everybody who could welcome everything with so

much gusto and say how wonderful it was half a dozen
times on end.

He went out to the kitchen after supper and offered to
wash up for Joan. 'I always do it for Mum,' he said. 'I
won't break a thing.' So he did the washing up and Anne
did the drying. Julian thought it was a good thing to give
her as much to do as possible, to stop her worrying.

Sid looked a bit taken-aback when he was asked to play
games later on. 'Well – I dunno,' he said. 'I'm not much
good at games. I did try to learn draughts, but all that
jumping over one another got me muddled. If I want to
jump over things I'll play leap-frog and do the thing
properly.'

'Well – we did think of playing Snap,' said Julian,
and Sid brightened up at once.

'Snap! That's right up my street!' he said. And so it
was. His habit of shouting snap and collecting all the
cards at the same moment as his shout, led to his winning
quite a lot of games. He was delighted.

'This is a smasher of an evening,' he kept saying.
'Don't know when I've enjoyed myself so much. Wonder
how that brother of yours is getting on – hope he brings
my bike back all right.'

'Oh, he will,' said Julian, dealing out the cards for the
sixth game of Snap. They were all in the lighted sitting-
room now, sitting round a table in the window – Julian,
Joan, Anne and Sid. Anyone watching would see them
clearly – and would certainly not guess that Sid, the
fourth one, was the paper-boy and not Dick.

At eleven o'clock Julian left to put the parcel that Anne

had carefully wrapped up under the stone at the bottom of the garden. She had found a big notebook she thought would do, one that didn't seem at all important, and had wrapped it in paper and tied it with string. Julian had slipped a note inside.

Here is the notebook. Please release our cousin at once. You will get into serious trouble if you hold her any longer.

He slipped down the garden and shone his torch on the crazy paving there. When he came to the last stone he found that it had been loosened. He lifted it up easily and put the parcel into a hollow that seemed to have been prepared ready for it. He took a cautious look round, wondering if Dick was hidden anywhere about, but could see no one.

He was back in the lighted sitting-room in under two minutes, yelling 'Snap' with the others. He played stupidly, partly because he wanted the delighted Sid to win and partly because he was wondering about Dick. Was he all right?

An outbreak of owls hooting loudly made them all jump. Julian glanced at Joan and Anne, and they nodded. They guessed that it was the signal to tell them that the parcel had been found and collected. Now they could get rid of Sid, and wait for Dick.

Joan disappeared and came back with cups of chocolate and some buns. Sid's eyes gleamed. Talk about an evening!

Another hour was spent in eating and drinking and hearing Sid relate details of all the most exciting games of Snap he had ever played. He then went on to talk of Happy Families and seemed inclined to stay a bit longer and have a game at that.

'Your Mum will be getting worried about you,' said Julian, looking at the clock. 'It's very late.'

'Where's my bike?' said Sid, realizing with sorrow that his 'smasher of an evening' was now over. 'Hasn't that brother of yours come back yet? Well, you tell him to leave it at my house in time for my paper-round tomorrow morning. And my cap, too. That's my Special Cap, that is. I'm very partial to that cap – it's a bit of a smasher.'

'It certainly is,' agreed Julian, who was now feeling very tired. 'Now listen, Sid. It's very late, and there may be bad folks about. If anyone speaks to you, run for your life, and don't stop till you get home.'

'Coo,' said Sid, his eyes nearly falling out of his head. 'Yes, I'll run all right.'

He shook hands solemnly with each of them and departed. He whistled loudly to keep his spirits up. The village policeman came unexpectedly round a corner on rubber soles and made him jump.

'Now then, young Sid,' said the policeman, sternly. 'What you doing out this time of night?'

Sid didn't wait to answer. He fled and when he got home there was his bicycle by the front gate, complete with checked cap and paper-bag. 'That was a bit of all right!' thought Sid.

He glanced in disappointment at the dark windows of his house. Mum was in bed and asleep. Now he would have to wait till morning to tell her of his most remarkable evening.

And now, what had happened to Dick? He had shot out of the house and sailed away on Sid's bicycle, with Sid's dazzling cap on his head. He thought he saw a movement in the hedge nearby and guessed someone was hidden there, watching. He deliberately slowed down, got off his bicycle and pretended to do something to the wheel. Let the watcher see his bag of papers and be deceived into thinking he was without any doubt the paper-boy.

He rode to the farm and delivered the two papers there, then down to the village where he left Sid's things outside his house. Then he went into the cinema for a long while – until it was dark and he could safely creep back to Kirrin Cottage.

He set off at last, going a very roundabout way indeed. He came to the back of Kirrin garden. Where should he hide? Was anyone already hidden there? If so, the game was up – and he'd be caught, too!

Chapter Eleven

DICK MAKES A CAPTURE

DICK stood and listened, holding his breath. He could
hear no sound except for the rustling of the trees around,
and the sudden squeak of a field-mouse. It was a dark
night and cloudy. Was there anyone hidden nearby, or
could he find a hiding-place in safety and wait?

He thought for a few minutes, and decided that there
wouldn't be anyone watching the back of the house now
that it was dark. Julian and the others would be in full
view of any watcher at the front, seated as they were in
the lighted sitting-room – there would be no need for
anyone to watch the back.

He debated where to hide and then made a quick
decision. 'I'll climb a tree,' he thought. 'What about that
one just near the crazy paving path? If the clouds clear
away I could perhaps catch a glimpse of what the man's
like who comes to collect the parcel. Then I'll shin quietly
down the tree and stalk him.'

He climbed up into an oak tree that spread its broad
branches over the path. He wriggled down in a comfortable fork and set himself to wait patiently.

What time had that note said? Eleven o'clock. Yes –

Julian was to go down at eleven o'clock and put the parcel under the stone. He listened for the church clock to strike. If the wind was in the right direction he would hear it clearly.

It struck just then. Half-past ten. Half an hour to wait. The waiting was the worst part. Dick put his hand into his pocket and brought out a bar of half-melted chocolate. He began to nibble it very gently, to make it last a long time.

The church clock struck a quarter to eleven. Dick finished the chocolate, and wondered if Julian would soon be along. Just as the clock began to chime the hour at eleven, the kitchen door opened and Dick saw Julian outlined in the opening. He had the parcel under his arm.

He saw Julian go swiftly down the path and sensed him looking all about. He dared not give the slightest hint to him that he was just above his head!

He heard Julian scrabble about in the path, and then drop the big stone back into its place. He watched the light of Julian's torch bobbing back up the path to the kitchen door. Then the door shut with a bang.

And now Dick could hardly breathe! Who would come for the parcel? He listened, stiff with excitement. The wind blew and a leaf rustled against the back of his neck making him jump. It felt as if a finger had touched him.

Five minutes went by and nobody came. Then he heard the slightest sound. Was that somebody crawling through the hedge? Dick strained his eyes but could only make out a deeper shadow that seemed to be moving. Then he could most distinctly hear somebody breathing hard as they tugged at the heavy stone! The parcel was being collected as arranged!

The stone plopped back. A shadow crept over to the hedge again. Whoever had the parcel was now going off with it.

Dick dropped quietly down. He had rubber shoes on and made no noise. He slipped through a big gap in the hedge nearby and stood straining his eyes to find the man he wanted to follow. Ah – there was a shadow moving steadily down the field-path to the stile. Dick followed, keeping close to the hedge.

He kept well behind the moving shadow till it reached the stile, got over it and went into the lane beyond. When it got there it stopped, and a perfect fusillade of loud owl-hoots came to Dick's startled ears.

Of course! That was the signal that the parcel had been collected. Dick admired the excellent imitation of a little owl's loud, excited hooting.

The shadow stopped hooting and went on again. It obviously did not suspect that it might be followed and, although it moved quietly, it did not attempt to keep under cover. Down the lane it went and into a field.

Dick was about to follow when he heard the sound of voices. They were very low, and he couldn't hear a word. He crouched in the shadow of the gate, which was swung right back, leaving an entry into the field.

A loud noise made him jump. Then a brilliant light dazzled him and he felt glad he could duck down behind the gate. There was a car in the field. A car that had just started up its engine and switched on its lights. It was going, moving slowly down to the gate!

Dick tried his hardest to see who was in the car. He could make out only one man, and he was driving. It didn't seem as if anyone else was in the car at all. Where was the other fellow, then – the one who must have collected the parcel and given it to the man in the car? Had he been left behind? If so, Dick had better be careful!

The car was soon out in the lane. It gained speed and then Dick heard it roaring off in the distance. He couldn't stalk a car, that was certain! He held his breath, listening for some movement of the other man who, he felt certain, was still there.

He heard a sniff and crouched lower still. Then a shadow passed quickly through the gate, turned back in the direction of Kirrin Cottage and was lost in the darkness of the lane.

In a trice Dick was after it again. At least he could track down *this* fellow! He must be going somewhere!

Down the lane to the stile. Over the stile and into the field. Across the field and back at the hedge that grew at the bottom of Kirrin Cottage.

Why was this fellow going back there? Dick was puzzled. He heard the shadow creeping through the hedge and he followed. He watched it go silently up the path and peer in at a darkened window.

'Going to get into the house again and ransack it, I suppose!' thought Dick, in a rage. He considered the shadowy figure by the window. It didn't look big. It must be a small man – one that Dick could tackle and bring to the ground. He could yell loudly for Julian, and maybe he could hold the fellow down till Julian came.

'And then perhaps *we* could do a little kidnapping, and a little bargaining, too,' thought Dick grimly. 'If *they* hold George as a hostage, we'll hold one of them, too! Tit for tat!'

He waited till the shadow left the window, and then he pounced. His victim went down at once with a yell.

Dick was surprised how small he was – but how he fought! He bit and scratched and heaved and kicked, and the two of them rolled over and over and over, breaking down Michaelmas daisies in the beds, and scratching legs and arms and faces on rose bushes. Dick yelled for Julian all the time.

'Julian! JULIAN! Help! JULIAN!'

Julian heard. He tore out at once. 'Dick, Dick, where are you? What is it?'

He flashed his torch towards the shouting and saw

Dick rolling on top of somebody. He ran to help at once, throwing his torch on the grass so that both hands were free.

It wasn't long before they had the struggling figure firmly in their grasp and dragged it, wailing, to the back door. Dick recognized that wailing voice! Good gracious – no, it couldn't be – it couldn't be Jo!

But it was! When they dragged her inside she collapsed completely, sobbing and wailing, rubbing her scratched and bruised legs, calling both boys all the names she could think of. Anne and Joan looked on in complete amazement. *Now* what had happened?

'Put her upstairs,' said Julian. 'Get her to bed. She's in a awful state now. So am I! I wouldn't have lammed her like that if I'd known it was only Jo.'

'I never guessed,' said Dick, wiping his filthy face with his handkerchief. 'My word, what a wild-cat! See how she's bitten me!'

'I didn't know it was you, Dick; I didn't know,' wailed Jo. 'You pounced on me, and I fought back. I wouldn't have bitten you like that.'

'You're a savage, deceitful, double-dealing little wild-cat,' said Dick, looking at his bites and scratches. 'Pretending you know nothing about the man who gave you that note – and all the time you're in with that crooked lot of thieves and kidnappers, whoever they are.'

'I'm not in with them,' wept Jo.

'Don't tell lies,' shouted Dick, in a fury. 'I was up in a tree when you came and took that parcel from under the stone – yes, and I followed you right to that car – and followed you back again! You came back here to steal again, I suppose?'

Jo gulped. 'No, I didn't.'

'You did! You'll be handed over to the police to-morrow,' said Dick, still furious.

'I *didn't* come back to steal. I came back for something else,' insisted Jo, her eyes peering through her tangled hair like a frightened animal's.

'Ho! So you say! And what did you come back for? To find another dog to dope?' jeered Dick.

'No,' said Jo, miserably. 'I came back to tell you I'd take you to where George was, if you wouldn't tell on me. My Dad would half kill me if he thought I'd split on him. I know I took the parcel – I had to. I didn't know what it was or anything. I took it to the place I was told to. Jake told me. And then I came back to tell you all I could. And you set on me like that.'

Four pairs of eyes bored into Jo, and she covered her face. Dick took her hands away and made her look at him.

'Look here,' he said, 'this matters a lot to us, whether you are speaking the truth or not. Do you know where George is?'

Jo nodded.

'And will you take us there?' said Julian, his voice stern and cold.

Jo nodded again. 'Yes I will. You've been mean to me, but I'll show you I'm not as bad as you make out. I'll take you to George.'

Chapter Twelve

JO BEGINS TO TALK

THE hall clock suddenly struck loudly. DONG!'

'One o'clock,' said Joan. 'One o'clock in the morning! Master Julian, we can't do any more tonight. This gipsy child here, she's not fit to take you trapesing out anywhere else. She's done for – she can hardly stand.'

'Yes, you're right Joan,' said Julian, at once giving up the idea of going out to find George that night. 'We'll have to wait till tomorrow. It's a pity the telphone wires are cut. I do really think we ought to let the police know something about all this.'

Jo looked up at once. 'Then I won't tell you where George is,' she said. 'Do you know what the police will do to me if they get hold of me? They'll put me into a Home for Bad Girls, and I'll never get out again – because I *am* a bad girl and I do bad things. I've never had a chance.'

'Every one gets a chance sooner or later,' said Julian gently. 'You'll get yours, Jo – but see you take it when it comes. All right – we'll leave the police out of it if you promise you'll take us to where George is. That's a bargain.'

Jo understood bargains. She nodded. Joan pulled her to her feet and half led, half carried her upstairs.

'There's a couch in my room,' she told Julian. 'She can bed down there for the night – but late or not she's going to have a bath first. She smells like something the dog brought in!'

In half an hour's time Jo was tucked up on the couch in Joan's room, perfectly clean, though marked with scratches and bruises from top to toe, hair washed, dried, and brushed so that it stood up in wiry curls like George's. A basin of steaming bread and milk was on a tray in front of her.

Joan went to the landing and called across to Julian's room. 'Master Julian! Jo's in bed. She wants to say something to you and Master Dick.'

Dick and Julian put on dressing-gowns and went into Joan's neat room. They hardly recognized Jo. She was wearing one of Anne's old nightgowns and looked very clean and childish and somehow pathetic.

Jo looked at them and gave them a very small smile. 'What do you want to say to us?' asked Julian.

'I've got some things to tell you,' said Jo, stirring the bread round and round in the basin. 'I feel good now – good and clean and – and all that. But maybe tomorrow I'll feel like I always do – and then I wouldn't tell you everything. So I'd better tell you now.'

'Go ahead,' said Julian.

'Well, I let the men into your house here, the night they came,' said Jo. Julian and Dick stared in astonishment. Jo went on stirring her bread round and round.

'It's true,' she said. 'I got in at that tiny window that was left unfastened, and then I went to the back door and opened it and let the men in. They did make a mess of that room, didn't they? I watched them. They took a lot of papers.'

'You couldn't possibly squeeze through that window,' said Dick at once.

'Well, I did,' said Jo. 'I've – I've squeezed through quite a lot of little windows. I know how to wriggle, you see. I can't get through such tiny ones as I used to, because I keep on growing. But yours was easy.'

'Phew!' said Julian, and let out a long breath. He hardly knew what to say. 'Well, go on. I suppose when the men had finished you locked and bolted the kitchen door after them and then squeezed out of the pantry window again?'

'Yes,' said Jo, and put a piece of milky bread into her mouth.

'What about Timmy? Who doped him so that he slept all that night?' demanded Dick.

'I did,' said Jo. 'That was easy, too.'

Both boys were speechless. To think that Jo did that, too! The wicked little misery!

'I made friends with Timmy on the beach, don't you remember?' said Jo. 'George was cross about it. I like dogs. We always had dozens till Mum died, and they'd do anything I told them. Dad told me what I was to do – make friends with Timmy so that I could meet him that night and give him meat with something in it.'

'I see. And it was very, very easy, because we sent Timmy out alone – straight into your hands,' said Dick bitterly.

'Yes. He came to me at once, he was glad to see me. I took him quite a long walk, letting him sniff the meat I'd got. When I gave it to him, he swallowed it all at once with hardly a chew!'

'And slept all night long so that your precious friends could break into the house,' said Julian. 'All I can say is that you are a hardened little rogue. Aren't you ashamed of anything?'

'I don't know,' said Jo, who wasn't really quite certain what feeling ashamed meant. 'Shall I stop telling you things?'

'No. For goodness' sake go on,' said Dick, hastily. 'Had you anything to do with George's kidnapping?'

'I just had to hoot like an owl when she and Timmy were coming,' said Jo. 'They were ready for her with a sack to put over her head – and they were going to bang Timmy on the head with a stick to knock him out – then put him into a sack too. That's what I heard them say. But I didn't see them. I had to creep back here and shut the front door, so that if nobody missed George till morning they'd just think she'd gone out early somewhere.'

'Which is what we did think,' groaned Dick. 'What mutts we are! The only clever thing we thought of was to stalk the person who collected the parcel.'

'It was only me, though,' said Jo. 'And anyway, I was coming back to tell you I would take you to George. Not because I like her – I don't. I think she's rude and horrible. I'd like her to stay kidnapped for years!'

'What a nice, kind nature!' said Julian to Dick, helplessly. 'What can you do with a kid like this?' He turned

to Jo again. 'Seeing that you wish George would stay kidnapped for years, what made you decide to come and
tell us where to find her?' he asked, puzzled.

'Well, I don't like George – but I do like *him*!' said
Jo, pointing with her spoon at Dick. 'He was nice to me,
so I wanted to be nice back. I don't often feel like that,'
she added hurriedly, as if being kind was some sort of
weakness not really to be admired. 'I wanted him to go on
liking me,' she said.

Dick looked at her. 'I shall like you if you take us to
George,' he said. 'Not unless. If you deceive us, I shall
think you're like one of those sour damson stones – only
fit to be spat out as far away as possible.'

'I'll take you tomorrow,' said Jo.

'Where *is* George?' asked Julian, bluntly, thinking it
would be as well to know now, in case Jo changed her
mind by the morning, and became her wicked little self
again.

Jo hesitated. She looked at Dick. 'It would be very nice
of you to tell us,' said Dick, in a kind voice. Jo loved a
bit of kindness and couldn't resist this.

'Well,' she whispered, 'you know I told you my Dad
had gone off and left me to Jake. Dad didn't tell me why –
but Jake did. He shut George and Timmy into our
caravan, harnessed Blackie the horse, and drove away in
the night with them both. And I guess I know where he's
gone – where he always goes when he wants to hide.'

'Where?' asked Julian, feeling so astounded at these
extraordinary revelations that he really began to wonder
if he was dreaming.

'In the middle of Ravens Wood,' said Jo. 'You don't know where that is, but I do. I'll take you tomorrow. I can't tell you any more now.' She began to spoon up her bread and milk very fast indeed, watching the boys through her long eyelashes.

Dick considered her. He felt pretty sure she had told them the truth, though he was equally certain she would have told lies if she could have got more by doing so.

He thought her a bad, cold-blooded, savage little monkey, but he pitied her, and admired her unwillingly for her courage.

He caught sight of her bruises and grazes, and bit his lip as he remembered how he had pounced on her and pummelled her, giving her back kick for kick and blow for blow – he hadn't guessed for one moment it was Jo.

'I'm sorry I hurt you so,' he said. 'You know I didn't mean to. It was a mistake.'

Jo looked at him as a slave might look at a king. 'I don't mind,' she said. 'I'd do anything for you, straight I would. You're kind.'

Joan knocked impatiently at the door. 'Aren't you ready yet, you boys?' she said. 'I want to come to bed. Tell Jo to stop talking, and you come on out too, and go to bed.'

The boys opened the door. Joan took one look at their solemn faces and guessed that what Jo had told them was important. She took the empty basin from the girl's hands and pushed her down on the couch.

'Now you go straight off to sleep – and mind, if I hear any hanky-panky from you in the night I'll get up and give you such a spanking you won't be able to sit down for a month of Sundays,' she said roughly, but not unkindly.

Jo grinned. She understood that kind of talk. She snuggled down into the rugs, marvelling at the warmth and softness. She was already half-asleep. Joan got into bed and switched off her light.

'Two o'clock in the morning!' she muttered as she heard the hall clock strike. 'Such goings-on! I'll never wake up in time to tell the milkman I want more milk.'

Soon only Julian was awake. He worried about whether he was doing right or not. Poor George – was she safe? Would that scamp of a Jo really lead them to the caravan next day – or might she lead them right into the lion's mouth, and get them all captured? Julian simply didn't know.

Chapter Thirteen

OFF TO FIND GEORGE

JOAN was the only one in the household who woke up reasonably early the next morning – but even she was too late to catch the milkman. She scurried downstairs at half-past seven, an hour later than usual, tying up her apron as she went.

'Half-past seven – what a time to wake up!' she muttered, as she began to do the kitchen fire. She thought of all the happenings of the night before – the queer evening with young Sid, Dick's capture of Jo – and Jo's extraordinary tale. She had had a look at Jo before she went down, half expecting that lively young rogue to have disappeared in the night.

But Jo was curled up like a kitten, her brown cheek on her brown paw, her hair, unusually bright and tidy, falling over her tightly-shut eyes. She didn't even stir when Joan scurried about the bedroom, washing and dressing.

The others were fast asleep, too. Julian woke first, but not till eight o'clock. He remembered immediately all that had happened, and jumped out of bed at once.

He went to Joan's room. He could hear Joan downstairs talking to herself as usual. He peeped round the open door of her bedroom. Thank goodness – Jo was still there.

95

He went and shook her gently. She wriggled away, turned over and buried her face in the pillow. Julian shook her more vigorously. He meant to get her up and make her take them to where George was as soon as possible!

Most miraculously everyone was down at half-past eight, eating porridge and looking rather subdued. Jo had hers in the kitchen, and the others could hear Joan scolding her for her manners.

'Have you got to stuff yourself like that, as if the dog's going to come and lick your plate before you've finished? And who told you to stick your fingers into the syrup and lick them? I've eyes in the back of my head, so just you be careful what you're doing!'

Jo liked Joan. She knew where she was with her. If she kept on Joan's right side and did what she was told, Joan would feed her well and not interfere too much – but if she didn't, then she could expect something else she understood very well indeed – scoldings and a sharp slap. Joan was good-hearted but impatient, and no child was ever afraid of her. Jo followed her about like a little dog when she had finished her breakfast.

Julian came out into the kitchen at nine o'clock. 'Where's Jo?' he said. 'Oh, there you are. Now, what about taking us to where you father's caravan is? You're sure you know the way?'

Jo laughed scornfully. 'Course I do! I know everywhere round here for miles.'

'Right,' said Julian, and he produced a map, which he spread out on the kitchen table. He put a finger on one spot. 'That's Kirrin,' he said. 'And here's a place called

Ravens Wood. Is that the place you mean? How do you
propose to get there – by this road, or that one?'

Jo looked at the map. It meant nothing to her at all.
She gazed vaguely at the spot that Julian had pointed to.

'Well?' said Julian, impatiently. 'Is that the Ravens
Wood you mean?'

'I don't know,' said Jo, helplessly. 'The one I mean is
a real wood – I don't know anything about yours on this
map.'

Joan gave a little snort. 'Master Julian, maps are
wasted on her. I don't expect she's ever seen one in her
life! She can't even read!'

'*Can't* she?' said Julian, amazed. 'Then she can't write
either.' He looked questioningly at Jo.

She shook her head. 'Mum tried to learn me to read,'
she said, 'but Mum wasn't very good herself. What's the
good of reading, anyway? Won't help you to trap rabbits
or catch fish for your dinner, will it?'

'No. It's used for other things,' said Julian, amused.
'Well – maps are no good to *you*, I can see.' He rolled his
map up, looking thoughtful. It was very difficult to know
exactly how to deal with a person like Jo, who knew so
little of some things and so much of others.

'She'll know the way all right,' said Joan, scraping
out a saucepan. 'They're like dogs, these folk – they can
smell out any road they want.'

'*Do* you smell out your way like a dog?' asked Anne,
curiously. She had come in to see what was going on, and
was quite willing to believe that Jo really could smell her
way here and there, as Timmy did.

'No, I don't,' said Jo. 'I just know the way I have to
go. And I don't go by the roads, either! They take too
long to get to a place. I take the shortest way, see?'

'How do you know it's the shortest way?' asked Anne.

Jo shrugged her thin shoulders. All this was very boring
to her.

'Where's that other boy?' she said. 'Isn't he coming? I want to see him.'

'She's just crazy on Dick,' said Joan, taking up another saucepan. 'Here he is – now you can go and lick his boots if you want to, young Jo!'

'Hallo, Jo!' said Dick, with one of his amiable grins. 'Ready to take us travelling?'

'Better go at night,' said Jo, staring at Dick.

'Oh, no!' said Dick. 'We're going *now*. We're not going to be put off like that. *Now*, Jo, now!'

'If my Dad sees us coming he'll be mad,' said Jo obstinately.

'Very well,' said Dick, looking at Julian. 'We'll go by ourselves. We've found Ravens Wood on the map. We can easily get there.'

'Pooh,' said Jo, rudely. 'You can get there all right – but it's a big place, Ravens Wood is – and nobody but me and Dad knows where we hide the caravan there. And if Dad wants to keep George quite safe, he'll take her to our hidey-hole in the middle of the wood, see? You can't go without me.'

'Right. Then we'll get the police to take us,' said Julian, quite cheerfully. 'They will help us to comb the wood from end to end. We'll soon find George.'

'No!' cried Jo, in alarm. 'You said you wouldn't! You promised!'

'*You* made a promise too,' said Julian. 'It was a bargain. But I see you're not really to be trusted. I'll just get on my bike and ride down to the police-station.'

But before he could go out of the room Jo flung herself

on him and clung to his arm like a cat. 'No, no! I'll take you. I'll keep my promise! But it *would* be best to go at night!'

'I'm not putting things off any more,' said Julian, shaking Jo off his arm. 'If you mean what you say, you'll come with us now. Make up your mind.'

'I'll come,' said Jo.

'Hadn't we better give her another pair of shorts or something?' said Anne, suddenly seeing a tremendous hole in Jo's grubby shorts. 'She can't go out like that. And look at her awful jersey. It's full of holes.'

The boys looked at it. 'She'd smell a bit better if she had clean clothes,' said Joan. 'There's that old pair of shorts I washed for George last week, and mended up. Jo could have those. And there's an old shirt of hers she could have, too.'

In five minutes' time Jo was proudly wearing a pair of perfectly clean, much-mended shorts of George's, and a shirt like the one Anne had on. Anne looked at her and laughed.

'Now she's more like George than ever! They might be sisters.'

'Brothers, you mean,' said Dick. 'George and Jo – what a pair!'

Jo scowled. She didn't like George, and she didn't want to look like her.

'She's even got George's scowl!' said Anne. Jo turned her back at once, and Joan then got the benefit of the scowl.

'My word, what an ugly creature you are!' said Joan.

'You be careful the wind doesn't change – you might get your face stuck like that!'

'Oh, come on,' said Julian, impatiently. 'Jo! Do you hear me? Come along now and take us to Ravens Wood.'

'Jake might see us,' said Jo, sulkily. She was determined to put off going as long as she could.

'Yes, he might,' said Julian, who hadn't thought of that. 'Well – you go on a long way ahead, and we'll follow. We won't let Jake know you're leading us anywhere.'

At last they set off. Joan had packed them up a meal in case they wanted one. Julian slipped the package into a bag and slid it over his shoulder.

Jo slipped out the back way, went down to the bottom of the garden and made her way out to the lane through a little thicket. The others went out of the front gate and walked up the lane slowly, watching for Jo to appear.

'There she is,' said Julian. 'Come on. We must keep the little wretch in sight. I wouldn't be surprised if she gave us the slip even now!'

Jo danced on in front, a good way ahead. She took no notice of the others behind, and they followed steadily.

Then suddenly something happened. A dark figure strode out from the hedge, stood in front of Jo, and said something to her. She screamed and tried to dodge away. But the man caught hold of her and firmly pulled her into the hedge.

'It was Jake!' said Dick. 'I'm sure it was Jake. He was watching out for her. *Now* what do we do?'

Chapter Fourteen

SIMMY'S CARAVAN

THEY all hurried up to the place where Jake had caught hold of Jo. There was absolutely nothing to be seen except a few broken twigs in the hedge there. No Jake, no Jo. There was not a sound to be heard, either. Not a scream from Jo, not a shout from Jake. It was as if both had faded into the hedge and disappeared.

Dick squeezed through the hedge and into the field beyond. Nobody was there either, except a few cows who looked at him in surprise, their tails whisking.

'There's a little copse at the end of the field,' called back Dick. 'I bet they're there. I'll go and see.'

He ran across the field to the copse. But there was nobody there either. Beyond the copse was a row of huddled-up cottages. Dick looked along the untidy row, exasperated.

'I suppose Jake's taken her to one of those,' he thought, angrily. 'Probably lives there! Well, he won't let her go, that's certain. He most likely guesses that she's in with us now. Poor Jo!'

He went back to the others and they had a low-voiced conference in the lane. 'Let's tell the police now,' begged Anne.

'No. Let's go to Ravens Wood ourselves,' said Dick. 'We know where it is. We wouldn't be able to go the way Jo would have taken us – but at least we can go by the map.'

'Yes. I think we will,' said Julian. 'Come on, then. Quick march!'

They went on up the lane, took a field path and came out eventually on to a road. A bus passed them in the opposite direction to which they were going.

'When we come to a bus stop we'll find out if one goes anywhere near Raven's Wood,' said Julian. 'It would save a lot of time if we caught a bus. We'd be there long before Jake, if he thinks of going to warn Jo's father we're on the way! I bet Jo will tell him. You might as well trust a snake as that slippery little thing.'

'I hate Jo!' said Anne, almost in tears. 'I don't trust her a bit. Do you, Dick?'

'I don't know,' said Dick. 'I can't make up my mind. She hasn't really proved whether she's trustable or not yet. Anyway, she came back to tell us all she knew last night, didn't she?'

'I don't believe she *did* come back for that,' said Anne obstinately. 'I believe she was coming back to pry and snoop.'

'You may be right,' said Dick. 'Look, here's a bus-stop – and a time-table!'

A bus did apparently go quite near Ravens Wood, and was due in five minutes' time. They sat down on the bus-stop seat and waited. The bus was punctual and came rumbling down the road, full of women going to Ravens

Market. They all seemed very plump women and had enormous baskets, so it was difficult to squeeze inside.

Everyone got out at Ravens Market. Julian asked his way to Ravens Wood. 'There it is,' said the conductor, pointing down the hill to where trees grew thickly in the valley. 'It's a big place. Don't get lost! And look out for the gipsies. There's usually hordes of them there!'

'Thanks,' said Julian, and the three of them set off down the hill into the valley. They came to the wood.

'It's a proper wood,' said Anne. 'Nothing but trees and trees. I should think it gets very thick in the middle – like a forest.'

They came to a clearing where there was a little gipsy camp. Three rather dirty-looking caravans stood together, and a crowd of brown gipsy children were playing some sort of a game with a rope. Julian took a quick look at the caravans. All had their doors open.

'No George here,' he said in a low voice to the others. 'I wish I knew exactly where to go! I suppose if we follow this broad pathway it would be best. After all, Jo's caravan must have a fairly broad way to go on.'

'Can't we ask if anyone knows if Jo's caravan is anywhere about?' said Anne.

'We don't know her father's name,' said Julian.

'But we could say it's a caravan drawn by a horse called Blackie, and that a girl called Jo lives in it with her father,' said Anne.

'Yes. I'd forgotten the horse,' said Julian. He went up to an old woman who was stirring something in a black pot over a fire of sticks. Julian thought she looked very like a witch. She peered up at him through tangled grey hair.

'Can you tell me if there's a caravan in the wood drawn by a horse called Blackie?' he asked politely. 'A girl called Jo lives in it with her father. We want to see her.'

The old woman blinked. She took an iron spoon out of the pot and waved it to the right.

'Simmy's gone down-away there,' she said. 'I never saw Jo this time – but the caravan door was shut so maybe she was inside. What you want with Jo?'

'Oh – only just to see her,' said Julian, quite unable to think up a good reason for going to visit a gipsy-child on the spur of the moment. 'Is Simmy her father?'

The old woman nodded and began to stir her pot again. Julian went back to the others.

'This way,' he said, and they went down the rutted path. It was just wide enough for a caravan to go down. Anne looked up. Tree branches waved overhead.

'I should think they brush against the roof of a caravan all the time,' she said. 'What a queer life to live – in a little caravan day in and day out, hiding yourself away in woods and fields!'

They walked on down the path, which wound about through the trees, following the clear spaces. Sometimes the trees were so close together that it seemed impossible for a caravan to go between. But the wheel-ruts showed that caravans did go down the path.

After a time the wood became thicker, and the sunlight could hardly pierce through the branches. Still the path went on, but now it seemed as if only one set of wheel-ruts was marked on it. They were probably the wheels of Simmy's caravan.

Here and there a tree was shorn of one of its branches, and a bush uprooted and thrown to one side.

'Simmy meant to go deep into the wood last time he came,' said Julian, pointing to where a bush lay dying by the side of the path. 'He's cleared the way here and there. Actually we aren't on a proper path any longer – we're only following wheel-ruts.'

It was true. The path had faded out. They were now

in a thick part of the wood, with only the ruts of the caravan wheels to guide them.

They fell silent. The wood was very quiet. There were no birds singing, and the branches of the trees were so thick that there was a kind of green twilight round them.

'I wish we had Timmy with us,' half-whispered Anne at last.

Julian nodded. He had been wishing that a long time. He was also wishing he hadn't brought Anne – but when they had started out, they had Jo with them to guide them, and warn them of any danger. Now they hadn't.

'I think we'd better go very cautiously,' he said, in a low voice. 'We may come on the caravan unexpectedly. We don't want Simmy to hear us and lie in wait.'

'I'll go a little way in front and warn you if I hear or see anything,' said Dick. Julian nodded to him and he went on ahead, peering round the trees when he came to any curve in the wheel-rut path. Julian began to think of what they would do when they reached the caravan. He was pretty certain that both George and Timmy would be found locked up securely inside.

'If we can undo the door and let them out, Timmy will do the rest,' he thought. 'He's as good as three policemen! Yes – that's the best plan.'

Dick suddenly stopped and lifted up his hand in warning. He peered round the bole of a big tree, and then turned and nodded excitedly.

'He's found the caravan!' said Anne, and her heart began its usual thump-thump-thump of excitement.

'Stay here,' said Julian to Anne, and went on quietly

to join Dick. Anne crept under a bush. She didn't like this dark, silent wood, with the green light all round. She peered out, watching the boys.

Dick had suddenly seen the caravan. It was small, badly needed painting, and appeared quite deserted. No fire burned outside. No Simmy was sitting anywhere about. Not even Blackie the horse was to be seen.

The boys watched intently for a few minutes, not daring to move or speak. There was absolutely no sound or movement from the tiny clearing in which the caravan stood.

Windows and doors were shut. The shafts rested crookedly on the ground. The whole place seemed deserted.

'Dick,' whispered Julian at last, 'Simmy doesn't seem to be about. This is our chance! We'll creep over to the caravan and look into the window. We'll attract George's attention, and get her out as soon as we can. Timmy, too.'

'Funny he doesn't bark,' said Dick, also in a whisper. 'I suppose he can't have heard us. Well – shall we get over to the caravan now?'

They ran quietly to the little caravan, and Julian peered through the dirty window. It was too dark inside to see anything at all.

'George!' he whispered. 'George! Are you there?'

Chapter Fifteen

ANNE DOESN'T LIKE ADVENTURES

THERE was no answer from inside the caravan. Perhaps George was asleep – or drugged! And Timmy, too. Julian's heart sank. It would be dreadful if George had been ill-treated. He tried to peer inside the window again, but what with the darkness of the wood and the dirt on the pane, it really was impossible to see inside.

'Shall we bang on the door?' asked Dick.

'No. That would only bring Simmy if he's anywhere about – and if George is inside and awake, our voices would have attracted her attention,' said Julian.

They went quietly round the carvan to the door at the back. It had no key in the lock. Julian frowned.

Simmy must have got the key with him. That would mean breaking down the door and making a noise. He went up the few steps and pushed at the door. It seemed very solid indeed. How could he break it down, anyway? He had no tools, and it didn't look as if kicking and shoving would burst it in.

He knocked gently on the door – rap-rap-rap. Not a movement from inside. It seemed very strange. He tried the round handle, and it turned easily.

It not only turned easily – but the door opened! 'Dick! It's not locked!' said Julian, forgetting to whisper in his surprise. He went inside the dark caravan, hardly hoping now to see George or Timmy.

Dick pushed in after him. There was a nasty sour smell and it was very untidy. Nobody was there. It was quite empty, as Julian had feared.

He groaned. 'All this way for nothing. They've taken George somewhere else. We're done, now, Dick – we haven't a clue where to go next.'

Dick fished his torch out of his pocket. He flashed it over the untidy jumble of things in the caravan, looking for some sign that George had been there. But there was nothing at all that he could see to show him that either Timmy or George had been there.

'It's quite likely that Jo made the whole story up about her father taking George away,' he groaned. 'It doesn't look as if they've been here at all.'

His torch flashed on to the wooden wall of the caravan, and Dick saw something that arrested his attention. Somebody had written something on the wall!

He looked more closely. 'Julian! Isn't that George's writing? Look! What's written there?'

Both boys bent towards the dirty wall. 'Red Tower, Red Tower, Red Tower,' was written again and again, in very small writing.

'Red Tower!' said Dick. 'What does that mean? *Is* it George's writing?'

'Yes, I think so,' said Julian. 'But why should she keep writing that? Do you suppose that's where they have taken her to? She might have heard them saying something and scribbled it down quickly – just in *case* we found the caravan and examined it. Red Tower! It sounds queer.'

'It must be a house with a red tower, I should think,' said Dick. 'Well – we'd better get back and tell the police now – and they'll have to hunt for a red tower somewhere.'

Bitterly disappointed the boys went back to Anne. She scrambled out from under her bush as they came.

'George is not there,' said Dick. 'She's gone. But she *has* been there – we saw some scribbled writing on the wall of the caravan inside.'

'How do you know it's hers?' said Anne.

'Well, she's written "Red Tower" ever so many times, and the R's and the T's are just like hers,' said Dick. 'We think she must have heard someone talking and say they were taking her to Red Tower, wherever it is. We're going straight back to the police now. I wish we hadn't trusted Jo. We've wasted such a lot of time.'

'Let's have something to eat,' said Julian. 'We won't sit down. We'll eat as we go. Come on.'

But somehow nobody wanted anything to eat. Anne said she felt sick. Julian was too worried to eat, and Dick was so anxious to go that he felt he couldn't even wait to unpack sandwiches! So they started back down the path, following the wheel-ruts as before.

It suddenly grew very dark indeed, and on the leaves of the trees heavy rain fell with a loud, pattering sound. Thunder suddenly rolled.

Anne caught hold of Julian's arm, startled. 'Julian! It's dangerous to be in a wood, isn't it, in a storm? Oh, Julian, we'll be struck by lightning.'

'No, we shan't,' said Julian. 'A wood's no more dangerous than anywhere else. It's sheltering under a lone tree somewhere that's dangerous. Look – there's a little clearing over there; we'll go to that, if you like.'

But when they got to the little clearing the rain was falling down in such heavy torrents that Julian could see that they would immediately be soaked through. He hurried Anne to a clump of bushes, and they crouched underneath, waiting for the storm to pass.

Soon the rain stopped, and the thunder rolled away to the east. There had been no lightning that they could see. The wood grew just a little lighter, as if somewhere above the thick green branches the sun might be shining!

'I hate this wood,' said Dick, crawling out from the bushes. 'Come on, for goodness' sake. Let's get back to the wheel-rut path.'

He led the way through the trees. Julian called to him. 'Wait, Dick. Are you sure this is right?'

Dick stopped, anxious at once. 'Well,' he said uncertainly. 'I thought it was. But I don't know. Do you?'

'*I* thought it was through those trees there,' said Julian. 'Where that little clearing is.'

They went to it. 'It's not the same clearing, though,' said Anne at once. 'The other clearing had a dead tree at one side. There's no dead tree here.'

'Blow!' said Julian. 'Well – try *this* way, then.'

They went to the left, and soon found themselves in a

thicker part of the wood than ever. Julian's heart went cold. What an absolute idiot he was! He might have known that it was madness to leave the only path they knew without marking it in some way.

Now he hadn't the very faintest idea where the wheel-rut way was. It might be in any direction! He hadn't even the sun to guide him.

He looked gloomily at Dick. 'Bad show!' said Dick. 'Well – we'll have to make up our minds which way to go! We can't just stay here.'

'We might go deeper and deeper and deeper,' said Anne, with a sudden little gulp of fear. Julian put his arm round her shoulder.

'Well, if we go deeper and deeper, we shall come out on the other side!' he said. 'It's not an endless wood, you know.'

'Well, let's go straight on through the wood, then,' said Anne. 'We'll *have* to come out the other side some time.'

The boys didn't tell her that it was impossible to go straight through a wood. It was necessary to go round clumps of bushes, to double back sometimes when they came to an impenetrable part, and to go either to the left or right when clumps of trees barred their way. It was quite impossible to go *straight* through.

'For all I know we're probably going round and round in circles, like people do when they're lost in the desert,' he thought. He blamed himself bitterly for having left the wheel-ruts.

They made their way on and on for about two or three

hours, and then Anne stumbled and fell. 'I can't go on any further,' she wept. 'I must have a rest.'

Dick glanced at his watch and whistled. Where ever had the time gone? It was almost three o'clock. He sat down by Anne and pulled her close to him. 'What we want is a jolly good meal,' he said. 'We've had nothing since breakfast.'

Anne said she still wasn't hungry, but when she smelt the meat sandwiches that Joan had made she changed her mind. She was soon eating with the others, and feeling much better.

'There's nothing to drink, unfortunately,' said Dick. 'But Joan's packed tomatoes and plums, too – so we'll have those instead of a drink. They're nice and juicy.'

They ate everything, though secretly Julian wondered if it was a good thing to wolf all their food at once. There was no telling how long they might be lost in Ravens Wood! Joan might get worried sooner or later and tell the police they had gone there, and a search would be made. But it might be ages before they were found.

Anne fell asleep after her meal. The boys talked softly over her head. 'I don't much like this,' said Dick. 'We set out to find George – and all we've done is to lose ourselves. We don't seem to be managing this adventure as well as we usually do.'

'If we don't get out before dark we'll have to make up some kind of bed under a bush,' said Julian. 'We'll have another go when Anne wakes – and we'll do a bit of yelling, too. Then if we're still lost, we'll bed down for the night.'

But when darkness came – and it came very early in that thick wood, they were still as much lost as ever. They were all hoarse with shouting, too.

In silence they pulled bracken from an open space and piled it under a sheltering bush. 'Thank goodness it's warm tonight,' said Dick, trying to sound cheerful. 'Well – we'll all feel much more lively in the morning. Cuddle up to me, Anne, and keep warm. That's right. Julian's on the other side of you! This is quite an adventure.'

'I don't like adventures,' said Anne, in a small voice, and immediately fell asleep.

Chapter Sixteen

VISITOR IN THE NIGHT

IT took a long time for Julian and Dick to fall asleep. They were both worried – worried about George and worried about themselves, too. They were also very hungry, and their hunger kept them awake as much as their anxiety.

Dick fell asleep at last. Julian still lay awake, hoping that Anne was nice and warm between them. He didn't feel very warm himself.

He heard the whisper of the leaves in the trees, and then the scamper of tiny paws behind his head. He wondered what animal it was – a mouse?

Something ran lightly over his hair and he shivered. A spider, perhaps. Well he couldn't move, or he would disturb Anne. If it wanted to make a web over his hair it would have to. He shut his eyes and began to doze off. Soon he was dreaming.

He awoke very suddenly, with a jump. He heard the hoot of an owl. That must have been what wakened him. Now it would be ages before he slept again.

He shut his eyes. The owl hooted again and Julian frowned, hoping that Anne would not wake. She stirred and muttered in her sleep. Julian touched her lightly. She felt quite warm.

He settled down again and shut his eyes. Then he

opened them. He had heard something! Not an owl or
the pattering of some little animal's feet – but another
sound, a bigger one. He listened. There was a rustling
going on somewhere. Some much bigger animal was
about.

Julian was suddenly panic-stricken. Then he reasoned
sternly with himself. There were no dangerous wild
animals in this country, not even a wolf. It was probably
a badger out on a nightly prowl. He listened for any
snuffling sound, but he heard none, only the rustling as
the animal moved about through the bushes.

It came nearer. It came right over to him! He felt
warm breath on his ear and made a quick movement of
revulsion. He sat up swiftly and put out his hand. It fell
on something warm and hairy. He withdrew his hand at

once, feeling for his torch in panic. To touch something warm and hairy in the pitch darkness was too much even for Julian!

Something caught hold of his arm, and he gave a yell and fought it off. Then he got the surprise of his life. The animal spoke.

'Julian!' said a voice. 'It's me!'

Julian, his hands trembling, flashed his torch round. The light fell on a dirty dark face, with tangled hair over its eyes.

'Jo!' said Julian. 'JO! What on earth are you doing here? You scared me stiff. I thought you were some horrible hairy animal. I must have touched your head.'

'You did,' said Jo, squeezing in under the bush. Anne and Dick, who had both wakened up at Julian's yell, gazed at her, speechless with surprise. Jo of all people, here in the middle of the wood. How had she got there?

'You're surprised to see me, aren't you?' said Jo. 'I got caught by Jake. But he didn't know you were following behind. He dragged me off to the cottage he lives in and locked me up. He knew I'd spent the night at Kirrin Cottage, and he said he was going to take me to my Dad, who would give me the worst hiding I'd ever had in my life. So he would, too.'

'So that's what happened to you!' said Dick.

'Then I broke the window and got out,' said Jo. 'That Jake! I'll never do a thing he tells me again – locking me up like that. I hate that worse than anything! Well, then I came to look for you.'

'How did you find us?' said Julian, in wonder.

'Well, first I went to the caravan,' said Jo. 'Old Ma Smith – the one who always sits stirring a pot – she told me you'd been asking for my Dad's caravan. I guessed you'd go off to find it. So along I went after you – but there was the caravan all by itself, and nobody there. Not even George.'

'Where *is* George, do you know?' asked Anne.

'No. I don't,' said Jo. 'Dad's taken her somewhere else. I expect he put her on Blackie, because Blackie's gone, too.'

'What about Timmy?' asked Dick.

Jo looked away. 'I reckon they've done Timmy in,' she said. Nobody said anything. The thought that Timmy might have come to harm was too dreadful to speak about.

'How did you find us here?' asked Julian at last.

'That was easy,' said Jo. 'I can follow anybody's trail. I'd have come quicker, but it got dark. My, you did wander round, didn't you?'

'Yes. We did,' said Dick. 'Do you mean to say you followed all our wanderings in and out and round about?'

'Oh, yes,' said Jo. 'Properly tired me out, you did, with all your messing round and round. Why did you leave the wheel-ruts?'

Julian told her. 'You're daft,' said Jo. 'If you're going somewhere off the path, just mark the trees with a nick as you go along – one here and one there – and then you can always find your way back.'

'We didn't even know we were lost till we were,' said Anne. She took Jo's hand and squeezed it. She was so very, very glad to see her. Now they would be able to get out of this horrible wood.

Jo was surprised and touched, but she withdrew her hand at once. She didn't like being fondled, though she would not have minded Dick taking her hand. Dick was her hero, someone above all others. He had been kind to her, and she was glad she had found him.

'We found something written on the caravan wall,' said Julian. 'We think we know where George has been taken. It's a place called Red Tower. Do you know it?'

'There's no place called Red Tower,' said Jo at once. 'It's . . .'

'Don't be silly, Jo. You can't possibly know if there's no place called Red Tower,' said Dick, impatiently. 'There may be hundreds of places with that name. That's the place we've got to find, anyway. The police will know it.'

Jo gave a frightened movement. 'You promised you wouldn't tell the police.'

'Yes – we promised that – but only if you took us to George,' said Dick. 'And you didn't. And anyway if you *had* taken us to the caravan George wouldn't have been there. So we'll jolly well have to call in the police now and find out where Red Tower is.'

'*Was* it Red Tower George had written down?' asked Jo. 'Well, then – I *can* take you to George!'

'How can you, when you say there's no place called Red Tower?' began Julian, exasperated. 'I don't believe a word you say, Jo. You're a fraud – and I half-believe you're still working for our enemies too!'

'I'm not,' said Jo. 'I'm NOT! You're mean. I tell you
Red Tower isn't a place. Red Tower is a man.'

There was a most surprised silence after this astonishing
remark. A man! Nobody had thought of that.

Jo spoke again, pleased at the surprise she had caused.
'His name's Tower, and he's got red hair, flaming red –
so he's called Red Tower. See?'

'Are you making this up, by any chance?' asked Dick,
after a pause. 'You have made up things before, you
know.'

'All right. You can think I made it up, then,' said Jo,
sulkily. 'I'll go. Get yourselves out of this the best you
can. You're mean.'

She wriggled away, but Julian caught hold of her arm.
'Oh, no, you don't! You'll just stay with us now, if I have
to tie you to me all night long! You see, we find it difficult to trust you, Jo – and that's your fault, not ours. But
we'll trust you just this once. Tell us about Red Tower,
and take us to where he lives. If you do that, we'll trust
you for evermore.'

'Will Dick trust me, too?' said Jo, trying to get away
from Julian's hand.

'Yes,' said Dick shortly. He felt as if he would dearly
like to smack this unpredictable, annoying, extraordinary,
yet somehow likeable ragamuffin girl. 'But I don't feel
as if I *like* you very much at present. If you want us to
like you as well as to trust you, you'll have to help us a
lot more than you have done.'

'All right,' said Jo, and she wriggled down again. 'I'm

tired. I'll show you the way out in the morning, and then I'll take you to Red's. But you won't like Red. He's a beast.'

She would say nothing more, so once again they tried to sleep. They felt happier now that Jo was with them and would show them the right way out of the wood. Julian hardly thought she would leave them in the lurch now. He shut his eyes and was soon dreaming.

Jo woke first. She uncurled like an animal and stretched, forgetting where she was. She woke up the others, and they all sat up, feeling stiff, dirty and hungry.

'I'm thirsty as well as hungry,' complained Anne. 'Where can we get something to eat and drink?'

'Better get back home for a wash and a meal, and to let Joan know where we are,' said Julian. 'Come on, Jo – show us the way.'

Jo led the way immediately. The others wondered how in the world she knew it. They were even more astonished when they found themselves on the wheel-rut path in about two minutes.

'Gracious! We were as near to it as that!' said Dick. 'And yet we seemed to walk for miles through this horrible wood.'

'You did,' said Jo. 'You went round in an enormous circle, and you were almost back where you started. Come on – I'll take you *my* way back to your house now – it's much better than any bus!'

Chapter Seventeen

OFF IN GEORGE'S BOAT

JOAN was extremely thankful to see them. She had been so worried the night before that if the telephone wires in the house had been mended, she would most certainly have rung up the police. As it was, she couldn't telephone, and the night was so dark that she was really afraid of walking all the way down to the village.

'I haven't slept all night,' she declared. 'This mustn't happen again, Master Julian. It's worrying me to death. And now you haven't got George or Timmy. I tell you, if they don't turn up soon I'll take matters into my own hands. I haven't heard from your uncle and aunt either – let's hope they're not lost, too!'

She bustled about after this outburst, and was soon frying sausages and tomatoes for them. They couldn't wait till they were cooked, and helped themselves to great hunks of bread and butter.

'I can't even go and wash till I've had something,' said Anne. 'I'm glad you knew so many short cuts back here, Jo – the way didn't seem nearly so long as when we came by bus.'

It had really been amazing to see the deft, confident manner in which Jo had taken them home, through fields and little narrow paths, over stiles and across allotments. She was never once at a loss.

They had arrived not long after Joan had got up, and she had almost cried with surprise and relief when she had seen them walking up the front path.

'And a lot of dirty little tatterdemalions you looked,' she said, as she turned their breakfast out on to a big dish. 'And still do, for that matter. I'll get the kitchen fire going for a bath for you. You might all be sister and brothers to that ragamuffin Jo.'

Jo didn't mind remarks of this sort at all. She chewed her bread and grinned. She wolfed the breakfast with no manners at all – but the others were nearly as bad, they were so hungry!

'It's a spade and trowel you want for your food this morning, not a knife and fork,' said Joan, disapprovingly. 'You're just shovelling it in. No, I can't cook you any more, Master Julian. There's not a sausage left in the house nor a bit of bacon either. You fill up with toast and marmalade.'

The bath water ran vigorously after breakfast. All four had baths. Jo didn't want to, but Joan ran after her with a carpet beater, vowing and declaring she would beat the dust and dirt out of her if she didn't bath. So Jo bathed, and quite enjoyed it.

They had a conference after breakfast. 'About this fellow, Red Tower,' said Julian. 'Who is he, Jo? What do you know about him?'

'Not much,' said Jo. 'He's rich, and he talks queer, and I think he's mad. He gets fellows like Dad and Jake to do his dirty work for him.'

'What dirty work?' asked Dick.

'Oh – stealing and such,' said Jo, vaguely. 'I don't really know. Dad doesn't tell me much; I just do what I'm told, and don't ask questions. I don't want more slaps than I get!'

'Where does he live?' said Anne. 'Far away?'

'He's taken a house on the cliff,' said Jo. 'I don't know the way by land. Only by boat. It's a queer place – like a small castle almost, with very thick stone walls. Just the place for Red, my Dad says.'

'Have you been there?' asked Dick, eagerly.

Jo nodded. 'Oh, yes,' she said. 'Twice. My Dad took a big iron box there once, and another time he took something in a sack. I went with him.'

'Why?' asked Julian. 'I shouldn't have thought he'd wanted you messing round!'

'I rowed the boat,' said Jo. 'I told you, Red's place is up on the cliff. We got to it by boat; I don't know the way by road. There's a sort of cave behind a cove we landed at, and we went in there. Red met us. He came from his house on the cliff, he said, but I don't know how.'

Dick looked at Jo closely. 'I suppose you'll say next that there's a secret way from the cave to the house!' he said. 'Go on!'

'Must be,' said Jo. She suddenly glared at Dick. 'Don't you believe me? All right, find the place yourself!'

'Well – it does sound like a tale in a book,' said Julian. 'You're sure it *is* all true, Jo? We don't want to go on a wild-goose chase again, you know.'

'There's no wild goose in my story,' said Jo, puzzled. She hadn't the faintest idea what a wild-goose chase was. 'I'm telling you about Red. I'm ready to go when you are. We'll have to have a boat, though.'

'We'll take George's,' said Dick, getting up. 'Look, Jo – I think we'd better leave Anne behind this time. I don't like taking her into something that may be dangerous.'

'I want to come,' said Anne at once.

'No, you stay with me,' said Joan. 'I want company today. 'I'm getting scared of being by myself with all these things happening. You stay with me.'

So Anne stayed behind, really rather glad, and watched the other three go off together. Jo slipped into the hedge to avoid being seen by Jake, in case he was anywhere about. Julian and Dick went down to the beach and glanced round to make sure the gipsy was nowhere in sight.

They beckoned to Jo, and she came swiftly from hiding, and leapt into George's boat. She lay down in it so that she couldn't be seen. The boys hauled the boat down to the sea. Dick jumped in, and Julian pushed off when a big wave came. Then he jumped in too.

'How far up the coast is it?' he asked Jo, who was still at the bottom of the boat.

'I don't know,' said Jo, with her usual irritating vagueness. 'Two hours, three hours, maybe.'

Time didn't mean the same to Jo as it did to the others. For one thing Jo had no wrist-watch as they had, always there to be glanced at. She wouldn't have found one any use if she had, because she couldn't tell the time. Time was just day and night to her, nothing else.

Dick put up the little sail. The wind was in their favour, so he thought he might as well use it. They would get there all the more quickly.

'Did you bring the lunch that Joan put up for us?' said Julian to Dick. 'I can't see it anywhere.'

'Jo! You must be lying on it!' said Dick.

'It won't hurt it,' said Jo. She sat up as soon as they were well out to sea, and offered to take the tiller.

She was very deft with it, and the boys soon saw that they could leave her to guide the boat. Julian unfolded the map he had brought with him.

'I wonder whereabouts this place is where Red lives,' he said. 'It's pretty desolate all the way up to the next place, Port Limmersley. If there *is* a castle-like building, it must be a very lonely place to live in. There's not even a little fishing village shown for miles.'

The boat went on and on, scudding at times before a fairly strong wind. Julian took the tiller from Jo. 'We've come a long way already,' he said. 'Where *is* this place? Are you sure you'll know it, Jo?'

'Of course,' said Jo, scornfully. 'I think it's round that far-off rocky cliff.'

She was right. As they rounded the high cliff, which jutted fiercely with great slanting rocks, she pointed in triumph.

'There you are! See that place up there? That's Red's place.'

The boys looked at it. It was a dour, grey stone building, and was, as Jo had said, a little like a small castle. It brooded over the sea, with one square tower overlooking the waves.

'There's a cove before you come to the place,' said Jo.
'Watch out for it – it's very well hidden.'

It certainly was. The boat went right past it before
they saw it. 'There it is!' cried Jo, urgently.

They took the sail down and then rowed back. The
cove lay between two high layers of rock that jutted out
from the cliff. They rowed right into it. It was very quiet
and calm there, and their boat merely rose and fell as the
water swelled and subsided under it.

'Can anyone see us from the house above?' asked
Dick, as they rowed right to the back of the cove.

'I don't know,' said Jo. 'I shouldn't think so. Look –
pull the boat up behind that big rock. We don't know who
else might come here.'

They dragged the boat up. Dick draped it with great
armfuls of seaweed, and soon it looked almost like a rock
itself.

'Now, what next?' said Julian. 'Where's this cave you
were talking about?'

'Up here,' said Jo, and began to climb up the rocky
cliff like a monkey. Both the boys were very good climbers,
but soon they found it impossible to get any further.

Jo scrambled down to them. 'What's the matter?' she
said. 'If my Dad can climb up, surely you can!'

'Your Dad was an acrobat,' said Julian, sliding down
a few feet, much too suddenly. 'Oooh! I don't much like
this. I wish we had a rope.'

'There's one in the boat. I'll get it,' said Jo, and slith-
ered down the cliff to the cove below at a most alarming
rate. She climbed up again with the rope. She went on a

good bit higher, and tied the rope to something. It hung
down to where Dick and Julian stood clinging for dear
life.

It was much easier to climb up with the help of a rope.
Both boys were soon standing on a ledge, looking into a
curious shaped cave. It was oval-shaped, and very dark.

'In here,' said Jo, and led the way. Dick and Julian
followed stumblingly. Where in the world were they going
to now?

Chapter Eighteen

THINGS BEGIN TO HAPPEN

Jo led them into a narrow rocky tunnel, and then out
into a wider cave, whose walls dripped with damp. Julian
was thankful for his torch. It was eerie and chilly and
musty. He shivered. Something brushed his face and he
leapt back.

'What was that?' he said.

'Bats,' said Jo, 'there's hundreds of them here. That's
why the place smells so sour. Come on. We go round this
rocky bit here into a better cave.'

They squeezed round a rocky corner and came into a
drier cave that did not smell so strongly of bats. 'I haven't
been any farther than this,' said Jo. 'This is where me and
Dad came and waited for Red. He suddenly appeared,
but I don't know where from.'

'Well, he must have come from somewhere,' said Dick,
switching on his torch, too. 'There's a passage probably.
We'll soon find it.'

He and Julian began to hunt round the cave, looking
for a passage or little tunnel, or even a hole that led into
the cliff, upwards towards the house. Obviously Red

must have come down some such passage to reach the cave. Jo stayed in a corner, waiting. She had no torch.

Suddenly the boys had a tremendous shock. A voice boomed into their cave, a loud and angry voice that made their hearts beat painfully.

'SO! YOU DARE TO COME HERE!'

Jo slipped behind a rock immediately, like an animal going to cover. The boys stood where they were, rooted to the spot. Where did the voice come from?

'Who are you?' boomed the voice.

'Who are *you*?' shouted Julian. 'Come out and show yourself! We've come to see a man called Red. Take us to him.'

There was a moment's silence, as if the owner of the voice was rather taken aback. Then it boomed out again.

'Why do you want to see Red? Who sent you?'

'Nobody. We came because we want our cousin back, and her dog, too,' boomed Julian, making a funnel of his hands and trying to outdo the other voice.

There was another astonished silence. Then two legs appeared out of a hole in the low ceiling, and someone leapt lightly down beside them. The boys started back in surprise. They hadn't expected that the voice came from the roof of the cave!

Julian flashed his torch on the man. He was a giant-like fellow with flaming red hair. His eyebrows were red, too, and he had a red beard that partly hid a cruel mouth. Julian took one look into the man's eyes and then no more.

'He's mad,' he thought. 'So this is Red Tower. What is he? A scientist like Uncle Quentin, jealous of uncle's work? Or a thief working on a big scale, trying to get important papers and sell them? He's mad, whatever he is.'

Red was looking closely at the two boys. 'So you think I have your cousin,' he said. 'Who told you such a stupid tale?'

Julian didn't answer. Red took a threatening step towards him. 'Who told you?'

'I'll tell you that when the police come,' said Julian boldly.

Red stepped back.

'The police! What do they know? Why should they come here? Answer me, boy!'

'There's a lot to know about you, Mr. Red Tower,' said Julian. 'Who sent men to steal my uncle's papers? Who sent a note to ask for another lot? Who kidnapped our cousin, so that she could be held till the papers were sent? Who brought her here from Simmy's old caravan. Who...?'

'Aaaaaah!' said Red, and there was panic in his voice. 'How do you know all this? It isn't true! But the police – have they heard this fantastic tale, too?'

'What do you suppose?' said Julian, wishing with all his heart that the police *did* know, and that he was not merely bluffing. Red pulled at his beard. His green eyes gleamed as he thought quickly and urgently.

He suddenly called loudly, turning his head up to the hole in the ceiling. 'Markhoff! Come down!'

Two legs were swung down through the hole, and a short burly man leapt down beside the two startled boys.

'Go down the cliff. You will find a boat in the cove, somewhere – the boat we saw these boys coming in,' said Red sharply. 'Smash it to pieces. Then come back here and take the boys to the yard. Tie them up. We must leave quickly, and take the girl with us.'

The man stood listening, his face sullen. 'How can we go?' he said. 'You know the helicopter is not ready. You *know* that.'

'Make it ready then,' snapped Red. 'We leave tonight. The police will be here – do you hear that? This boy knows everything – he has told me – and the police must know everything too. I tell you, we must go.'

'What about the dog?' said the man.

'Shoot it,' ordered Red. 'Shoot it before we go. It's a brute of a dog. We should have shot it before. Now go and smash the boat.'

The man disappeared round the rocky corner that led into the cave of bats. Julian clenched his fist. He hated to think of George's boat being smashed to bits. Red stood there waiting, his eyes glinting in the light of the torches.

'I'd take you with us too, if there was room!' he suddenly snarled at Julian. 'Yes, and drop you into the sea!

'You can tell your uncle he'll hear from me about his precious daughter – we'll make an exchange. If he wants her back he can send me the notes I want. And many thanks for coming to warn me. I'll be off before the police break in.'

He began to pace up and down the cave, muttering. Dick and Julian watched in silence. They felt afraid for

George. Would Red really take her off in his helicopter?
He looked mad enough for anything.

The sullen man came back at last. 'It's smashed,' he
said.

'Right,' said Red. 'I'll go first. Then the boys. Then
you. And boot them if they make any trouble.'

Red swung himself up into the hole in the roof. Julian
and Dick followed, not seeing any point in resisting.
The man behind was too sulky to stand any nonsense.
He followed immediately.

There had been no sign of Jo. She had kept herself
well hidden, scared stiff. Julian didn't know what to do
about her. He couldn't possibly tell Red about her – and
yet it seemed terrible to leave her behind all alone.
Well – she was a sharp-brained little monkey. Maybe
she would think up something for herself.

Red led the way through another cave into a passage
with such a low roof that he had to walk bent almost
double.

The man behind had now switched on a very powerful
torch, and it was easier to see. The passage sloped upwards and was obviously leading to the building on the
cliff. At one part it was so steep that a hand-rail had been
put for the climber to help himself up.

Then came a flight of steps hewn out of the rock itself –
rough, badly-shaped steps, so steep that it was quite an
effort to climb from one to the next.

At the top of the steps was a stout door set on a broad
ledge. Red pushed it open and daylight flooded in.
Julian blinked. He was looking out on an enormous yard

paved with great flat stones with weeds growing in all the crevices and cracks.

In the middle stood a helicopter. It looked very strange and out-of-place in that old yard. The house, with its one tall square tower, was built round three sides of the yard. It was covered with creeper and thick-stemmed ivy.

A high wall ran along the fourth side, with an enormous gate in the middle. It was shut, and from where he stood Julian could see the huge bolts that were drawn across.

'It's almost like a small fort,' thought Julian, in astonishment. Then he felt himself seized and taken to a shed nearby. His arms were forced behind him and his wrists were tightly tied. Then the rope was run through an iron loop and tied again.

Julian glared at the burly fellow now doing the same to Dick. He twisted about to try to see how the rope was tied, but he couldn't even turn, he was so tightly tethered.

He looked up at the tower. A small, forlorn face was looking out of the window there. Julian's heart jumped and beat fast. That must be poor old George up there. He wondered if she had seen them. He hoped not, because she would know that he and Dick had been captured, and she would be very upset.

Where was Timmy? There seemed no sign of him. But wait a minute – what was that lying inside what looked like a summer-house on the opposite side of the yard? *Was* it Timmy? Surely he would have barked a welcome when he heard them coming into the yard, if it *was* Timmy!

'Is that my cousin's dog?' he asked the sullen man.

The man nodded. 'Yes. He's been doped half the time, he barked so. Savage brute, isn't he? *Ought* to be shot, I reckon.'

Red had gone across the yard and had disappeared through a stone archway. The sullen man now followed him. Julian and Dick were left by themselves.

'We've muddled things again,' said Julian, with a groan. 'Now these fellows will be off and away, and take George with them – they've been nicely warned!'

Dick said nothing. He felt very miserable, and his bound wrists hurt him, too. Both boys stood there, wondering what would happen to them.

'Psssssst!'

What was that? Julian turned round sharply and looked in the direction of the door that led from underground into the yard. Jo stood there, half-hidden by the archway over the door. 'Pssssst! I'll come and untie you. Is the coast clear?'

Chapter Nineteen

JO IS VERY SURPRISING

'Jo!' said the boys together, and their spirits lifted at once. 'Come on!'

There was no one about in the yard. Jo skipped lightly across from the doorway and slipped inside the shed.

'There's a knife in my back pocket,' said Julian. 'Get it out. It would be quicker to cut these ropes than to untie them. My word, Jo – I was never so pleased to see anyone in my life!'

Jo grinned as she hauled out Julian's sturdy pocket-knife. She opened it and ran her thumb lightly over the blade. It was beautifully sharp. She set to work to saw the blade across the thick rope. It cut easily through the fibres.

'I waited behind,' she said, rapidly. 'Then I followed when it was safe. But it was very dark and I didn't like it. Then I came to that door and peeped out. I was glad when I saw you.'

'Good thing the men didn't guess you were there,' said Dick. 'Good old Jo! I take back any nasty thing I've ever said about you!'

Jo beamed. She cut the last bit of rope that bound Julian, and he swung himself away from the iron loop and began to rub his stiff, aching wrists. Jo set to work on Dick's bonds. She soon had those cut through, too.

'Where's George?' she asked, after she had helped Dick to rub his wrists and arms.

'Up in that tower,' said Julian. 'If we dared to go out in that yard you could look up and see her. And there's poor old Tim, look – half-doped – lying in that summer-house place over there.'

'I shan't let him be shot,' said Jo. 'He's a nice dog. I shall go and drag him down into those caves underground.'

'Not now!' said Julian, horrified. 'If you're seen now, you'll spoil everything. We'll *all* be tied up then!'

But Jo had already darted over to the summer-house and was fondling poor old Timmy.

The slam of a door made the boys jump and sent Jo into the shadows at the back of the summer-house at once. It was Red, coming across the yard!

'Quick! He's coming over here!' said Dick, in a panic. 'Let's get back to the iron loops and put our hands behind us so that he thinks we're still bound.'

So, when Red came over to the door of the shed, it looked exactly as if the boys still had their hands tied behind them. He laughed.

'You can stay here till the police come!' he said. Then he shut the shed door and locked it. He strolled over to the helicopter and examined it thoroughly. Then back he went to the door he had come from, opened it, and slammed it shut. He was gone.

When everything was quiet Jo sped back from the

summer-house to the shed. She unlocked the door of the shed. 'Come out,' she said. 'And we'll lock it again. Then nobody will know you aren't here. Hurry !'

There was nothing for it but to come out and hope there was nobody looking. Jo locked the shed door after them and hurried them back to the door that led underground. They slipped through it and half-fell down the steep steps.

'Thanks, Jo,' said Dick.

They sat down. Julian scratched his head, and for the life of him could not think of anything sensible to do. The police were *not* coming because they didn't know a thing about Red, or where George was or anything. And before long George would be flown off in that helicopter, and Timmy would be shot.

Julian thought of the high square tower and groaned. 'There's no way of getting George out of that tower,' he said aloud. 'It'll be locked and barred, or George would have got out at once. We can't even get to her. It's no good trying to make our way into the house – we'd be seen and caught at once.'

Jo looked at Dick. 'Do you badly want George to be rescued ?' she said.

'That's a silly question,' said Dick. 'I want it more than anything else in the world.'

'Well – I'll go and get her, then,' said Jo, and she got up as if she really meant it.

'Don't make jokes now,' said Julian. 'This really is serious, Jo.'

'Well, so am I,' retorted Jo. 'I'll get her out, you see

if I don't. Then you'll know I'm trustable, won't you?
You think I'm mean and thieving and not worth a penny,
and I expect you're right. But I can do some things you
can't, and if you want this thing, I'll do it for you.'

'How?' said Julian, astonished and disbelieving.

Jo sat down again.

'You saw that tower, didn't you?' she began. 'Well,
it's a big one, so I reckon there's more than one room in
it – and if I can get into the room next to George's I could
undo her door and set her free.'

'And how do you think you're going to get into the
room next to hers?' said Dick, scornfully.

'Climb up the wall, of course,' said Jo. 'It's set thick
with ivy. I've often climbed up walls like that.'

The boys looked at her. 'Were you the Face at the
Window by any chance?' said Julian, remembering
Anne's fright. 'I bet you were. You're like a monkey,
climbing and darting about. But you can't climb up that
great high wall, so don't think it. You'd fall and be killed.
We couldn't let you.'

'Pooh!' said Jo, with great scorn. 'Fall off a wall like
that! I've climbed up a wall without any ivy at all!
There's always holes and cracks to hold on to. That one
would be easy!'

Julian was quite dumbfounded to think that Jo really
meant all this. Dick remembered that Jo's father was an
acrobat. Perhaps that kind of thing was in the family.

'You just ought to see me on a tight-rope,' said Jo
earnestly. 'I can dance on it – and I never have a safety-
net underneath – that's baby-play! Well, I'm going.'

Without another word she climbed
the steep steps lightly as a goat
and stood poised in the archway
of the door. All was quiet. Like
a squirrel she leapt and bounded
over the courtyard and came
to the foot of the ivy-covered
tower. Julian and Dick were now
at the doorway that led into the
yard, watching her.

'She'll be killed,' said Julian.

'Talk about pluck!' said Dick.
'I never saw such a kid in my life.
There she goes – just like a monkey.'

And, sure enough, up the ivy went
Jo, climbing lightly and steadily.
Her hands reached out and tested
each ivy-stem before she threw her
weight on it, and her feet tried
each one, too, before she stood on it.

Once she slipped when an ivy-stem came away from
the wall. Julian and Dick watched, their hearts in their
mouths. But Jo merely clutched at another piece of stem
and steadied herself once. Then up she went again.

Up and up. Past the first storey, past the second, and
up to the third. Only one more now and she would be
up to the topmost one. She seemed very small as she
neared the top.

'I can't bear to look and I can't bear not to,' said Dick,
pretending to shield his eyes and almost trembling with

nervousness. 'If she fell now – what should we do?'

'Do shut up,' said Julian, between his teeth. 'She won't fall. She's like a cat. There – she's making for the window next to George's. It's open at the bottom.'

Jo now sat triumphantly on the broad window-sill of the room next to George's. She waved impudently to the boys far below. Then she pushed with all her might at the window to open it a little more. It wouldn't budge.

So Jo laid herself flat, and by dint of much wriggling and squeezing, she managed to slip through the narrow space between the bottom of the window-pane and the sill. She disappeared from sight.

Both boys heaved heartfelt sighs of relief. Dick found that his knees were shaking. He and Julian retired into the underground passage below the steep steps and sat there in silence.

'Worse than a circus,' said Dick at last. 'I'll never be able to watch acrobats again. What's she doing now, do you suppose?'

Jo was very busy. She had fallen off the inside window-sill with a bump, and bruised herself on the floor below. But she was used to bruises.

She picked herself up and shot behind a chair in case anyone had heard her. Nobody seemed to have heard anything, so she peeped cautiously out. The room was furnished with enormous pieces of furniture, old and heavy. Dust was on everything, and cobwebs hung down from the stone ceiling.

Jo tiptoed to the door. Her feet were bare and made no sound at all. She looked out. There was a spiral stone stairway nearby going downwards, and on each side was a door – there must be four rooms in the tower then, one for each corner, two windows in each. She looked at the door next to the room she was in. That must be the door of George's room.

There was a very large key in the lock, and a great bolt had been drawn across. Jo leapt across and dragged at the bolt. It made a loud noise and she darted back into the room again. But still nobody came. Back she went to the door again, and this time turned the enormous key. It was well oiled and turned easily.

Jo pushed open the door and put her head cautiously round. George was there – a thin and unhappy George, sitting by the window. She stared at Jo as if she couldn't believe her eyes!

'Psssst!' said Jo, enjoying all this very much indeed. 'I've come to get you out!'

Chapter Twenty

THE ADVENTURE BOILS UP

GEORGE looked as if she had seen a ghost. 'Jo!' she whispered. 'It can't really be you.'

'It is. Feel,' said Jo, and pattered across the room to give George quite a hard pinch. Then she pulled at her arm.

'Come on,' she said. 'We must go before Red comes. Hurry! I don't want to be caught.'

George got up as if she was in a dream. She went across to the door. She and Jo slipped out, and stood at the top of the spiral staircase.

'Have to go down here, I suppose,' said Jo. She cocked her head and listened. Then she went down a few steps and turned the first spiral bend.

But before she had gone down more than a dozen steps she stopped in fright. Somebody was coming up!

In panic Jo ran up again and pushed George roughly into the room she had climbed into first of all.

'Someone's coming,' she panted. 'Now we're finished.'

'It's that red-haired man, I expect,' said George. 'He

comes up three or four times a day and tries to make me tell him about my father's work. But I don't know a thing. What are we to do?'

The slow steps came up and up, sounding hollowly on the stone stairs. They could hear a panting breath now, too.

An idea came to Jo. She put her mouth close to George's ear. 'Listen! We look awfully alike. I'll let myself be caught and locked up in that room – and you take the chance to slip down and go to Dick and Julian. Red will never know I'm not you – we've even got the same clothes on now, because Joan gave me old ones of yours.'

'No,' said George, astounded. 'You'll be caught. I don't want you to do that.'

'You've *got* to,' whispered Jo, fiercely. 'Don't be daft. I can open the window and climb down the ivy, easy as winking, when Red's gone. It's your only chance. They're going to take you off in that helicopter tonight.'

The footsteps were now at the top. Jo pushed George well behind a curtain and whispered fiercely again: 'Anyway, I'm not really doing this for you. I'm doing it for Dick. You keep there and I'll do the rest.'

There was a loud exclamation when the man outside discovered the door of George's room open. He went in quickly and found nobody there. Out he came and yelled down the stairs.

'Markhoff! The door's open and the girl's gone! Who opened the door?'

Markhoff came up two steps at a time, looking bewildered. 'No one! Who could? Anyway, the girl can't be far off! I've been in the room below all the time since I locked her in last time. I'd have seen her if she's gone.'

'Who unlocked the door?' screamed Red, quite beside himself with anger. 'We've *got* to have that girl to bargain with.'

'Well, she must be in one of the other rooms,' said Markhoff, stolidly, quite unmoved by his master's fury. He went into one on the opposite side to the room where Jo and George crouched trembling. Then he came into their room, and at once saw the top of Jo's head showing behind the chair.

He pounced on her and dragged her out. 'Here she is!' he said, and didn't seem to realize that it was not George at all, but Jo. With their short hair, freckled faces and their similar clothes they really were alike. Jo yelled and struggled most realistically. Nobody would have guessed that she had planned to be caught and locked up!

George shook and shivered behind the curtain, longing to go to Jo's help, but knowing that it wouldn't be of the least use. Besides – there might be a chance now of finding Timmy. It had almost broken George's heart to be parted from him for so long.

Jo was dragged yelling and kicking into the room and locked in again. Red and Markhoff began to quarrel about which of them must have left the door unlocked.

'You were there last,' said Red.

'Well, if I was, I tell you I didn't leave the door unlocked,' Markhoff raged back. 'I wouldn't be so fatheaded. That's the kind of thing *you* do.'

'That'll do,' snapped Red. 'Have you shot that dog

yet? No, you haven't! Go down and do it before *he* escapes too!'

George's heart went stone-cold. Shoot Timmy! Oh *no*! Dear darling old Timmy. She couldn't let him be shot!

She didn't know what to do. She heard Red and Markhoff go down the stone stairway, their boots making a terrific noise at first, and then gradually becoming fainter.

She slipped down after them. They went into a nearby room, still arguing. George risked being seen and shot past the open door. She came to another stairway, not a spiral one this time, and went down it so fast that she almost lost her footing. Down and down and down. She met nobody at all. What a very strange place this was!

She came into a dark, enormous hall that smelt musty and old. She ran to the great door at the front and tried to open it. It was very heavy, but at last it swung slowly back.

She stood there in the bright sunlight, peering out cautiously. She knew where Timmy was. She had been able to see him sometimes, flopping queerly in and out of the summer-house. She knew that because of his continual barking he had been doped. Red had told her that when she had asked him. He enjoyed making her miserable. Poor George!

She tore across the courtyard and came to the summer-house. Timmy was there, lying as if he were asleep. George flung herself on him, her arms round his thick neck.

'Timmy, oh Timmy!' she cried, and couldn't see him for tears. Timmy, far away in some drugged dream, heard the voice he loved best in all the world. He stirred. He opened his eyes and saw George!

He was too heavy with his sleep to do more than lick her face. Then his eyes closed again. George was in despair. She was afraid Markhoff would come and shoot him in a very short time.

'Timmy!' she called in his ear. 'TIMMY! Do wake up. TIMMY!'

Tim opened his eyes again. What – his mistress still here! Then it couldn't be a dream. Perhaps his world would soon be right again. Timmy didn't understand at all what had been happening the last few days. He staggered to his feet somehow and stood swaying there, shaking his head. George put her hand on his collar. 'That's right, Tim,' she said. 'Now you come with me. Quick!'

But Timmy couldn't walk, though he had managed to stand. In despair George glanced over the courtyard, fearful that she would see Markhoff coming at any moment.

She saw somebody else. She saw Julian standing in an archway opposite, staring at her. She was too upset about Timmy even to feel much astonishment.

'Ju!' she called. 'Come and help me with Timmy. They're going to shoot him!'

In a trice Julian and Dick shot across the courtyard to George. 'What happened, Jo?' said Julian. 'Did you find George?'

'Ju – it's me, George!' said George, and Julian suddenly saw that indeed it was George herself. He had been so certain that it was still Jo that he hadn't known it was George!

'Help me with Timmy,' said George, and she pulled at the heavy dog. 'Where shall we hide him?'

'Down underground,' said Dick. 'It's the only place. Come on!'

How they managed it they never quite knew, but they did drag the heavy, stupid Timmy all the way across the yard and into the archway. They opened the door and shoved him inside. Poor Timmy fell over and immediately rolled down the steep steps, landing at the bottom with a frightful thud. George gave a little scream.

'He'll be hurt!'

But astonishingly enough Timmy didn't seem to be hurt at all. In fact the shaking seemed to have done him good. He got up and looked round him in rather a surprised way. Then he whined and looked up at George. He tried to climb the steep steps, but wasn't lively enough.

George was down beside him in a moment, patting him and stroking him. The two boys joined in. Timmy began to feel that things might be all right again, if only he could get rid of the dreadful, heavy feeling in his head. He couldn't understand why he kept wanting to lie down and go to sleep.

'Bring him right down to the caves,' said Dick. 'Those men are sure to hunt for him and for us too when they find Timmy gone, and us not in the shed.'

So down the narrow passages and into the little cave

with the hole in the roof they all went, Timmy feeling as if he didn't quite know which of his legs to use next.

They all sat down in a heap together when they got there, and George got as close to Timmy as she could. She was glad when the boys switched off their torches. She badly wanted to cry, and as she never did cry it was most embarrassing if anyone saw her.

She told the boys in a low voice all that had happened with Jo. 'She *made* me stay hidden so that she could be caught,' she said. 'She's wonderful. She's the bravest girl I ever knew. And she did it all even though she doesn't like me.'

'She's a queer one,' said Dick. 'She's all right at heart, though – very much all right.'

They talked quickly, in low voices, exchanging their news. George told them how she had been caught and taken to the caravan with Timmy, who had been knocked out with a cudgel.

'We saw where you had written Red's name,' said Dick. 'That gave us the clue to come here!'

'Listen,' said Julian, suddenly. 'I think we ought to make a plan quickly. I keep thinking I hear things. We're sure to be looked for soon, you know. What can we *do*?'

Chapter Twenty-One

A FEW SURPRISES

As soon as Julian had said that he kept hearing noises, the others felt as if they could hear some, too. They sat and listened intently, George's heart beating so loudly that she was certain the boys would be able to hear it.

'I think perhaps it's the sound of the sea, echoing in through the caves and the tunnels,' said Julian at last. 'In the ordinary way, of course, we wouldn't need to bother to listen – Timmy would growl at once! But, poor old chap, he's so doped and sleepy that I don't believe he hears anything.'

'Will he get all right again?' asked George, anxiously, fondling Timmy's silky ears.

'Oh, yes,' said Julian, sounding much more certain than he really felt. Poor Timmy – he really did seem ill! There wasn't even a growl in him.

'You've had an awful time these last few days, haven't you George?' asked Dick.

'Yes,' said George. 'I don't much want to talk about it. If I'd had Timmy with me it wouldn't have been so bad, but at first, when they brought me here, all I knew of Timmy was hearing him bark and snarl and bark and snarl down below in that yard. Then Red told me he had doped him.'

'How did you get to Red's place?' asked Julian.

'Well, you know I was locked in that horrible-smelling caravan,' said George. 'Then suddenly a man called Simmy – he's Jo's father, I think – came and dragged us out. Timmy was all stupid with the blow they'd given him – and they put him in a sack and put us both on the caravan horse and took us through the wood and along a desolate path by the coast till we came here. That was in the middle of the night.'

'Poor old George!' said Julian. 'I wish Tim was himself again – I'd love to set him loose on Red and the other fellow!'

'I wonder what's happening to Jo,' said Dick, suddenly remembering that Jo was now imprisoned in the tower room where George had been kept so long.

'And do you suppose Red and Markhoff have discovered that we've got out of that shed, and that Timmy has disappeared, too?' said Julian. 'They'll be in a fury when they do discover it!'

'Can't we get away?' said George, feeling suddenly scared. 'You came in a boat, didn't you? Well, can't we get away in that and go and fetch help for Jo?'

There was a silence. Neither of the boys liked to tell George that her beloved boat had been smashed to pieces by Markhoff. But she had to know, of course, and Julian told her in a few short words.

George said nothing at all. They all sat silently for a few minutes, hearing nothing but Timmy's heavy, almost snoring, breathing.

'Would it be possible, when it's dark, to creep up into the courtyard, and go round the walls to the big gate?

said Dick, breaking the silence. 'We can't escape anywhere down here, it's certain – not without a boat,
anyhow.'

'Should we wait till Red and Markhoff have gone off
in the helicopter?' said Julian. 'Then we'd be much safer.'

'Yes – but what about Jo?' asked Dick. 'They think
she's George, don't they? – and they'll take her away
with them, just as they planned to do with George. I
don't see how we can try to escape ourselves without first
trying to save Jo. She's been a brick about George.'

They talked round and round the idea of trying to save
Jo, but nobody could think of any really sensible plan at
all. Time went on, and they all felt hungry and rather
cold. 'If only we could *do* something, it wouldn't be so
bad!' groaned Dick. 'I wonder what's happening up at
the house.'

Up at the grey stone house with its big square-tower,
plenty was happening!

To begin with, Markhoff had gone to shoot Timmy,
as Red had ordered. But when he got to the summer-
house there was no dog there!

Markhoff stared in the greatest amazement! The dog
had been tied up, even though he was doped – and now,
there was the loose rope, and no dog attached to it!

Markhoff gazed round the summer-house in astonishment. Who could have loosed Timmy? He darted across
to the locked shed where he had tied Julian and Dick
with rope to the iron staples. The door was still locked, of
course – and Markhoff turned the key and pushed it
open.

'Here, you . . .' he began, shouting roughly. Then he stopped dead. Nobody was there! Again there was loose rope – this time cut here and there, so that it lay in short pieces – and again the prisoners had gone. No dog. No boys.

Markhoff couldn't believe his eyes. He looked all round the shed. 'But it was locked from the outside!' he muttered. 'What's all this? Who's freed the dog and the boys? What will Red say?'

Markhoff looked at the helicopter standing ready for flight in the middle of the yard, and half decided to desert Red and get away himself. Then, remembering Red's mad tempers, and his cruel revenges on anyone who dared to let him down, he changed his mind.

'We'd better get off now, before it's dark,' he thought. 'There's something queer going on here. There must be somebody else here that we know nothing about. I'd better find Red and tell him.'

He went in through the massive front door, and in the hall he came face to face with two men waiting there. At first he couldn't see who they were, and he stepped back hurriedly. Then he saw it was Simmy and Jake.

'What are you doing here?' shouted Markhoff. 'Weren't you told to keep watch on Kirrin Cottage and make sure the police weren't told anything?'

'Yes,' said Jake, sulkily. 'And we've come to say that that cook – woman called Joan – went down to the police this morning. She had one of the kids with her – a girl. The boys don't seem to be about.'

'No. They're here – at least, they were,' said Markhoff. 'They've disappeared again. As for the police, we've heard they're on the way, and we've made our plans. You're a bit late with your news! Lot of good you are, with your spying! Clear off now – we're taking the girl off in the helicopter before the police come. How did any-one know where the girl was? Have you been spilling the beans?'

'Pah!' said Simmy, contemptuously. 'Think we want to be messed up with the police? You must be mad. We want some money. We've done all your dirty work, and you've only paid us half you promised. Give us the rest.'

'You can ask Red for it!' growled Markhoff. 'What's the good of asking me? Go and ask *him*!'

'Right. We will,' said Jake, his face as black as thun-der. 'We've done all he told us – took the papers for him, took the girl – and that savage brute of a dog too – see where he bit me on my hand? And all we get is half our money! I reckon we've only just come in time, too. Plan-ning to go off in that there heli-thing and do us out of our pay. Pah!'

'Where's Red?' demanded Simmy.

'Upstairs,' said Markhoff. 'I've got some bad news for him, so he won't be pleased to see you and your ugly mugs. Better let me find him for you and say what I've got to say – then you can chip in with your polite little speeches.'

'Funny, aren't you?' said Jake, in a dangerous voice. Neither he nor Simmy liked Markhoff. They followed him up the broad stairway, and then up again till they came to the room that lay below the spiral staircase.

Red was there, scanning through the papers that had been stolen from the study of George's father. He was in a black temper. He flung down the papers as Markhoff came in.

'These aren't the notes I wanted!' he began, loudly. 'Well, I'll hold the girl till I get . . . why, Markhoff, what's up? Anything wrong?'

'Plenty,' said Markhoff. 'The dog's gone – he wasn't there when I went to shoot him – and the two boys have gone too – yes, escaped out of a locked shed. Beats me!

'And here are two visitors for you – they want money! They've come to tell you what you already know – the police have been told about you.'

Red went purple in the face, and his strange eyes shone with rage. He stared first at Markhoff, then at Simmy and Jake. Markhoff looked uneasy, but Simmy and Jake looked back insolently.

'You – you – you *dare* to come here when I told you to keep away!' he shouted. 'You've BEEN paid. You can't blackmail me for any more money.'

What he would have said next nobody knew because from up the spiral stairs there came yells and screams and the noise of someone apparently trying to batter down a door.

'That's that girl, I suppose,' muttered Markhoff. 'What's up with her? She's been quiet enough before.'

'We'd better get her out now and go,' said Red, his face still purple. 'Jake, go and get her. Bring her down here, and knock some sense into her if she goes on screaming.'

'Fetch her yourself,' said Jake, insolently.

Red looked at Markhoff, who immediately produced a revolver.

'My orders are always obeyed,' said Red in a suddenly cold voice. '*Always*, you understand?'

Not only Jake scuttled up the stairs then but also Simmy! They went to the locked and bolted room at the top and unlocked the door. They pulled back the bolt and door. Simmy stepped into the room to deal with the imprisoned girl.

But he stopped dead and gaped. He blinked, rubbed his eyes and gaped again. Jake gaped too.

'Hallo, Dad!' said Jo. 'You *do* seem surprised to see me!'

Chapter Twenty-Two

JO IS VERY SMART

'Jo' said Simmy. 'Well, of all the . . . well . . . JO!' Jake recovered first. 'What's all this?' he said, roughly, to Simmy. 'What's Jo doing here? How did *she* get here? Where's the other kid, the one we caught?'

'How do *I* know?' said Simmy, still staring at Jo. 'Look here, Jo – what are you doing here? Go on, tell us. And where's the other kid?'

'Hunt round the room and see if you can find her!' said Jo, brightly, keeping on her toes in case her father or Jake was going to pounce on her. The two men looked hurriedly round the room. Jake went to a big cupboard.

'Yes – she might be in there,' said Jo, enjoying herself. 'You have a good look.'

The two bewildered men didn't know what to think. They had come to get George – and had only found Jo!

But how – why – what had happened? They didn't know what to do. Neither of them wanted to go back and tell Red. So they began to search the room feverishly, looking into likely and unlikely places, with Jo jeering at them all the time.

'Better take the drawers out of that chest and see if

she's here. And don't forget to look under the rug.
That's right, Jake, poke your head up the chimney. Mind
George doesn't kick soot down into your eyes.'

'I'll lam you in a minute!' growled Jake, furiously,
opening a small cupboard door.

An angry voice came up the stairway. 'Jake! What
are you doing up there? Bring that kid down.'

'She's not here!' yelled back Jake, suddenly losing
his temper. 'What have you done with her? She's gone!'

Red came tearing up, two steps at a time, his eyes narrow with anger. The first thing he saw in the room was
Jo – and, of course, he thought she was George.

'What do you mean – saying she's not here!' he raged.
'Are you mad?'

'Nope,' said Jake, his eyes narrow too. 'Not so mad as
you are, anyway, Red. This kid isn't that fellow's daughter – the scientist chap we took the papers from – this is
Simmy's kid – Jo.'

Red looked at Jake as if he had gone off his head. Then
he looked at Jo. He could see no difference between Jo
and the absent George at all – short hair, freckles, turned-
up nose – he couldn't believe that she was Simmy's
daughter.

In fact, he didn't believe it. He thought Jake and
Simmy were suddenly deceiving him for some strange
reason.

But Jo had a word to say, too. 'Yes, I'm Jo,' she said.
'I'm not Georgina. She's gone. I'm just Jo, and Simmy's
my Dad. You've come to save me, haven't you, Dad?'

Simmy hadn't come to do anything of the sort, of

course. He stared helplessly at Jo, completely bewildered.

Red completely lost his temper. As soon as he heard Jo's voice he realized she was not George. Somehow or other he had been deceived – and seeing that this was Simmy's daughter, then it must be Simmy who had had a hand in the deception!

He went suddenly over to Simmy and struck him hard, his eyes blazing. 'Have you double-crossed me?' he shouted.

Simmy was sent flying to the floor. Jake came up immediately to help him. He tripped up Red, and leapt on him.

Jo looked at the three struggling, shouting men, and shrugged her shoulders. Let them fight! They had forgotten all about her, and that suited her very well. She ran to the door and was just going down the stairs, when an idea came into her sharp little mind. With an impish grin she turned back. She pulled the door to quietly – and then she turned the key in the lock, and shot the bolt.

The three men inside heard the key turn, and in a trice Jake was at the door, pulling at the handle.

'She's locked us in!' he raged. 'And shot the bolt, too.'

'Yell for Markhoff!' shouted Red, trembling with fury. And Markhoff, left down in the room at the bottom of the stairs, suddenly heard yells and shouts and tremendous hammerings at the door! He tore up at once, wondering what in the world had happened.

Jo was hiding in the next room. As soon as Markhoff went to the door and shot back the bolt she slipped out and was down the spiral stairway in a trice, unseen by Markhoff. She grinned to herself and hugged something to her thin little chest.

It was the big key belonging to the door upstairs. Nobody could unlock that door now – the key was missing. Jo had it!

'Unlock the door!' shouted Red. 'That kid's gone.'

'There's no key!' yelled back Markhoff. 'She must have taken it. I'll go after her.'

But it was one thing to go after Jo and quite another to find her. She seemed to have disappeared into thin air.

Markhoff raged through every room, but she was nowhere to be seen. He went out into the courtyard and looked round there.

Actually she had made her way to the kitchen and found the larder. She was very hungry and wanted something to eat. There was nobody in the kitchen at all, though a fine fire burned in the big range there.

She slipped into the larder, took the key from the outer side of the door and locked herself in. She saw that there was a small window, and she carefully unfastened it so that she could make her escape if anyone discovered that she was locked in the larder.

Then she tucked in. Three sausage rolls, a large piece of cheese, a hunk of bread, half a meat pie and two jam tarts went the same way. After that Jo felt a lot better. She remembered the others and thought how hungry they must be feeling, too.

She found a rush bag hanging on a nail and slipped some food into it – more sausage rolls, some rock-buns, some cheese and bread. Now, if only she could find the others, how they would welcome her!

Jo put the big key at the bottom of the rush basket. She was feeling very, very pleased with herself. Red and Simmy and Jake were all nicely locked up and out of the way. She didn't fear Markhoff as much as Red. She was sure she could get away from him.

She wasn't even sorry for her father, Simmy.

She had no love for him and no respect, because he was everything that a father shouldn't be.

She heard Markhoff come raging into the kitchen and she clambered quickly up on the larder shelf, ready to drop out of the window if he tried the door. But he didn't. He raged out again, and she heard him no more.

Jo unlocked the door very cautiously. There was now an old woman in the kitchen, standing by the table, folding some clothes she had brought in from the clothes line in the yard. She stared in the greatest surprise at Jo peeping out of the larder.

'What . . .?' she began, indignantly; but Jo was out of the room before she had even got out the next word. The old dame waddled over to the larder and began to wail as she saw all the empty plates and dishes.

Jo went cautiously into the front hall. She could hear Markhoff upstairs, still tearing about. She smiled delightedly and slipped over to the door.

She undid it and pulled it open. Then, keeping to the wall, she sidled like a weasel to the door that led underground. She opened it and went through, shutting it softly behind her.

Now to find the others. She felt sure they must be down in the caves. How pleased they would be with the food in her bag!

She half-fell down the steep steps, and made her way as quickly as she could down the slanting passage. She had no torch and had to feel her way in the dark. She wasn't in the least afraid. Only when she trod on a sharp stone with her bare foot did she make a sound.

The other three – Julian, Dick and George – were still sitting crouched together with Timmy in the centre. Julian had been once up to the door that led into the yard and had cautiously peered out to see what was to be seen – but had seen nothing at all except for an old woman hanging out some clothes on a line.

The three had decided to wait till night before they did anything. They thought maybe Timmy might have recovered a little then, and would be of some help in protecting them against Red or Markhoff. They half-dozed, sitting together for warmth, enjoying the heat of Timmy's big body.

Timmy growled! Yes, he actually growled – a thing he hadn't done at all so far. George put a warning hand on him. They all sat up, listening. A voice came to them.

'Julian! Dick! Where are you? I've lost my way!'

'It's Jo!' cried Dick, and switched on his torch at once. 'Here we are, Jo! How did you escape? What's happened?'

'Heaps,' said Jo, and came gladly over to them. 'My, it was dark up in those passages without a torch. Somehow I went the wrong way. That's why I yelled. But I hadn't gone far wrong. Have a sausage roll?'

'*What?*' cried three hungry voices, and even Timmy lifted his head and began to sniff at the rush basket that Jo carried.

Jo laughed and opened the basket. She handed out all the food and the three of them fell on it like wolves. 'Jo, you're the eighth wonder of the world,' said Dick. 'Is there anything left in the basket?'

'Yes,' said Jo, and took out the enormous key. 'This, look! I locked Red and Jake and Simmy into that tower room, and here's the key. What do you think of *that*?'

Chapter Twenty-Three

MARKHOFF GOES HUNTING

GEORGE took the big key and looked at it with awe. 'Jo! Is this really the key – and you've locked them all in? Honestly, I think you're a marvel.'

'She is,' said Dick, and to Jo's enormous delight he gave her a sudden quick hug. 'I never knew such a girl in my life. Never. She's got the pluck of twenty!'

'It was easy, really,' said Jo, her eyes shining joyfully in the light of the torch. 'You trust me now, Dick, don't you? You won't be mean to me any more, any of you, will you?'

'Of course not,' said Julian. 'You're our friend for ever!'

'Not George's,' said Jo at once.

'Oh yes you are,' said George. 'I take back every single mean thing I said about you. You're as good as a boy.'

This was the very highest compliment that George could ever pay any girl. Jo beamed and gave George a light punch.

'I did it all for Dick, really,' she said. 'But next time I'll do it for you!'

'Goodness, I hope there won't *be* a next time,' said

George, with a shiver. 'I can't say I enjoyed one single minute of the last few days.'

Timmy suddenly put his head on Jo's knee. She stroked him. 'Look at that!' she said. 'He remembers me. He's better, isn't he, George?'

George carefully removed Timmy's head from Jo's knee to her own. She felt decidedly friendly towards Jo now, but not to the extent of having Timmy put his head on Jo's knee. She patted him.

'Yes, he's better,' she said. 'He ate half the sausage roll I gave him, though he sniffed at it like anything first. I think he knows something has been put into his food and now he's suspicious of it. Good old Timmy.'

They all felt much more lively and cheerful now that they were no longer so dreadfully empty. Julian looked at his watch. 'It's getting on towards evening now,' he said. 'I wonder what all those fellows are doing.'

Three of them were still locked up! No matter how Markhoff had tried to batter in the door, it held. It was old and immensely strong, and the lock held without showing any sign of giving way even an eighth of an inch. Two other men had been called in from the garage to help, but except that the door looked decidedly worse for wear, it stood there just the same, sturdy and unbreakable.

Simmy and Jake watched Red as he walked up and down the tower room like a caged lion. They were glad they were two against one. He seemed like a madman to them as he raged and paced up and down.

Markhoff, outside with the other two men he had

brought up to help, was getting very worried. No police had arrived as yet (and wouldn't either, because Joan hadn't been able to tell them anything except that she knew Julian and Dick had gone to see a man called Red – but where he lived she had no idea!).

But Red and Markhoff didn't know this – they felt sure that a police ambush was somewhere nearby. If only they could get away in the helicopter before anything else happened!

'Markhoff! Take Carl and Tom and go down into those underground caves,' ordered Red at last. 'Those children are sure to be there – it's the only place for them to hide. They can't get out of here because the front gate is locked and bolted, and the wall's too high to climb. Get hold of the kids and search them for the key.'

So Markhoff and two burly fellows went downstairs and out of the door. They crossed the yard to the door that led to the caves.

They got down the steep steps and were soon stumbling along the narrow, slanting passage, their nailed boots making a great noise as they went. They hung on to the hand-rail when they came to the difficult stretch of tunnel, and finally came out into the cave that had the hole in the floor.

There was nobody there. The children had heard the noise of the coming men, and had hurriedly swung themselves down through the hole into the cave below.

They ran through into another cave, the sour smelling one where bats lived and slept. Then round the rocky corner into the first cave, the curious oval-shaped one that led out to the ledge of rock overlooking the steep cliff.

'There's nowhere to hide,' groaned Julian. He looked back into the cave. At least it was better in there than out on this ledge, outlined by the daylight. He pulled the others back into the cave, and shone his torch up and down the walls to find some corner that they could squeeze behind.

Half-way up the wall was a shelf of rock. He hoisted George up there, and she dragged Timmy up too. Poor Timmy – he wasn't much use to them; he was still so bemused and so very sleepy. He had growled at the noise made by the coming men, but had dropped his head again almost immediately.

Dick got up beside George. Julian found a jutting-out rock and tried to hide behind it, while Jo lay down in a hole beside one wall and covered herself cleverly with sand. Julian couldn't help thinking how sharp Jo was. She always seemed to know the best thing to do.

But as it happened, Jo was the only one to be discovered! It was quite by accident – Markhoff trod on her. He and the other two men had let themselves down through the hole into the cave below, had then gone into the cave of bats, seen no sign of anyone there, and were now in the cave that led to the cliff.

'Those kids aren't here,' said one of the men. 'They've gone to hide somewhere else. What a horrible place this is – let's go back.'

Markhoff was flashing his torch up and down the walls to see if any of the children were crouching behind a jutting rock – and he trod heavily on Jo's hand. She gave an agonized yell, and Markhoff almost dropped his torch!

In a trice he had pulled the girl out of her bed of sand and was shaking her like a rat. 'This is the one we want!' he said to the others. 'She's got the key. Where is it, you little rat? Give it to me or I'll throw you down the cliff!'

Julian was horrified. He felt quite certain that Markhoff really would throw Jo down the cliff, and he was just about to jump down to help her, when he heard her speak.

'All right. Let me go, you brute. Here's the key! You go and let my Dad out before the police come! I don't want him caught!'

Markhoff gave an exclamation of triumph, and snatched a shining key out of Jo's hand. He gave her a resounding box on the ear.

'You little toad! You can just stay down here with the others, and it'll be a very, very long stay! Do you know what we're going to do? We're going to roll a big rock over the hole in that other cave's roof – and you'll be prisoners!

'You can't escape upwards – and you won't be able to escape downwards. You'll be dashed on the rocks by the sea if you try to swim away. That'll teach you to interfere!'

The other two men guffawed. 'Good idea Mark,' said one. 'They'll all be nicely boxed up here and nobody will know where they are! Come on – we've no time to lose. If Red isn't unlocked soon he'll go mad!'

They made their way into the heart of the cliff again, and the listening children heard their footsteps getting fainter. Finally they ceased altogether, as one by one the men levered themselves up through the hole in the roof of the last cave, and disappeared up the narrow, low-roofed tunnel that led to the courtyard.

Julian came out from his hiding-place, looking grim and rather scared. 'That's done it!' he said. 'If those fellows really do block up that hole – and I bet they have already – it looks as if we're here for keeps! As he said, we can't get up, and we can't escape down – the sea's too rough for us to attempt any swimming, and the cliff's unclimbable above the ledge!'

'I'll go and have a look and see if they *have* blocked up that hole,' said Dick. 'They may be bluffing.'

But it hadn't been bluff. When Julian and Dick shone their torches on to the hole in the roof, they saw that a great rock was now blocking it up.

They could not get through the hole again. It was impossible to move the rock from below. They went soberly back to the front cave and sat out on the ledge in the light of the sinking sun.

'It's a pity poor Jo was found,' said George. 'And an even greater pity she had to give up the key! Now Red and the others will go free.'

'They won't,' said Jo, surprisingly. 'I didn't give them the key of the tower room. I'd another key with me – the key of the kitchen larder! And I gave them that.'

'Well, I'm blessed!' said Julian, astounded. 'The things

you do, Jo! But how on earth did you happen to have the key of the *larder*?'

Jo told them how she had taken it out and locked herself in when she was having a meal there.

'I had to unlock the door to get out again, of course,' she said. 'And I thought I'd take that key, too, because, who knows? – I might have wanted to get into that larder again and lock myself in with the food!'

'No one will ever get the better of you, Jo,' said Dick with the utmost conviction. 'Never. You're as cute as a bagful of monkeys. So you've still got the right key with you?'

'Yes,' said Jo. 'And Red and my Dad and Jake are still locked up in the tower room!'

But suddenly a most disagreeable thought struck Dick. 'Wait a bit!' he said. 'What's going to happen when they find they've got the *wrong* key? They'll be down here again, and my word, what'll happen to us all then!'

Chapter Twenty-Four

A GRAND SURPRISE

THE thought that the men might soon return even angrier than they had been before was most unpleasant.

'As soon as Markhoff tries the key in the door of the tower room he'll find it won't unlock it, and he'll know that Jo has tricked him!' said George.

'And then he'll be in such a fury that he'll tear down here again, and goodness knows what will happen to us!' groaned Julian. 'What shall we do? Hide again?'

'No,' said Dick. 'Let's get out of here and climb down the cliff to the sea. I'd feel safer there than up here in this cave. We might be able to find a better hiding-place down on the rocks in that little cove.'

'It's a pity my boat's smashed,' said George, with a sigh for her lovely boat. 'And, I say – how are we going to get old Timmy down?'

There was a conference about this. Timmy couldn't climb down, that was certain. Jo remembered the rope still hanging down the side of the cliff to the ledges below – the one she had tied there to help Julian and Dick climb up the steep sides of the cliff.

'I know,' she said, her quick mind working hard again. 'You go down first, Julian, then Dick. Then

George can go – each of you holding on to the rope as you climb down, in case you fall.

'Then I'll haul up the rope and tie old Timmy to it, round his waist – and I'll lower him down to you. He's so sleepy still, he won't struggle. He won't even know what's happening!'

'But what about you?' said Dick. 'You'll be last of all. Will you mind? You'll be all alone up on this ledge, with the men coming behind you at any minute.'

'No, I don't mind,' said Jo. 'But let's be quick.'

Julian went down first, glad of the rope to hold to as his feet and hands searched for crevices and cracks. Then came Dick, almost slipping in his anxiety to get down.

Then George climbed down, slowly and anxiously, not at all liking the steep cliff. Once she glanced down to the sea below, and felt sick. She shut her eyes for a moment and clung with one hand to the rope.

It was a dreadful business getting Timmy down. George stood below, anxiously waiting. Jo found it very difficult to tie Timmy safely. He was big and heavy, and didn't like being tied up at all, though he really seemed hardly to know what was going on. At last Jo had got the knots well and securely tied, and called out to the others.

'Here he comes. Watch out that the rope doesn't break. Oh, dear – I wish he wouldn't struggle – now he's bumped himself against the cliff!'

It was not at all a nice experience for poor Timmy. He swung to and fro on the rope as he was slowly let down, and was amazed to find that he was suspended in mid air. Above him Jo panted and puffed.

'Oh, he's so awfully heavy! I hope I shan't have to let go. Look out for him!' she screamed.

The weight was too much for her just at the last, and the rope was let out with rather a rush. Fortunately Timmy was only about six feet up then, and Julian and George managed to catch him as he suddenly descended.

'I'm coming now,' called Jo, and without even holding the rope, or looking at it, she climbed down like a monkey, seeming to find handholds and footholds by magic. The others watched her admiringly. Soon she was standing beside them. George was untying Timmy.

'Thanks awfully, Jo,' said George, looking up gratefully at Jo. 'You're a wonder. Tim must have been frightfully heavy.'

'He was,' said Jo, giving him a pat. 'I nearly dropped him. Well – what's the next move?'

'We'll hunt round this queer little cove a bit and see if there's any place we can hide,' said Julian. 'You go that way, George, and we'll go this.'

They parted, and began to hunt for a hiding-place. As far as Julian and Dick could see there was none at all, at least on the side they were exploring. The sea swept into the cove, swelling and subsiding – and just outside the great waves battered on to the rocks. There was certainly no chance of swimming out.

There was suddenly an excited shriek from George. 'JU! Come here. Look what I've found!'

They all rushed round to where George was standing, behind a big ledge of rock. She pointed to a great mass of something draped with seaweed.

'A boat! It's covered with seaweed – but it's a boat!'

'It's *your* boat!' yelled Dick, suddenly, and began to pull the fronds of seaweed madly off the hidden boat. 'Markhoff *didn't* smash it! It's here, perfectly all right. He couldn't find it – it was hidden so well with seaweed – so he just came back to Red and told him a lie.'

'He didn't smash it!' shouted Jo, and she, too, began to pull away the seaweed. 'It's quite all right – there's nothing wrong with it. He didn't smash it!'

The four children were so tremendously surprised and joyful that they thumped each other ridiculously on the back, and leapt about like mad things. They had their boat after all – George's good, sound boat. They could escape, hip hip hurrah!

A roar from above made them fall silent.

They gazed up, startled. Markhoff and the other two men were on the ledge far above, shouting and shaking their fists.

'You wait till we get you!' yelled Markhoff.

'Quick, quick!' said Julian, urgently, pulling at the boat. 'We've got just a chance. Pull her down to the water, pull hard!'

Markhoff was now coming down the cliff, and Jo wished she had untied the rope before she herself had climbed down, for Markhoff was finding it very useful. She tugged at the boat with the others, wishing it wasn't so heavy.

The boat was almost down to the water when something happened. Timmy, who had been gazing at everything in a most bewildered manner, suddenly slid off the

ledge he was on and fell straight into the sea. George gave
a scream.

'Oh, Timmy! He's in the water, quick, quick – he's
too doped to swim! He'll drown!'

Julian and Dick didn't dare to stop heaving at the
boat, because they could see that Markhoff would soon
be down beside them. George rushed to Timmy, who
was splashing around in the waves, still looking surprised
and bemused.

But the water had an amazing effect on him. It was
cold and it seemed to bring him to his senses quite suddenly. He became much more lively and swam strongly
to the rock off which he had slipped. He clambered out
with George's help, barking loudly.

The boat slid into the water, and Julian grabbed at
George. 'Come on. In you get. Buck up!'

Jo was in the boat and so was Dick. George, trying to
clutch at Timmy, was hauled in, too. Julian took a des-
pairing look at Markhoff, who was almost at the end
of the rope, about to jump down. They just wouldn't
get off in time!

Timmy suddenly slipped out of George's grasp and
tore madly over to the cliff barking warningly. He seemed
to be perfectly all right. The sudden coldness of the sea
had washed away all his dopeyness and sleepiness. Timmy
was himself again!

Markhoff was about five feet above the ledge when he
heard Timmy barking. He looked down in horror and
saw the big dog trying to jump up at him. He tried to
climb up quickly, out of Timmy's reach.

'Woof!' barked Timmy. 'Woof, woof, woof! Grrrrrrr!'

'Look out – he'll have your foot off!' yelled one of the men above on the ledge

'He's mad – angry – he's savage. Look out Mark!'

Markhoff *was* looking out! He was terrified. He clambered up another few feet, and then found that Timmy was making runs at the cliff to try and get up after him. He went up a bit further and clung to the rope with one hand, afraid of falling and being pounced on by the furious Timmy.

'Come on, Timmy!' suddenly cried George. 'Come on!'

The four of them had now got the boat on the waves, and if only they had Timmy they could set off and row round the rocks at the cave entrance before Markhoff could possibly reach them.

'Timmy! Timmy!'

Timmy heard, cast a last regretful look at Markhoff's legs, and bounded across to the boat. He leapt right in and stood there, still barking madly.

Markhoff dropped down the rope to the ledge – but he was too late. The boat shot out to the entrance of the cove and rounded it. In half a minute it had disappeared round the rocky corner and was out at sea.

Julian and Dick rowed steadily. George put her arms round Timmy and buried her face in his fur. Jo did the same.

'He's all right again, quite all right,' said George, happily.

'Yes, falling into the cold water did it,' agreed Jo, ruffling up his fur. 'Good old Timmy!'

Timmy was now snuffling about in the bottom of the boat joyfully. He had smelt a lovely smell. Jo wondered what he had found. Then she knew.

'It's the packet of sandwiches we brought with us in the boat and never ate!' she cried. 'Good old Timmy – he's wolfing the lot!'

'Let him!' said Julian, pulling hard at the oars. 'He deserves them all! My word, it's nice to hear his bark again and see his tail wagging.'

And wag it certainly did. It never stopped. The world had come right again for Timmy, he could see and hear properly again, he could bark and caper and jump – and he had his beloved George with him once more.

'Now for home,' said Julian. 'Anne *will* be pleased to see us. Gosh, what a time we've had!'

Chapter Twenty-Five

EVERYTHING OKAY

IT was getting dark as George's boat came into Kirrin Bay. It had seemed a very long pull indeed, and everyone was tired out. The girls had helped in the rowing when the boys had almost collapsed from exhaustion, and Timmy had cheered everyone up by his sudden high spirits.

'Honestly, his tail hasn't stopped wagging since he got into the boat,' said George. 'He's so pleased to be himself again!'

A small figure was on the beach as they came in, half-lost in the darkness. It was Anne. She called out to them in a trembling voice.

'Is it really you? I've been watching for you all day long! Are you all right?'

'Rather! And we've got George and Timmy, too!' shouted back Dick, as the boat scraped on the shingle. 'We're fine!'

They jumped out, Timmy too, and hauled the boat up the beach. Anne gave a hand, almost crying with joy to have them all again.

'It's bad enough being in the middle of an adventure,' she said, 'but it's much, much worse when you're left out. I'll never be left out again!'

'Woof,' said Timmy, wagging his tail in full agreement. He never wanted to be left out of adventures either!

They all went home – rather slowly, because they were so tired. Joan was on the look-out for them, as she had been all day. She screamed for joy when she saw George. 'George! You've got George at last! Oh, you bad children, you've been away all day and I didn't know where and I've been worried to death. George, are you all right?'

'Yes, thank you,' said George, who felt as if she was about to fall asleep at any moment. 'I just want something to eat before I fall absolutely sound asleep!'

'But where have you been all day? What have you been doing?' cried Joan, as she bustled off to get them a meal. 'I got so worked up I went to the police – and what a silly I felt – I couldn't tell them where you'd gone or anything. All I could say was you'd gone to find a man called Red, and had rowed away in George's boat!'

'The police have been up and down the coast in a motor-boat ever since,' said Anne. 'Trying to spot you, but they couldn't.'

'No. Our boat was well hidden,' said Dick. 'And so were we! So well hidden that I began to think we'd stay hidden for the rest of our lives.'

The telephone bell rang. Julian jumped. 'Oh, good – you've had the telephone mended. I'll go and 'phone the police when you've answered this call, Joan.'

But it was the police themselves on the telephone, very pleased to hear Joan saying excitedly that all the children were back safely. 'We'll be up in ten minutes,' they said.

In ten minutes' time the five children and Timmy were tucking into a good meal. 'Don't stop,' said the police sergeant, when he came into the room with the constable the children had seen before. 'Just talk while you're eating.'

So they talked. They told about every single thing. First George told a bit, then Jo, then Dick then Julian. At first the sergeant was bewildered, but then the bits of information began to piece themselves together in his mind like a jigsaw puzzle.

'Will my father go to prison?' asked Jo.

'I'm afraid so,' said the sergeant.

'Bad luck, Jo,' said Dick.

'I don't mind,' said Jo. 'I'm better off when he's away – I don't have to do things he tells me then.'

'We'll see if we can't fix you up with a nice home,' said the sergeant kindly. 'You've run wild, Jo – you want looking after.'

'I don't want to go to a Home for Bad Girls,' said Jo, looking scared.

'I shan't let you,' said Dick. 'You're one of the pluckiest kids I've ever known. We'll none of us let you go to a Home. We'll find someone who'll be kind to you someone like – like . . .'

'Like *me*,' said Joan, who was listening, and she put her arm rouund Jo and gave her a squeeze. 'I've got a

cousin who'd like a ragamuffin like you – a bad little girl
with a very good heart. Don't you fret. We'll look after
you.'

'I wouldn't mind living with somebody like you,' said
Jo, in an offhand way. 'I wouldn't be mean any more
then, and I daresay I wouldn't be bad. I'd like to see
Dick and all of you sometimes, though.'

'You will if you're good,' said Dick, with a grin. 'But
mind – if I ever hear you've got in at anyone's pantry
window again, or anything like that, I'll never see you
again!'

Jo grinned. She was very happy. She suddenly remembered something and put her hand into the little rush
basket she still carried. She took out an enormous key.

'Here you are,' she said to the sergeant. 'Here's the
key to the tower room. I bet Red and the others are still
locked up there, ready for you to catch! My, won't they
get a shock when *you* unlock the door and walk in!'

'Quite a lot of people are going to get shocks,' said the
sergeant, putting away his very full note-book. 'Miss
Georgina, you're lucky to get away unharmed, you and
your dog. By the way, we got in touch with a friend of
your father's, when we tried to find out about those papers
that were stolen. He says your father gave him all his
important American papers before he went – so this fellow
Red hasn't anything of value at all. He went to all his
trouble for nothing.'

'Do you know anything about Red?' asked Julian.
'He seemed a bit mad to me.'

'If he's the fellow we think he is, he's not very sane,'

said the sergeant. 'We'll be glad to have him under lock and key – and that man Markhoff too. He's not as clever as Red, but he's dangerous.'

'I hope he hasn't escaped in that helicopter,' said Dick. 'He meant to go tonight.'

'Well, we'll be there in under an hour or so,' said the sergeant. 'I'll just use your telephone, if I may, and set things going'

Things were certainly set going that night! Cars roared up to Red's house, and the gate was broken in when no one came to open it. The helicopter was still in the yard – but alas! it was on its side, smashed beyond repair. The children were told afterwards that Markhoff and the other two men had tried to set off in it, but there was something wrong – and it had risen some way and then fallen back to the yard.

The old woman was trying to look after the three hurt men, who had crawled from their seats and gone to bathe their cuts and bruises. Markhoff had hurt his head, and showed no fight at all.

'And what about Red?' the sergeant asked Markhoff. 'Is he still locked up?'

'Yes,' said Markhoff, savagely. 'And a good thing, too. You'll have to break that door down with a batter-ing-ram to get him and the others out.'

'Oh no, we shan't,' said the sergeant, and produced the key. Markhoff stared at it.

'That kid!' he said. 'She gave me the key of the lar-der. Wait till I get her – she'll be sorry.'

'It'll be a long wait, Markhoff,' said the sergeant. 'A

long, long wait. We'll have to take you off with us, I'm
afraid.'

Red, Simmy and Jake were still locked up, and were
mad with rage. But they saw that the game was up, and
it wasn't long before all of them were safely tucked away
in police cars.

'A very, very nice little haul,' said the sergeant to one
of his men. 'Very neat, too – three of them all locked up
ready for us!'

'What about that kid, Jo?' said the man. 'She seems
a bad lot, and as clever as they make them!'

'She's going to have a chance now,' said the sergeant.
'Everybody has a chance sometimes, and this is hers. She's
just about half-and-half. I reckon – half bad and half
good. But she'll be all right now she's got a chance!'

Jo was sleeping in Joan's room again. The rest were
in their own bedrooms, getting ready for bed. They
suddenly didn't feel sleepy any more. Timmy especially
was very lively, darting in and out of the rooms, and
sending the landing mats sliding about all over the place.

'Timmy! If you jump on my bed again I'll slam the
door on you!' threatened Anne. But she didn't, of course.
It was so lovely to see old Timmy quite himself once more.

The telephone bell suddenly rang, and made everyone
jump.

'*Now* what's up?' said Julian, and went down in the
hall to answer it. A voice spoke in his ear.

'Is that Kirrin 011? This is Telegrams. There is a
cable for you, with reply prepaid. I am now going to read
it.'

'Go ahead,' said Julian.

'It is from Seville in Spain,' said the voice, 'and reads as follows:

"HERE IS OUR ADDRESS. PLEASE CABLE BACK SAY-ING IF EVERYTHING ALL RIGHT – UNCLE QUENTIN".'

Julian repeated the message to the others, who had now crowded round him in the hall. 'What reply shall I give?' he asked. 'No good upsetting them now everything is over!'

'Not a bit of good,' said Dick. 'Say what you like!'

'Right!' said Julian, and turned to the telephone again. 'Hallo – here is the reply message, please. Ready?

"HAVING A MOST EXCITING TIME, WITH LOTS OF FUN AND GAMES. EVERYTHING OKAY – JULIAN".'

'Everything okay,' repeated Anne, as they went up-stairs to bed once more 'That's what I like to hear at the end of an adventure. Everything okay.'

ENID BLYTON

FIVE ON A HIKE TOGETHER

Illustrated by Betty Maxey

KNIGHT BOOKS
Hodder and Stoughton

Printed and bound in Great Britain
for Hodder and Stoughton Children's
Books, a division of Hodder and
Stoughton Ltd., Mill Road,
Dunton Green, Sevenoaks, Kent
TN13 2YA.
Editorial Office: 47 Bedford Square,
London WC1B 3DP) by
Cox & Wyman Ltd., Reading

ISBN 0 340 04144 7

FIVE ON A HIKE
TOGETHER

CONTENTS

Chapter One

A LETTER FROM JULIAN

'ANNE!' shouted George, running after her cousin
as she went along to her classroom. 'Anne! I've just
been down to the letterboard and there's a letter from
your brother Julian. I've brought it for you.'

Anne stopped. 'Oh thanks,' she said. 'What *can*
Julian want? He only wrote a few days ago – it's most
extraordinary for him to write again so soon. It must
be something important.'

'Well, open it and see,' said George. 'Hurry up –
I've got a maths class to go to.'

Anne ripped open the envelope. She pulled out a
sheet of notepaper and read it quickly. She looked
up at George, her eyes shining.

'George! Julian and Dick have got a few days off
at our half-term week-end! Somebody's won a
wonderful scholarship or something, and the boys have
got two days tacked on to a week-end to celebrate!
They want us to join them in a hike, and all go off
together.'

'What a glorious idea!' said George. 'Good old
Julian. I bet he thought of that. Let's read the letter,
Anne.'

But before she could read it a mistress came along.

'Georgina! You should be in class – and you too, Anne.'

George scowled. She hated to be called by her full name. She went off without a word. Anne tucked the letter into her pocket and rushed off joyfully. Half-term with her brothers, Julian and Dick – and with George and Timmy the dog. Could anything be better?

She and George talked about it again after morning school. 'We get from Friday morning till Tuesday,' said George. 'The boys are getting the same. What luck! They don't usually have a half-term in the winter term.'

'They can't go home because the painters are in our house,' said Anne. 'That's why I was going home with you, of course. But I'm sure your mother won't mind if we go off with the boys. Your father never likes us in the middle of the term.'

'No, he doesn't,' said George. 'He's always deep in the middle of some wonderful idea, and he hates to be disturbed. It will suit everyone if we go off on a hike.'

'Julian says he will telephone to us tonight and arrange everything,' said Anne. 'I hope it will be a nice fine week-end. It will still be October, so there's a chance of a bit of warm sunshine.'

'The woods will be beautiful,' said George. 'And won't Timmy enjoy himself. Let's go and tell him the news.'

The boarding-school that the two girls were at was one that allowed the children to bring their own pets to school. There were kennels down in the yard for various dogs, and Timmy lived there during term-time. The two girls went to get him.

He heard their footsteps at once and began to bark excitedly. He scraped at the gate of the kennel yard, wishing for the thousandth time that he could find out how to open it.

He flung himself on the two girls, licking and pawing and barking.

'Silly dog. Mad dog!' said George, and thumped his back affectionately. 'Listen, Tim – we're going off for the week-end with Julian and Dick! What do you think of that? We're going on a hike, so you'll love it. All through the woods and up the hills and goodness knows where!'

Timmy seemed to understand every word. He cocked up his ears, put his head on one side and listened intently while George was speaking.

'Woof,' he said, at the end, as if he approved thoroughly. Then off he went with the girls for his walk, his plumy tail wagging happily. He didn't like term-time nearly as much as the holidays – but he was quite prepared to put up with kennel life so long as he could be near his beloved George.

Julian rang up that night as he had promised. He had got everything planned already. Anne listened, thrilled.

'It sounds super,' she said. 'Yes – we can meet where you say, and we'll be there as near as we can on time. Anyway, we can wait about if you others aren't there. Yes – we'll bring the things you say. Oh Julian, won't it be fun?'

'What's he say?' asked George impatiently when at last Anne put the receiver down. 'You might have let me have a word with Julian. I wanted to tell him all about Timmy.'

'He doesn't want to waste an expensive telephone call listening to you raving about Timmy,' said Anne. 'He asked how he was and I said "fine", and that's all he wanted to know about Tim. He's made all the arrangements. I'll tell you what they are.'

The girls went off to a corner of their common-room and sat down. Timmy was there too. He was allowed in at certain times, and so were three other dogs belonging to the girls. Each dog behaved well – he knew that if he didn't he would be taken back to the kennels at once!

'Julian says that he and Dick can get off immediately after breakfast,' said Anne. 'So can we, so that's all right. He says we've got to take very little with us – just night-things, tooth-brush, hair-brush and flannel and a rolled-up mac. And any biscuits or chocolate we can buy. Have you any money left?'

'A bit,' said George. 'Not much. Enough to buy a few bars of chocolate, I think. Anyway, you've got all the biscuits your mother sent last week. We can take some of those.'

'Yes. And the barley sugar one of my aunts sent,' said Anne. 'But Julian says we're not to take much because this is to be a proper hike, and we'll get tired if we have to carry a heavy load. Oh, he said put in two pairs of extra socks.'

'Right,' said George, and she patted Timmy who was lying close beside her. 'There's going to be a long walky-walk, Tim. Won't you love that!'

Timmy grunted comfortably. He wondered if there would be any rabbits on the walk. A walk wasn't really exciting unless there were rabbits all over the place. Timmy thought it was a pity that rabbits were allowed to live down holes. They always disappeared most unfairly just when he had nearly caught one!

Anne and George went to see their house-mistress to tell her that they were not going to Kirrin Cottage after all, but were going walking.

'My brother says he has written to you,' said Anne. 'So you'll know all about it tomorrow, Miss Peters. And George's mother will be writing too. We can go, can't we?'

'Oh, yes – it will be a lovely half-term for you!' said Miss Peters. 'Especially if this sunny weather lasts. Where are you going?'

'Over the moors,' said Anne. 'In the very loneliest, most deserted parts that Julian can find! We might see deer and wild ponies and perhaps even a few badgers. We shall walk and walk.'

'But where will you sleep if the parts you are going to are so very lonely?' asked Miss Peters.

'Oh Julian is arranging all that,' said George. 'He's been looking up little inns and farm-houses on the map, and we shall make for those at night. It will be too cold to sleep out of doors.'

'It certainly will!' said Miss Peters. 'Well don't get into trouble, that's all. I know what you five are when you get together. I imagine Timmy is going with you too?'

'Of *course*!' said George. 'I wouldn't go if he didn't go! I couldn't leave him here alone.'

The two girls got their things ready as Friday came near. The biscuits were taken out of the tin and put into paper bags. The barley sugar was put into a bag too, and the bars of chocolate.

Both girls had rucksacks with straps for their shoulders. They packed and repacked them several times. One by one more and more things were added. Anne felt she must take a book to read. George said they must each take a torch with a new battery.

'And what about biscuits for Timmy?' she said. 'I simply must take something for him. He'd like a bone too – a big one that he can chew and chew and that I can put back into the bag for another time.'

'Well, let me carry all the biscuits and chocolate then if you're going to put a smelly old bone into your bag,' said Anne. 'I don't see why you want to take *anything* for Timmy – he can always have something to eat when we do – wherever we have a meal.'

George decided not to take the bone. She had fetched one from his kennel, and it certainly was big and heavy, and equally certainly it was smelly. She took it back to the kennel again, Timmy following her rather puzzled. Why keep carrying his bone here and there? He didn't approve at all.

It seemed a long time till Friday, but at last it came. Both girls woke up very early indeed. George was out in the kennels before breakfast, brushing and combing Timmy to make him look spruce and tidy for Julian and Dick. He knew it was the day they were to set off and he was as excited as the two girls.

'We'd better eat a good breakfast,' said Anne. 'We might have to wait some time before our next meal. Let's slip off immediately after breakfast. It's lovely to feel free of school and bells and time-tables – but I shan't feel *really* free till I'm outside the school grounds!'

They ate an enormous breakfast though really they
were too excited to want much. Then they got their
rucksacks, ready-packed the night before, said good-
bye to Miss Peters, and went to fetch Timmy.

He was waiting impatiently for them, and barked
madly when they came near. In a trice he was out of
his kennel-yard and capering round them, almost trip-
ping them up.

'Good-bye, Anne and George!' yelled one of their
friends. 'Have a good time on your hike – and it's no
good coming back on Tuesday and telling us you've
had one of your usual hair-raising adventures, because
we just shan't believe it!'

'Woof,' said Timmy. 'Woof, woof!' Which meant
that *he* was going to have adventures with hundreds
of rabbits, anyway!

Chapter Two

SETTING OFF

JULIAN and Dick were also on their way, very pleased
to have such an unexpectedly long week-end.

'I never liked Willis or Johnson much,' said Dick,
as they walked out of the school grounds. 'Awful
swotters they were – never had any time for games or
fun. But I take my hat off to them today! Because of
their swotting they've won medals and scholarships
and goodness knows what – and we've got a week-end
off in celebration! Good old Willis and Johnson!'

'Hear hear,' said Dick. 'But I bet they'll sit in a
corner with their books all the week-end – they won't
know if it's a brilliant day like this, or pouring with
rain like yesterday! Poor mutts!'

'They'd hate to go off on a hike,' said Julian. 'It
would be utter misery to them. Do you remember how
awful Johnson was at rugger? He never knew which
goal he was playing against – always ran the wrong
way!'

'Yes. But he must have got terrific brains,' said Dick.
'Why are we talking about Willis and Johnson? I can
think of plenty of more interesting things. Anne and
George, for instance – and old Tim. I hope they'll
manage to get off in time all right.'

Julian had carefully looked up a large-scale map

of the moors that lay between the two schools that he
and the girls went to. They were vast stretches of lonely
heathery land, dotted with farms here and there, with
a few small cottages, and some inns.

'We'll keep right off the main roads, and the second-
and third-grades,' he said. 'We'll take the little lanes
and paths. I wonder what Timmy will say if we see
deer. He'll wonder what in the world they are!'

'He'll only be interested in rabbits,' said Dick. 'I
hope he's not as fat as he was last hols. I think we must
have given him too many ice-creams and too much
chocolate!'

'Well, he won't get that in term-time!' said Julian.
'The girls don't get as much pocket money as we do.
Buck up – there's the bus!'

They ran for the little country bus that rumbled
along the country lanes, taking people to market, or
to the tiny villages that lay here and there tucked away
in the moor. It stopped most obligingly for them, and
they leapt in.

'Ha! Running away from school?' said the conductor. 'Have to report you, you know!'

'Very funny,' said Julian, bored at this joke, which
the conductor produced regularly every time a boy
got on board with a rucksack over his shoulders.

They had to get out at the next village and cut across
country to get to another bus-route. They managed to
catch a bus there easily and settled down comfortably
in their seats. It was half an hour's run from there to
where they had planned to meet the girls.

'Here you are, young sirs,' called the conductor, as the bus ran into a village. It had a wide green on which geese cackled, and a small pond for ducks. 'You wanted Pippin Village, didn't you? We don't go any farther – we just turn round and go back.'

'Thanks,' said the boys and got out. 'Now – are the girls here or not?' said Julian. 'They have to walk from a tiny railway station about two miles away.'

They were not there. Julian and Dick went to have a drink of orangeade at the village store. They had hardly finished when they saw the two girls looking in at the door.

'Julian! Dick! We guessed you'd be eating or drinking!' said Anne, and she rushed at her brothers. 'We came as quickly as we could. The engine broke down – it was such a funny little train! All the passengers got out and advised the engine-driver what to do!'

'Hallo!' said Julian, and gave Anne a hug He was very fond of his young sister. 'Hallo, George! My, you've grown fat, haven't you?'

'I have not,' said George, indignantly. 'And Timmy isn't fat either, so don't tell him he is.'

'Julian's pulling your leg as usual,' said Dick, giving George a friendly slap on the back. 'All the same, you've grown a bit – you'll soon be as tall as I am. Hallo, Timmy! Good dog, fine dog! Tongue as wet as usual? Yes, it is! I never knew a dog with a wetter tongue than yours!'

Timmy went nearly mad with joy at being with all four of his friends. He leapt round them, barking,

wagging his long tail and sending a pile of tins crashing
to the floor in his delight.

'Now, now!' said the shop-woman, emerging from
a dark little room at the back. 'Take that dog out. He's
gone mad!'

'Don't you girls want a drink of ginger-beer or something?' asked Julian, getting hold of Timmy's collar.
'You'd better, because we don't want to have to carry
heavy bottles of drinkables with us.'

'Where are we going to set off to?' asked George.
'Yes, I'd like ginger-beer please. Get down, Timmy.
Anyone would think you'd been away from Julian and
Dick for at least ten years!'

'It probably does seem like ten years to him,' said
Anne. 'I say – are those sandwiches?'

She pointed to a ledge at the back of the counter.
There was a little pile of sandwiches there, looking
most appetizing.

'Yes, they're sandwiches, Miss,' said the shop-
woman, opening two bottles of ginger-beer. 'I've made
them for my son who works over at Blackbush Farm –
he'll be in for them soon.'

'I suppose you couldn't make *us* some, could you?'
asked Julian. 'We wouldn't need to bother about trying
to get to some village at lunch time then. They look
jolly good.'

'Yes. I can make you all you want,' said the shop-
woman, putting two glasses down in front of the girls.
'What do you want – cheese, egg, ham or pork?'

'Well – we'd like some of all of those,' said Julian.

'The bread looks so nice too.'

'I make it myself,' said the woman, pleased. 'All right – I'll go and make you some. You tell me if any-one comes into the shop while I'm gone.'

She disappeared. 'That's good,' said Julian. 'If she makes plenty of those we can avoid villages all the day and have a really good day of exploration – treading where no foot has trod before and all that!'

'How many can you manage each?' asked the woman, suddenly reappearing. 'My son, he has six – that's twelve rounds of bread.'

'Well – could you manage eight sandwiches for each of us?' said Julian. The woman looked astonished. 'It's to last us all day,' he explained, and she nodded and disappeared again.

'That's a nice little sum for her,' said Anne. 'Eight sandwiches each, making sixteen rounds of bread – for four people!'

'Well, let's hope she's got a bread-cutting machine!' said Dick. 'Or we'll be here for keeps! Hallo – who's this?'

A tall man appeared at the entrance of the shop, a bicycle in his hand. 'Ma!' he called.

The children guessed who he was at once – the son who worked over at Blackbush Farm. He had come for his sandwiches!

'Your mother is hard at work cutting sixty-four rounds of bread,' said Dick. 'Shall I get her for you?'

'No. I'm in a hurry,' said the man and he set his bicycle by the door, came in, reached over the counter for his sandwiches and then went back to his bicycle.

'Tell my mother I've been in,' he said. 'And you might tell her I'll be late home today – got to take some stuff to the prison.'

He was off at once, sailing away down the road on

his bicycle. The old woman suddenly came in, a knife in one hand, a loaf in the other.

'Did I hear Jim?' she said. 'Oh yes – he's got his sandwiches. You should have told me he was in!'

'He said he was in a hurry,' explained Julian. 'And he said we were to tell you he'd be late today because he had to take some stuff to the prison.'

'I've got another son there,' said the woman. The four looked at her. Did she mean he was a prisoner? And what prison?

She guessed their thoughts and smiled. 'Oh, my Tom isn't a prisoner!' she said. 'He's a warder – a fine fellow. Not a nice job there though – I'm always afraid of those men in prison – a fierce lot, a bad lot!'

'Yes – I've heard there is a big prison on this moor,' said Julian. 'It's marked on our map too. We're not going near it, of course.'

'No. Don't you take the girls near there,' said the woman, disappearing again. 'If I don't get on with your sandwiches you'll not have them before to-morrow morning.'

Only one customer came in while the children were waiting – a solemn old man smoking a clay pipe. He looked round the shop, couldn't see the woman, took a packet of blancmange powder, which he slipped into his pocket, and put the money down on the counter.

'Tell 'er when 'er comes,' he mumbled with his pipe still in his mouth, and out he shuffled. Timmy growled. The old man smelt very unwashed and Timmy didn't like him.

At last the sandwiches were finished and the old woman appeared again. She had packed them up neatly in four parcels of grease-proof paper, and had pencilled on each what they were. Julian read what she had written and winked at the others.

'My word – we're in for a grand time!' he said. 'Cheese, Pork, Ham and Egg – and what's this?'

'Oh, that's four slices of my home-made fruit cake,' said the old woman. 'I'm not charging you for that. It's just so that you can taste it!'

'It looks like half the cake!' said Julian, touched. 'But we shall pay for it, with many thanks. How much is all that?'

She told him. Julian put down the money and added some extra for the cake. 'There you are, and many thanks,' he said. 'And that money there was left by an old fellow with a clay pipe who took a packet of blanc-mange powder.'

'That would be Old Man Gupps,' said the woman. 'Well, I hope you'll enjoy your tour. Come back here if you want any more sandwiches cut! If you eat all those today you won't do badly!'

'Woof,' said Timmy, hoping that he too would share a few. The woman produced a bone for him, and he took it up in his mouth.

'Thanks!' Julian said. 'Come on – now we'll really start!'

Chapter Three

ACROSS THE COUNTRYSIDE

They set off at last, Timmy running in front. School already seemed far behind them. The October sun shone down warmly, and the trees in the village glowed yellow and red and golden, dressed in their autumn colourings. A few leaves floated down in the breeze, but not until there was a real frost would many come whirling down.

'It's a heavenly day,' said George. 'I wish I hadn't got my blazer on. I'm cooked already.'

'Well, take it off and carry it over your shoulder,' said Julian. 'I'm going to do the same. Our jerseys are quite warm enough today !'

They took off their thick blazers and carried them. Each of them had a rucksack, a mac rolled up tightly and tied to it, and now a blazer to carry. But none of them noticed the weight at the outset of their day.

'I'm glad you girls took my advice and wore your thickest shoes,' said Julian, looking with approval at their brogues. 'Some of our walking may be wet. Have you got changes of socks?'

'Yes. We brought everything you told us to,' said Anne. 'Your rucksack looks a bit fuller than ours, Ju !'

'Well, I've got maps and things in it,' said Julian. 'It's a queer place, this moor – miles and miles and miles of it! Queer names on it too – Blind Valley – Rabbit Hill – Lost Lake – Coney Copse!'

'Rabbit Hill! Timmy would love that,' said George, and Timmy pricked up his ears. Rabbits? Ah, that was the kind of place he liked!

'Well, actually we're going towards Rabbit Hill now,' said Julian. 'And after that there's Coney Copse, and as coney is a country word for rabbit, Timmy ought to enjoy himself!'

'Woof,' said Timmy joyfully and bounded ahead. He felt very happy. His four friends were with him, their rucksacks were full of delicious-smelling sandwiches, and a long, long walk lay ahead, teeming, he hoped with rabbits!

It was lovely walking along in the sun. They soon left the little village behind and took a winding lane. The hedges on either side became so high that the four couldn't see over the tops at all.

'What a sunken lane!' said Dick. 'I feel as if I'm walking in a tunnel! And how narrow! I wouldn't like to drive a car along this lane. If I met another car I might have to back for miles!'

'We shan't meet anyone much,' said Julian. 'It's only in the summer that cars come along these lanes – people on holiday, touring round the countryside. Look – we take that path now – it leads to Rabbit Hill, according to the map!'

They climbed over a stile in the high hedge and

walked over a field towards a curious little hill. Timmy
suddenly went mad with excitement. He could smell
rabbits – and he could see them too!

'You don't often see so many rabbits out in the day-
time,' said George, surprised. 'Big ones and little ones
too – what a scampering.'

They came to the hill and sat down quietly to watch
the rabbits. But it was quite impossible to make Timmy
do the same. The sight and smell of so many made him
quite wild. He pulled away from George's hand and
went bounding madly up the hill, scattering rabbits by
the dozen.

'Timmy!' yelled George, but for once Timmy paid
no attention. He rushed here and rushed there, getting

very angry as first one rabbit and then another neatly popped down a hole.

'It's no use calling him,' said Dick. 'He won't catch one, anyway – see how nippy they are. It's my belief they're having a game with our Timmy!'

It did look rather like it. As soon as Timmy had chased two or three rabbits down one hole, a few more would pop up from another behind him. The children laughed. It was as good as a pantomime.

'Where do you mean to have lunch?' asked Anne. 'If we stay here much longer I shall really have to have something to eat – and it's not nearly time yet. I wish I didn't always feel so hungry in the open air.'

'Well, come on then,' said Julian. 'We've got some way to go before we get to our lunch-place. I've made a pretty good time-table of our tour – we're going to go all round the moors and finish at the place we started at! I've really marked it all out pretty well.'

'Do we sleep at farm-houses or something at night?' asked George. 'I should like that. Will they mind having us, do you think? Or do we go to inns?'

'Farm-houses for two nights and inns for the other nights,' said Julian. 'I've marked them all.'

They went up Rabbit Hill and down the other side. There were just as many rabbits there. Timmy chased them till he panted like an engine going uphill! His tongue hung out, dripping wet.

'You've had enough, Tim,' said George. 'Be sensible now.'

But Timmy couldn't be sensible with so many

rabbits about. So they left him to chase and dart and race at top speed and went on down the hill. Timmy came rushing after them when they got to the bottom.

'*Now* perhaps you'll stop tearing about like a mad thing and walk with us,' scolded George. But she spoke too soon, for soon they were in a small wood which Julian informed them was Coney Copse.

'And as I told you, coney means rabbit, so you can't expect Timmy to stop being mad just yet,' said Julian.

They very nearly lost Timmy in Coney Copse. A rabbit disappeared down a very big hole, and Timmy was actually able to get down a little way. Then he got stuck. He scrabbled violently with his feet but it was no good. He was well and truly stuck.

The others soon discovered he wasn't with them and went back, calling. Quite by chance they came on the hole he was in and heard the sound of panting and scraping. A shower of sand flew out of the hole.

'There he is! The idiot, he's down a hole,' said George in alarm. 'Timmy! TIMMY! Come on out!'

There was nothing that Timmy would have liked better, but he couldn't come out, however much he tried. A root of a tree had got wedged into his back, and he couldn't seem to push himself out again, past the annoying root.

It took the four children twenty minutes to get Timmy out. Anne had to lie down and wriggle in a little way to reach him. She was the only one small enough to get into the hole.

She caught hold of Timmy's back legs and pulled

hard. Somehow the root slid off his back and he came backwards. He whined loudly.

'Oh Anne, you're hurting him, you're hurting him !' shouted George. 'Let him go !'

'I can't !' yelled back Anne. 'He'll only go down deeper, if I leave go his legs. Can you pull me out? If so Timmy will come too – he'll have to because I've got his legs !'

Poor Anne was pulled out by her legs, and poor Timmy came too, pulled by his. He whined and went to George.

'He's hurt himself somewhere,' said George anxiously. 'I know he has. He wouldn't whine like that if he wasn't hurt.'

She ran her fingers over him, pressing here and there. She examined each leg and each paw. She looked at his head. Still he whined. Where could he have hurt himself?

'Leave him,' said Julian, at last. 'I can't see that he's hurt anywhere – except in his feelings ! He probably didn't like Anne hauling him out by his hind legs. Most undignified !'

George wasn't satisfied. Although she could find nothing wrong, she couldn't help being sure that Timmy had hurt himself somewhere. Ought he to see a vet?

'Don't be silly, George,' said Julian. 'Vets don't grow on trees in a moorland country like this ! Let's go on walking. You'll see Timmy will follow quite all right, and soon forget to whine. I tell you, he's hurt his doggy feelings, that's all. His vanity is wounded !'

They left Coney Copse and went on, George rather silent. Timmy trotted beside her, also rather quiet. Still, there really didn't seem anything the matter with him, except that he gave sudden little whines now and again.

'Now here's where I thought we might have our lunch,' said Julian, at last. 'Fallaway Hill! It's a good name for it too – it falls away steeply, and we've got a marvellous view.'

So they had. They had come to the top of a steep hill, not guessing that it fell away on the other side. They could sit on the tip and see the sun shining on miles and miles of lonely heather-grown moor. They might see shy deer in the distance – or little wild ponies.

'This is heavenly,' said Anne, sitting down on a great tuft of heather. 'It's as warm as summer too! I do hope it's like this all over the week-end. We shall all be burnt brown!'

'It will also be heavenly having some of those sandwiches,' said Dick, choosing a lump of heather too. 'What comfortable seats are provided for us! I've a good mind to take a tuft of this heather back to school with me to put on the very hard chair that goes with my desk!'

Julian put the four packets of sandwiches down in the heather. Anne undid them. They looked wonderful!

'Super!' said Anne. 'What do you want first?'

'Well, speaking for myself I'm going to have one of each, put them all on top of one another, and have a huge bite of cheese, ham, pork and egg at once,' said Dick. Anne laughed.

'Even *your* mouth isn't big enough for that,' she said. But somehow Dick managed, though it was difficult.

'Disgusting behaviour,' he said, when he had managed the first mouthful. 'I think on the whole that one at a time is more economical. Hie, Timmy – have a bit?'

Timmy obliged. He was very quiet, and George was still anxious about him. Still, his appetite seemed remarkably good, so nobody but George wondered any more if he had hurt himself. He lay beside George, occasionally putting a great paw on her knee if he wanted another bit of sandwich.

'Timmy does jolly well,' said Dick, with his mouth full. 'He gets bits from us all. I bet he eats more than any of us. I say – did anyone ever taste such smashing sandwiches? Have you tried the pork? It must have come from a super pig!'

It was lovely sitting there in the sun, looking over miles of countryside, eating hungrily. They all felt very happy. Except George. *Was* there anything wrong with Timmy? It would spoil the whole week-end if so!

Chapter Four

GEORGE IS WORRIED

THEY lazed for some time in the sun after they had finished their meal. There were three sandwiches each left, and half a piece each of the fruit cake. No one had been able to manage a whole piece, much as they would have liked to.

Timmy seemed to think he could finish all the cake that was left, but Julian said no. 'It's such a gorgeous cake it would be really wasted on Timmy,' he said. 'You've had enough, Tim. Greedy dog!'

'Woof,' said Timmy, wagging his tail, and eyeing the cake watchfully. He sighed when he saw it being packed up. He had only had a bit of George's half-slice – what a cake!

'I'll pack three sandwiches and a half-slice of the cake into each of four bags,' said Julian. 'Anyone can eat his or hers whenever they like. I expect we shall have a good meal at the farm-house I've chosen for to-night, so you can eat when you like before then.'

'I don't feel as if I could eat anything till tomorrow morning,' said Anne, putting her bag of food into her rucksack. 'But it's odd how hungry you keep on getting, even if you feel you can't possibly be for hours and hours.'

'Well, Timmy can wolf anything you don't want,' said Julian. 'Nothing wasted when Tim's about. Now are we all ready? We're going through a little village soon, where we'll stop for a drink. I could do with a ginger-beer. And then on we go to our farm-house. We ought to try and arrive about five, because it gets dark so soon.'

'What's the farm-house called?' asked Anne.

'Blue Pond Farm,' said Julian. 'Nice name, isn't it? I hope it's still got a blue pond.'

'Suppose they haven't room for us?' said Anne.

'Oh, they can always put a couple of girls somewhere,' said Julian. 'Dick and I can sleep in a barn if necessary. We're not particular!'

'*I'd* like to sleep in a barn too,' said Anne. 'I'd love to. Let's not ask for a bedroom, let's all sleep in a barn – on straw or hay or something.'

'No,' said Julian. 'You girls will have to be in the house. It gets cold at night, and we've brought no rugs. We boys will be all right with our macs over us. I'm not letting you two girls do that.'

'It's *stupid* being a girl!' said George, for about the millionth time in her life. 'Always having to be careful when boys can do as they like! I'm going to sleep in a barn, anyway. I don't care what you say, Ju!'

'Oh yes you do,' said Julian. 'You know quite well that if ever you go against the orders of the chief – that's me, my girl, in case you didn't know it – you won't come out with us again. You may look like a boy and behave like a boy, but you're a girl all the same.

And like it or not, girls have got to be taken care of.'

'I should have thought that boys hated having to take care of girls,' said George, sulkily. 'Especially girls like me who don't like it.'

'Well, decent boys like looking after their girl cousins or their sisters,' said Julian. 'And oddly enough decent girls like it. But I won't count you as a girl, George, decent or otherwise. I'll merely count you as a boy who's got to have an eye on him – my eye, see? So take that look off your face, and don't make yourself any more difficult than you already are.'

George couldn't help laughing, and the sulky look went at once. She gave Julian a punch. 'All right. You win. You're so jolly domineering these days I feel quite afraid of you!'

'You're not afraid of anyone,' said Dick. 'You're the bravest girl I ever knew! Aha! That's made old George blush like a girl! Let me warm my hands, George!'

And Dick held his hands up in front of George's scarlet face, pretending to warm them at her fiery blush. She didn't know whether to be pleased or angry. She pushed his hands away and got up, looking more like a boy than ever with her short tousled hair and her well-freckled face!

The others got up and stretched. Then they settled their rucksacks on their backs again, with their macs fastened to them, threw their blazers over their shoulders and set off down Fallaway Hill.

Timmy followed, but he didn't bound about as usual.

He went slowly and carefully. George looked round
for him, and frowned.

'What *is* the matter with Timmy?' she said. 'Look
at him! Not a jump or a scamper in him!'

They all stopped and watched him. He came towards them and they saw that he was limping slightly
with his left hind leg. George dropped down beside him
and felt the leg carefully.

'I think he must have twisted it – sprained it or
something, when he was down that rabbit-hole,' she
said. She patted him gently on the back and he winced.

'What's the matter, Tim?' said George, and she
parted the hair on his back, examining the white skin
underneath to see why he had winced when she had
patted him.

'He's got an awful bruise here,' she said at last, and
the others bent to see. 'Something must have hurt his
back down in that hole. And Anne must have hurt
one of his legs when she held on to them and dragged
him out. I *told* you not to hold on to his legs, Anne.'

'Well, how were we to get him out if I didn't?' demanded Anne, feeling cross but rather guilty. 'Did you
want him to stick there for days and days?'

'I don't think there's much damage done,' said Julian, feeling the hind leg. 'I honestly think he's only
just twisted it a bit, George. He'll be all right after tonight, I'm sure.'

'But I must be *certain*,' said George. 'Did you say
we come to a village soon, Ju?'

'Yes – Beacons Village,' said Julian. 'We can ask if

there's a vet anywhere in the district if you like. He'll
look at Timmy's leg and tell you if there's anything
much wrong. But I don't think there is.'

'We'll go on to the village then,' said George. 'Oh
dear – the only time I *ever* wish Timmy was a *little* dog
is when he's hurt – because he's so very very heavy to
carry.'

'Well, don't think of carrying him yet,' said Dick.
'He can walk on three legs even if he can't on four!
He's not as bad as all that, are you, Timmy?'

'Woof,' said Timmy, mournfully. He was rather enjoying all the fuss. George patted his head. 'Come on,'
she said, 'we'll soon get that leg put right. Come on,
Tim.'

They all went on, looking round to see how Timmy
was getting on. He followed slowly, and then began to
limp more badly. Finally he lifted his left hind leg up
from the ground and ran on three legs only.

'Poor boy,' said George. 'Poor Timmy! I do hope
his leg will be all right tomorrow. I can't possibly go
on with the hike if it isn't.'

It was rather a gloomy company that came to
Beacons Village. Julian made his way to a little inn
that stood in the middle, called Three Shepherds.

A woman was shaking a duster out of a window.
Julian called up to her.

'I say! Is there a vet anywhere in this district? I
want someone to have a look at our dog's leg.'

'No. No vet here,' answered the woman. 'Not one
nearer than Marlins over six miles away.'

George's heart sank. Timmy would never be able to
walk six miles.

'Is there a bus?' she called.

'No. Not to Marlins,' said the woman. 'No bus goes
there, missy. But if you want your dog's leg seen to,
you go up to Spiggy House, up along there. Mr.
Gaston lives there with his horses, and he knows about
dogs too. You take the dog there. He'll know what to
do.'

'Oh *thank* you,' said George, gratefully. 'Is it very far?'

'About half a mile,' said the woman. 'See that hill? You go up there, take the turning to the right and you'll see a big house. That's Spiggy House. You can't mistake it because of the stables built all round it. Ask for Mr. Gaston. He's nice, he is. Maybe you'll have to wait a little if he's out with his horses though – he may not be in till it's almost dark.'

The four held a little council. 'We'd better go up to this Mr. Gaston's, I think,' said Julian. 'But I think you and Anne, Dick, should go on to the farm-house I planned to stay in for the night, and make arrangements for us. We don't want to leave it till the last minute. I'll go with George and Timmy, of course.'

'Right,' said Dick. 'I'll take Anne now. It will be dark pretty soon. Got your torch, Julian?'

'Yes,' said Julian. 'And I'm pretty good at finding my way, as you know. I shall come back to this village after we've been to Mr. Gaston's, and then make straight for the farm-house. It's about a mile and a half away.'

'Thanks awfully for saying you'll come with me, Julian,' said George. 'Let's go now, shall we? Well, Dick and Anne – see you later!'

Julian set off with George and Timmy up the hill to Spiggy House. Timmy went on three legs, and still seemed very sorry for himself. Anne and Dick watched him, feeling sorry for him.

'I hope he's all right tomorrow,' said Dick. 'It will spoil our week-end if he's not, no doubt about that!'

They turned away and walked through the little village of Beacons. 'Now for Blue Pond Farm-house,' said Dick. 'Julian didn't give me very clear directions, I think I'll ask someone exactly where it is.'

But they met nobody except a man driving a little cart. Dick hailed him and he pulled up his horse.

'Are we on the right road for Blue Pond Farm-house?' shouted Dick.

'Ar,' answered the man, nodding his head.

'Is it straight on – or do we take any paths or little lanes?' asked Dick.

'Ar,' said the man, nodding again.

'What does he mean – "ar"?' said Dick. He raised his voice again.

'Is it this way?' and he pointed.

'Ar,' said the man again. He raised his whip and pointed up the road where the two were going, and then across to the west.

'Oh, I see – we turn to the right up there?' called Dick.

'Ar,' said the man, nodding, and drove on so suddenly that the horse almost stepped on Dick's foot.

'Well – if we find the farm-house after all those "ars" we'll be clever,' said Dick. 'Come on!'

Chapter Five

ANNE AND DICK

IT began to get dark very suddenly. The sun had gone, and a big black cloud slid smoothly over the sky. 'It's going to rain,' said Dick. 'Blow! I thought it was going to be a lovely evening.'

'We'd better hurry,' said Anne. 'I hate sheltering under a hedge in the pouring rain, with drips down my neck, and puddles round my feet!'

They hurried. They went up the road that led out of the village and then came to a turning on the right. This must be the one the man had meant. They stopped and looked down it. It seemed to be like one of the sunken lanes they had walked down in the morning, and it looked rather dark and tunnel-like now, in the twilight.

'I hope it's right,' said Dick. 'We'll ask the very first person we meet.'

'If we *do* meet anyone!' said Anne, feeling that they never would in this curious deep lane. They went up it. It wound round and about and then went downhill into a very muddy bit indeed. Anne found herself sloshing about in thick mud.

'A stream or something must run across the lane here,' she said. 'Ugh! The water's got into my shoes!

I'm sure we don't go this way, Dick. The water's quite deep farther on, I'm certain. I was up to my ankles just now.'

Dick looked about in the deepening twilight. He made out something above him in the high hedge that grew on the steep bank each side.

'Look – is that a stile?' he said, 'Where's my torch? At the bottom of my rucksack, of course! Can you get it out, Anne, to save me taking the thing off?'

Anne found the torch and gave it to Dick. He switched it on, and immediately the shadows round them grew blacker, and the lane seemed more tunnel-like than ever. Dick flashed the torch upwards to what he had thought was a stile.

'Yes – it is a stile,' he said. 'I expect that leads up to the farm-house – a short cut, probably. I've no doubt this lane is the one used by the farm-carts, and probably goes right round to the farm – but if this is a short cut we might as well take it. It must lead somewhere, anyway!'

They scrambled up the bank to the stile. Dick helped Anne over, and they found themselves in a wide field. In front of them was a narrow path, running between crops of some sort.

'Yes – this is obviously a short cut,' said Dick, pleased. 'I expect we'll see the lights of the farm-house in a minute.'

'Or fall into the blue pond first,' said Anne, rather dismally. It was just beginning to rain and she was wondering if it was worth while to untie her mac from her shoulder and put it on. Or was the farm-house really nearby? Julian had said it wasn't very far.

They walked across the field and came to another stile. The rain was coming down fast now. Anne decided to put on her mac. She stood under a thick bush and Dick helped her on with it. She had a small sou'wester in the pocket and put that on too. Dick put his on and they set off again.

The second stile led into another endless field, and the path then came at last to a big field-gate. They climbed over it and found themselves on what looked like a heathery moor – wild and uncultivated land! No farm-house was to be seen – though, indeed, they could not have seen anything of one unless they had been very close to it, because the night was on them, dark and rainy.

'If only we could see some lights somewhere – shining out of a window,' said Dick. He shone his torch on to the moor in front of them. 'I don't quite know what to do. There doesn't seem a path here – and I just hate the idea of going all the way back across those wet fields, and into that dark little lane.'

'Oh no – don't let's,' said Anne, with a shiver. 'I really didn't like that lane. There *must* be a path somewhere! It's silly for a gate to open on to moor-land!'

And then, as they stood there, with the rain dripping on them and not much else to be heard, another noise came to their ears.

It was so unexpected and so very startling that both

of them clutched the other in a start of alarm. It was certainly a strange noise to hear in that deserted bit of country.

Bells! Wild, clanging bells sounding without a stop, jangling out over the dark countryside in peal after peal. Anne held on tightly to Dick.

'What is it? Where are those bells? What are they ringing for?' whispered Anne.

Dick had no idea. He was as startled as Anne to hear this extraordinary noise. It sounded some distance away, but every now and again the wind blew hard and then the noise of the jangling swept round them, close to them it seemed.

'I wish they'd stop. Oh, I wish they'd stop!' said Anne, her heart beating fast. 'I don't like them. They frighten me. They're not church bells.'

'No. They're certainly not church bells,' said Dick. 'They're a warning of some kind. I'm sure – but what for? Fire? We'd see fire if there was one anywhere near us. War? No – bells and beacons were used to warn people of war long long ago. Not now.'

'That village was called Beacons,' said Anne, suddenly remembering. 'Do you suppose it has that name because long ago there was a nearby hill where people lighted a beacon, to send a warning to other towns telling them that the enemy was coming? Did they ring bells too? Are we hearing long-ago bells, Dick? They don't sound like bells I've ever heard in my life before.'

'Good gracious! They're certainly not long-ago

bells!' said Dick, speaking cheerfully, though he was really just as puzzled and alarmed as Anne. 'Those bells are being rung now, at this very minute!'

Quite suddenly the bells stopped and an enormous silence took the place of the wild ringing. The two children stood and listened for a minute or two and then heaved a sigh of relief.

'They've stopped at last,' said Anne. 'I hated them! *Why* did they ring out on this dark dark night? Oh do let's find Blue Pond Farm-house as soon as ever we can, Dick. I don't like being lost in the dark like this, with bells ringing madly for nothing at all!'

'Come on,' said Dick. 'Keep close to the hedge. As long as we follow that we must come to somewhere. We won't wander out on to the moorland.'

He took Anne's arm and the two of them kept close to the hedge. They came to another path at last and followed it. That led to a lane, but not a sunken one this time – and then, oh wonderful sight, – not far off they saw a light shining!

'That must be Blue Pond Farm-house!' said Dick, thankfully. 'Come on, Anne – not much farther now!'

They came to a low stone wall and followed it till they came to a broken-down gate. It opened with a squeak, and Anne stepped through – right into an enormous puddle!

'Blow!' she said. 'Now I'm wetter than ever! For a moment I thought I must have stepped into the blue pond!'

But it was only a puddle. They went round it and

followed a muddy path to a little door set in a white stone wall. Dick thought it must be the back door. Nearby was a window, and in it shone the light they had seen so thankfully.

An old woman sat near the light, her head bent over some sewing. The children could see her quite clearly as they stood by the door.

Dick looked for a bell or knocker but there was none. He knocked with his bare knuckles. Nobody answered. The door remained shut. They looked at the old woman by the lamp, and saw that she was still sewing.

'Perhaps she's deaf,' said Dick and he knocked again, much more loudly. Still the old woman sewed on placidly. She must indeed be deaf!

'We'll never get in at this rate!' said Dick, impatiently. He tried the handle of the door – it opened at once!

'We'll just have to walk in and announce ourselves,' said Dick, and he stepped on to the worn mat inside the door. He was in a narrow little passage that led to a stone stairway, steep and narrow at the farther end.

On his right was a door, a little ajar. It opened into the room where the old woman was sitting. The two children could see a streak of light coming through the crack.

Dick pushed the door open and walked boldly in, followed by Anne. Still the old woman didn't look up. She pushed her needle in and out of her sewing and seemed to hear and see nothing else whatsoever.

Dick had to walk right up to her before she knew he was in the room. Then she leapt up in such a fright that her chair fell over with a bang.

'I'm sorry,' said Dick, upset at frightening the old lady. 'We knocked but you didn't hear!'

She stared at them, her hand over her heart. 'You give me such a fright,' she said. 'Where did you come from, this dark night?'

Dick picked up her chair, and she sat down in it, panting a little.

'We've been looking for this place,' said Dick. 'Blue Pond Farm-house, isn't it? We wondered if we could stay the night here – and two others of us as well.'

The old woman pointed to her ears and shook her head. 'Deaf as a post,' she said. 'No good talking to me, my dear. You've lost your way, I suppose?'

Dick nodded.

'Well, you can't stay here,' said the old woman. 'My son won't have no one here at all. You'd best be gone before he comes. He have a nasty temper, he have.'

Dick shook his head. Then he pointed out to the dark rainy night, then pointed to Anne's wet shoes and clothes. The old woman knew what he meant.

'You've lost your way, you're wet and tired, and you don't want me to turn you out,' she said. 'But there's my son, you see. He don't like strangers here.'

Dick pointed to Anne, and then to a sofa in a corner of the room. Then he pointed to himself, and then outside. Again the old woman understood at once.

'You want me to give your sister shelter, but you'll
go out into the night?' she said. Dick nodded. He
thought he could easily find some shed or barn for
himself. But Anne really must be indoors.

'My son mustn't see either of you,' said the old
woman, and she pulled Anne to what the girl thought
was a cupboard. But when the door opened, she saw
a very small, steep wooden staircase leading upwards
into the roof.

'You go up there,' said the old woman to Anne.

'And don't you come down till I call you in the morning. I'll get into trouble if my son knows you're here.'

'Go up, Anne,' said Dick, rather troubled. 'I don't know what you'll find there. If it's too bad, come down. See if there's a window or something you can call out from, and then I'll know if you're all right.'

'Yes,' said Anne, in rather a trembling voice, and she went up the steep, dirty wooden stairs. They led straight into a little loft. There was a mattress there, fairly clean, and a chair. A rug was folded up on the chair and a jug of water stood on a shelf. Otherwise the room was bare.

A tiny window opened out of one side. Anne went to it and called out. 'Dick! Are you there? Dick!'

'Yes, I'm here,' said Dick. 'What's it like, Anne? Is it all right? Listen, I'll find somewhere nearby to shelter in – and you can always call me if you want me!'

Chapter Six

IN THE MIDDLE OF THE NIGHT

'It's not bad,' said Anne. 'There's a fairly clean mattress and a rug. I'll be all right. But what about if the others come, Dick? Will you look out for them? I almost think George will have to sleep in a barn with you and Julian if she comes. That old woman won't let anyone else in, I'm sure!'

'I'll look out for them and arrange something,' said Dick. 'You eat the rest of your sandwiches and your cake, and see if you can dry your wet feet and make yourself really comfortable. There's a shed or something out here. I shall be quite all right. Yell for me if you want me.'

Anne went back into the room. She felt wet and tired, hungry and thirsty. She ate all her food, and had a drink from the jug. Then she felt sleepy and lay down on the mattress, throwing the rug over her. She meant to listen for the others to come, but she was too tired. She fell fast asleep!

Dick was prowling about down below. He was careful because he didn't want to run into the old woman's son. He didn't like the sound of him somehow! He came to a small barn with piles of straw in one corner. He flashed his torch cautiously round.

'This will do for me,' he thought. 'I can be quite comfortable here in that straw. Poor Anne! I wish old George was with her. I'd better wait about and watch for the other two, or I'll fall asleep and miss them, once I bed down in that straw! It's only about six o'clock too – but we've had a long day. I wonder how Timmy is. I wish he was here!'

Dick thought that probably George and Julian would come in through the same gate as he and Anne had used. He found a broken-down shed near the gate and sat down on a box there, waiting for them to come.

He ate his sandwiches while he waited. They were very comforting! He ate every one and then the cake. He yawned. He felt very sleepy indeed, and his feet were wet and tired.

No one arrived at all – not even the old woman's son. She could still be seen sewing under the lamp. But after about two hours, when it was almost eight o'clock, and Dick was beginning to be very worried about George and Julian, the old woman got up and put away her work-basket.

She disappeared out of Dick's sight, and didn't come back. But the light was still there, shining out of the window. Left for her son, probably, thought Dick.

He tiptoed to the window. The rain had stopped now and the night was much clearer. The stars were out and a moon was coming up. Dick's spirits rose.

He peered in at the lighted room. Then he saw the

old woman lying on a broken-down sofa in a corner
A blanket was pulled right up to her chin and she
seemed to be asleep. Dick went back to his shed, but
now he felt there was no use in watching for George
and Julian. They must have lost their way completely!
Or else Mr. Gaston, or whatever his name was, must
have had to do something to Timmy's leg, and Julian
had decided to stay at the inn in Beacons Village for
the night.

He yawned again. 'I'm too sleepy to watch any
more,' he decided 'I shall fall off this box with sleep
if I don't go and lie down in that straw. Anyway I
think I'd hear if the others came.'

Using his torch cautiously again, he made his way
to the barn He shut the door behind him and bolted
it roughly from the inside by running a stick through
two hasps. He didn't know why he did that – perhaps
because he was still thinking of the old woman's bad-
tempered son!

He flung himself down on the straw, and immediately fell asleep. Outside the sky became clearer and
clearer. The moon came up, not fully, but large
enough to give some light. It shone down on the desolate little stone house and ill-kept out-buildings.

Dick slept soundly. He lay in the soft straw and
dreamed of Timmy and George and Blue Ponds and
bells. Especially bells.

He awoke suddenly, and lay for a moment wondering where he was. What was this prickly stuff
round him? Then he remembered – of course, it was

straw and he was in a barn! He was about to cuddle
down again when he heard a noise.

It was only a small noise – a scratching on the
wooden walls of the barn perhaps. Dick sat up. Were
there rats there? He hoped not!

He listened. The scratching seemed to come from
outside the barn, not inside. Then it stopped. After an
interval it began again. Then there came a gentle tapping at the broken window just above Dick's head.

He felt very startled. Rats scratched and scrabbled
about – but they didn't tap on windows. Who was tapping so very very cautiously on the little window? He
held his breath and listened, straining his ears.

And then he heard a voice – a hoarse whisper.

'Dick! Dick!'

Dick was amazed. Could it be Julian? If so, how
in the world did he know that he, Dick, was in the
barn? He sat listening, stiff with surprise.

The tapping came again, and then the voice, a little
louder. 'Dick! I know you're there. I saw you go in.
Come here to the window – quiet, now!'

Dick didn't know the voice. It wasn't Julian's, and
it certainly wasn't either George's or Anne's. Then
how did the owner know *his* name and that he was
there? It was astounding. Dick didn't know what to
do!

'Buck up!' said the voice. 'I've got to go in half a
tick. I've got that message for you.'

Dick decided to go nearer to the window. He was
quite certain that he didn't want whoever it was out-

side to come into the barn. He cautiously knelt up in
the straw and spoke just underneath the window.

'I'm here,' he said, trying to make his voice deep
and grown-up.

'You've been long enough coming,' grumbled the
one outside, and then Dick saw him through the window – just a face, dim and wild-eyed, with a round
bullet-like head. He crouched back, thankful that the
face couldn't see him in the darkness of the barn.

'Here's the message from Nailer,' said the voice.
'Two-Trees. Gloomy Water. Saucy Jane. And he says
Maggie knows. He sent you this. Maggie's got one
too.'

A bit of paper fluttered in at the broken pane. Dick
picked it up in a daze. What *was* all this? Was he
dreaming?

The voice came again, insistent and urgent. 'You
heard all that, Dick? Two-Trees. Gloomy Water.
Saucy Jane. And Maggie knows too. Now I'm going.'

There came the sound of someone cautiously creeping round the barn – and then there was silence. Dick
sat amazed and bewildered. Who was this wild-eyed
fellow, who called him by his name in the middle of
the night and gave him extraordinary messages that
meant nothing at all to a sleepy boy? But Dick was
wide awake now. He stood up and looked out of the
window. There was nothing and no one to be seen
except the lonely house and the sky.

Dick sat down again and thought. He put his torch
on cautiously and looked at the piece of paper he had

picked up. It was a dirty half sheet, with pencil marks on it that meant nothing to Dick at all. Words were printed here and there, but they were all nonsense to him. He simply couldn't make head or tail of his visitor, his message or the bit of paper!

'I'm sure I must be dreaming,' thought Dick, and put the paper into his pocket. He lay back in his straw, cuddling in deep, because he had got cold by the window. He lay and thought for a while, puzzling over the curious happenings, and then he felt his eyes closing.

But before he was quite asleep, he heard cautious footsteps again! Was that fellow back once more? This time someone tried the door – but the wooden stick was in the hasps. Whoever it was outside shook the door and the stick fell out at once. The man shook the door again as if thinking it had stuck, and then opened it. He came inside and shut the door behind him.

Dick caught a quick glimpse of him. No – this wasn't the same man as before. This was a man with a head of thick hair, Dick hoped and prayed that he wouldn't come over to the straw.

He didn't. He sat down on a sack and waited. He talked to himself after a while, but Dick could only make out a word or two.

'What's happened?' he heard. 'How much longer do I wait?' Then there was a mumble and Dick could not catch a word.

'Wait, wait – that's all I do,' muttered the man, and

he stood up and stretched himself. Then he went to
the door and looked out. He came back and sat down
on the sack again.

He sat still and quiet then, and Dick found his eyes
closing once more. Was this part of a dream too? He
didn't have time to think it out because he was suddenly in a real dream, walking along ringing bells and
seeing trees in twos everywhere round him!

He slept heavily all night long. When morning
came he awoke suddenly and sat up. He was alone in
the barn. Where had the second visitor gone? Or
could it all have been a dream?

Chapter Seven

IN THE MORNING

Dick stood up and stretched himself. He felt dirty and untidy. Also he was very hungry. He wondered if the old woman would let him buy some bread and cheese and a glass of milk.

'Anne must be hungry too,' he thought 'I wonder if she's all right.' He went cautiously outside and looked up at the tiny window of the loft where Anne had spent the night. Her anxious face was already there, watching for Dick!

'Are you all right, Anne?' called Dick, in a low tone. She pushed open the tiny window and smiled at him.

'Yes. But I daren't go down because that son is downstairs. I can hear him shouting at the deaf old woman every now and again. He sounds very bad-tempered.'

'I'll wait for him to go out to his work then, before I go and see the old woman,' said Dick. 'I must pay her something for letting you sleep up in that loft – and perhaps I can persuade her to let us have something to eat.'

'I wish you could,' said Anne. 'I've eaten all the chocolate I had in my bag. Shall I wait till I hear you call me?'

Dick nodded and disappeared into the barn in a hurry. He had heard footsteps!

A man came into sight – a broad, short, hunched-up man, with a shock of untidy hair. He was the man that Dick had seen in the barn the night before. He was muttering to himself and looked very bad-tempered indeed. Dick decided to keep out of his way. He crouched down in the barn.

But the man did not go in there. He walked past, still muttering. Dick listened for his footsteps to die away. He heard the opening of a gate somewhere, then it crashed behind the man.

'I'd better take my chance now,' thought Dick, and he went quickly out of the barn and up to the little white house. It looked very tumble-down and neglected in the daylight, and had a most forlorn air.

Dick knew that it was no good knocking, because the old woman wouldn't hear him. So he walked right into the house and found the woman washing up a few dishes in a cracked old sink. She stared at him in dismay.

'I'd forgotten about you! And the girl too! Is she still up there? Get her down quickly before my son comes back! And then go, both of you!'

'Can you sell us some bread and cheese?' shouted Dick. But the old woman really was stone deaf, and all she did was to push Dick away towards the door, jabbing at him with the wet cloth in her hand. Dick slipped aside and pointed to some bread on a table.

'No, no – I tell you, you're to go,' said the old woman, obviously terrified in case her son should come back. 'Get the girl, quickly!'

But before Dick could do anything, there were footsteps outside and in came the hunched-up fellow with
the shock of hair! He was back already, holding some
eggs he had been to find.

He walked into the kitchen and stared at Dick.
'Clear out!' he said, angrily. 'What do you want
here?'

Dick thought he had better not say he had slept the
night in the barn. There were queer goings-on here,
and the man might be very savage if he knew Dick
had slept the night nearby.

'I wanted to know if your mother could sell us some
bread,' he said, and could have bitten his tongue out.
He had said 'us'! Now the man would guess there was
someone with him.

'Us? Who's "us"?' said the man, looking round.
'You fetch him and I'll tell you both what I do to
boys who come stealing my eggs!'

'I'll go and fetch him,' said Dick, seizing the chance
to get away. He ran to the door. The man made a
clumsy dart at him and almost caught him. But Dick
was out and away, running down the path. He hid
behind a shed, his heart thumping. He had to wait for
Anne. Somehow he had to go back and get her.

The man stood at the door, shouting angrily after
Dick. But he didn't chase him. He went back into the
house and after a while came out again with a pail of
steaming food. Dick guessed he was going to feed the
chickens wherever they were.

He had to take this chance of fetching Anne. He

waited till he heard the crash of the distant gate again
and then he rushed to the house. Anne's face was at
the window, scared. She had heard all that the man
had said to Dick, and then to his mother about allow-
ing boys to come to the house.

'Anne! Come down at once. He's gone,' shouted
Dick. 'Hurry!'

Anne's face disappeared from the window. She ran
to the door, tumbled quickly down the stairs, and ran
through the kitchen. The old woman flapped a cloth
at her, screaming at her.

Dick ran into the kitchen and put twenty pence on
the table. Then he caught Anne's arm and both children tore out of the house and down the path. They
came to the hedge they had followed the night before.

Anne was quite scared. 'That awful man!' she said.
'Oh Dick – what a horrible place. Honestly I think
Julian must be mad to choose a place like that to
sleep in for the night – horrible little house! And it
didn't look a bit like a farm. There were no cows or
pigs that I could see and not even a farm-dog!'

'You know, Anne, I don't think it could possibly
have been Blue Pond Farm-house,' said Dick, as they
walked beside the hedge, looking for the gate that
they had come through the night before. 'We made a
mistake. It was an ordinary cottage. If we hadn't lost
our way we'd have come to the proper Blue Pond
Farm-house I'm sure.'

'Whatever will George and Julian be thinking?'
said Anne. 'They'll be dreadfully worried, won't they,

wondering what has become of us. Do you suppose
they're at the real Blue Pond Farm-house?'

'We'll have to find out,' said Dick. 'Do I look very
messy and untidy, Anne? I feel awful.'

'Yes. Haven't you a comb?' said Anne. 'Your hair's
all up on end. And your face is very dirty. Look, there's
a little stream over there. Let's get our flannels out
and wash our hands and faces with them.'

They did a little washing in the cold water of the stream, and Dick combed back his hair.

'You look a lot better,' said Anne. 'Oh dear – I wish we could have some breakfast. I'm really starving! I didn't sleep awfully well, did you, Dick? My mattress was so hard, and I was rather scared, up in that funny little room all alone.'

Before Dick could answer, a boy came whistling through the gate. He looked astonished to see Dick and Anne.

'Hallo!' he said. 'You hiking?'

'Yes,' said Dick. 'Can you tell me if that place up there is Blue Pond Farm-house?'

He pointed back to the old woman's house. The boy laughed.

'That's no farm-house. That's Mrs. Taggart's place, and a dirty old place it is. Don't you go there, or her son will drive you off. Dirty Dick we call him – he's a terror! Blue Pond Farm-house is down along there, see? Past the Three Shepherds Inn and away up to the left.'

'Thanks,' said Dick, feeling very angry indeed with the man who had said 'ar' and sent them all wrong the day before. The boy waved, and set off across a moorland path.

'We certainly went the wrong way last night,' said Dick, as they walked over the fields they had crossed in the dark the night before. 'Poor Anne! Dragging you all that way in the dark and the rain to a horrible place that wasn't Blue Pond Farm-house after all. I can't think what Julian is going to say to me.'

'Well, it was my fault too,' said Anne. 'Dick, let's go down to the Three Shepherds and telephone Blue Pond Farm-house from there, shall we? If it's on the phone, that is. I don't somehow feel as if I want to walk for miles and perhaps not find Blue Pond Farm-house again.'

'Good idea,' said Dick. 'The Three Shepherds was where that woman was shaking a duster out of the window, wasn't it? She told Julian the way to Spiggy House. I wonder how old Timmy is. I hope he's better. I say – this hike isn't as good as we hoped it would be, is it?'

'Well, there's still time for it to be all right!' said Anne, much more cheerfully than she felt. She so badly wanted her breakfast that she felt quite bad-tempered!

'We'll telephone to Julian from the Three Shepherds to say what happened to us,' said Dick, as they came to the lane where they had floundered in the mud the night before. He helped Anne over the stile and they jumped down to the narrow road 'And what's more, we'll have breakfast at the Three Shepherds – and I bet we eat more than ever the Three Shepherds did, whoever they were!'

Anne felt more cheerful at once. She had thought they would have to walk all the way to find Blue Pond Farm-house before they had breakfast!

'See – a stream does flow right across the road here,' she said. 'No wonder I got my feet wet yesterday!

Come on – the thought of breakfast makes my legs
want to run!'

They at last arrived in Beacons Village, and made
their way to the inn. On the sign three shepherds were
painted, looking rather gloomy.

'They look like I feel,' said Anne, 'but I shall soon
feel different. Oh Dick – think of porridge – and
bacon and eggs – and toast and marmalade!'

'We must telephone first,' said Dick, firmly – and
then he suddenly stopped, just as he was going into
the inn. Someone was calling him.

'DICK! DICK! ANNE! Look, there they are! Hey,
Dick, DICK!'

It was Julian's voice! Dick swung round in delight. He saw Julian, George and Timmy racing along
the village street, shouting and waving. Timmy was first
to reach them of course – and there was no sign of
limping either! He leapt on them, barking madly, and
licked every bare part of them he could reach.

'Oh, Ju! I'm so glad to see you!' said Anne, in
rather a trembling voice. 'We lost our way last night.
George, is Timmy all right?'

'Quite. Absolutely,' said George. 'You see . . .'

'Have you had breakfast?' interrupted Julian. 'We
haven't. We were so worried about you we were just
going to see the police. But now we can all have breakfast together and tell our news!'

Chapter Eight

ALL TOGETHER AGAIN

IT was wonderful to be all together again. Julian took
hold of Anne's arm and squeezed it. 'All right, Anne?'
he said, rather worried at her pale face.

Anne nodded. She felt better at once, now she had
Julian, George and Timmy, as well as Dick. 'I'm only
just terribly hungry,' she said.

'I'll ask for breakfast straight away,' said Julian.
'All news later!'

The woman who had leaned out of the window
shaking a duster the evening before, came up to them.
'I expect it's a bit late for you,' said Julian. 'But we
haven't had any breakfast. What have you got?'

'Porridge and cream,' said the woman. 'And our
own cured bacon and our own eggs. Our own honey
and the bread I bake myself. Will that do? And coffee
with cream?'

'I could hug you,' said Julian, beaming at her. The
others felt the same. They went into a small, cosy
dining-room and sat down to wait. Soon a smell of
frying bacon and hot strong coffee would come into
the room – what joy!

'Your news first,' said Dick, patting Timmy. 'Did
you get to Spiggy House? Was Mr. Gaston there?'

'No, he wasn't,' said Julian. 'He was out some-where. He had a very nice wife who made us wait for him, and said he wouldn't mind in the least look-ing at Timmy when he came back. So we waited and waited.'

'We waited till half past seven!' said George, 'and we felt rather awkward because we thought it might be getting near their meal-time. And then at last Mr. Gaston came.'

'He was awfully kind,' said Julian. 'He looked at Timmy's leg, and then he did something, I don't know what – put it back into place, I suppose – and Timmy gave a yell and George flung herself on him, and Mr. Gaston roared with laughter at George...'

'Well, he was very *rough* with Timmy's leg,' said George. 'But he knew what he was doing, of course, and now Timmy is perfectly all right, except for that bruise on his back, and even that is getting better. He can run as well as ever.'

'I'm glad,' said Anne. 'I kept thinking of poor old Tim all last night.' She patted him, and he licked her lavishly and wetly.

'What did you do then?' asked Dick.

'Well, Mrs. Gaston insisted on us staying to supper,' said Julian. 'She simply wouldn't take no for an answer, and I must say that by that time we were jolly hungry. So we stayed – and we had a jolly good meal too. So did Timmy! You should have seen his tummy afterwards – as round as a barrel. Good thing it's gone down today or I was thinking of changing his name to Tummy.' They all laughed, George especially.

'Idiot,' she said. 'Well, we didn't leave till about nine o'clock. We didn't worry about you because we felt sure you would be safely at Blue Pond Farm-house and would guess we'd had to wait about with Timmy. And when we got there and found you hadn't arrived – well, we *were* in a state!'

'And then we thought you must have found somewhere else for the night,' said Julian, 'but we thought if we heard nothing we'd go down to the police first thing this morning and report your disappearance!'

'So down we came – without any breakfast either!' said George. 'That shows how worried we were! Blue Pond Farm-house was nice. They gave us a bed each in two tiny little rooms, and Timmy slept with me, of course.'

A wonderful smell came creeping into the little dining-room, followed by the inn-woman carrying a large tray. On it was a steaming tureen of porridge, a bowl of golden syrup, a jug of very thick cream, and a dish of bacon and eggs, all piled high on crisp brown toast. Little mushrooms were on the same dish.

'It's like magic!' said Anne, staring. 'Just the very things I longed for!'

'Toast, marmalade and butter to come, and the coffee and hot milk,' said the woman, busily setting everything out. 'And if you want any more bacon and eggs, just ring the bell.'

'Too good to be true!' said Dick, looking at the table. 'For goodness' sake, help yourselves quickly, girls, or I shall forget my manners and grab.'

It was a wonderful breakfast – extra wonderful because they were all so ravenously hungry. There wasn't a word said as they spooned up their porridge and cream, sweetened with golden syrup. Timmy had a dishful too – he loved porridge, though he didn't like the syrup – it made his whiskers sticky!

'I feel better,' said Anne, looking at the porridge dish. 'The thing is – shall I have some more porridge and risk not enjoying my bacon and eggs so much – or shall I go straight on with bacon and eggs?'

'A difficult question,' said Dick. 'And one that I am faced with too. On the whole I think I'll go on with bacon and eggs – we can always have more of those if we want to – and those little mushrooms really do make my mouth water! Aren't we greedy? But how can anyone help that when they're so hungry?'

'You haven't told us a single word of what happened to *you* last night,' said Julian, serving out the bacon and eggs with a generous hand. 'Now that you've got something inside you, perhaps you feel able to tell us exactly why you ignored my instructions and didn't arrive where you were supposed to last night.'

'You sound like our headmaster at school!' said Dick. 'The plain fact is – we got lost! And when we did finally arrive somewhere, we thought it was Blue Pond Farm-house, and we stayed the night there.'

'I see,' said Julian. 'But didn't the people there tell you it wasn't the right place? Just so that you could have let us know? You must have known that we would worry about you.'

'Well, the old woman there was stone-deaf,' explained Anne, attacking her bacon and eggs vigorously. 'She didn't understand a word we said, and as we thought it *was* Blue Pond Farm-house, we stayed there – though it was a horrible place. And *we* were worried because *you* didn't arrive!'

'A chapter of accidents,' said Julian. 'All's well that ends well, however.'

'Don't sound so pompous!' said Dick. 'Actually we had a pretty poor time, Ju. Poor Anne had to sleep in a little loft, and I slept in straw in a barn – not that I minded that – but – well, peculiar things happened

in the night. At least – I *think* they did. I'm not really
sure it wasn't all a dream.'

'What peculiar things?' asked Julian at once.

'Well – I think perhaps I'll tell you when we're on
our way again,' said Dick. 'Now I think about it in
full daylight I feel that either it was all a silly dream –
or – well, as I said – something very peculiar.'

'You never told me, Dick!' said Anne, in surprise.

'Well, to tell you the truth I forgot about it because
other things happened,' said Dick. 'Having to get
away from that man, for instance – and wondering
about Julian and George – and feeling so hungry.'

'You don't sound as if you had a good night at all,'
said George. 'It must have been awful, too, trying
to find your way in the dark. It poured with rain,
didn't it?'

'Yes,' said Anne, 'but oh – the thing that frightened me more than anything was the bells! Did you
hear them Julian? They suddenly clanged out, and
they made me terribly scared. I couldn't think what
they were! Whatever were they ringing out for? They
were so loud.'

'Didn't you know what they were ringing for?'
said Julian. 'They were bells rung from the prison that
nice old woman told us about – they were rung to tell
everyone on the countryside that a prisoner had
escaped! Lock your doors. Guard your folk.'

Anne stared at Julian in silence. So that was why
the bells had made such a clamour and clangour. She
shivered.

'I'm glad I didn't know that,' she said. 'I would have slept in the straw with Dick if I'd known there was an escaped prisoner. Have they caught him?'

'I don't know,' said Julian. 'We'll ask the inn-woman when she comes.'

They asked her, and she shook her head. 'No. He's not caught yet. But he will be. All the roads from the moor are guarded and everyone is on the watch. He was a robber who broke into houses and attacked any-one who tried to prevent him. A dangerous fellow.'

'Julian – is it all right to go hiking on the moors if there's an escaped prisoner about?' said Anne. 'I shan't feel very comfortable.'

'We've got Timmy,' said Julian. 'He would be strong enough to protect us from three prisoners if necessary! You needn't worry.'

'Woof,' agreed Timmy, at once, and thumped his tail on the floor.

At last everyone had finished breakfast. Even starv-ing Anne couldn't manage the last bit of toast. She sighed happily. 'I feel myself again,' she announced. 'I can't say I feel very much like walking – but I know it would be good for me after that enormous meal.'

'Good or not, we're going on our way,' said Julian, getting up. 'I'll buy some sandwiches first.'

The inn-woman was delighted with their hearty praises. She gave them some packets of sandwiches and waved good-bye. 'You come again whenever you can,' she said. 'I'll always have something nice for you.'

The four went down the street and took a lane at

the bottom. It wound about for a short way and then came into a valley. A stream ran down the middle of the valley. The children could hear it gurgling from where they stood.

'Lovely!' said Anne. 'Are we going along by the stream? I'd like to.'

Julian looked at his map. 'Yes – we could,' he said. 'I've marked the path to follow, and the stream joins it some way on. So if you like we could go along by it, though it will be very rough walking.'

They made their way to the stream. 'Now Dick,' said Julian, when they had left the path. 'What about telling us all those peculiar things that happened in the night? There's nobody about to hear – not a soul in sight. Let's hear everything. We'll soon tell you whether it was a dream or not.'

'Right,' said Dick. 'Well, here's the tale. It does sound pretty queer. Listen . . .'

Chapter Nine

DICK SURPRISES THE OTHERS

DICK began his tale – but it really was very difficult to hear it because they couldn't walk four abreast, as there was no path to follow.

In the end Julian stopped and pointed to a thick clump of heather. 'Let's go and sit there and hear Dick's story properly. I keep missing bits. No one can hear us if we sit here.'

They sat down and Dick started again. He told about the old woman who was afraid her son would be angry if she let them stay the night. He told about his bed in the straw.

'And now here comes the bit I think must have been a dream,' he said. 'I woke up to hear a scratching noise on the wooden walls of the barn . . .'

'Rats or mice?' said George, and Timmy leapt up at once, of course. He was sure she had said the words to him!

'I thought that too,' said Dick. 'But then I heard a gentle tap-tap-tapping on the window.'

'How horrid,' said Anne. 'I shouldn't have liked that at all.'

'Neither did I,' said Dick. 'But the *next* thing I

heard was my name being called! "Dick! Dick!" Just
like that.'

'It *must* have been a dream then,' said Anne. 'There
was no one there who knew your name.'

Dick went on. 'Well, then the voice said – "Dick!
I know you're there. I saw you go in!" And it told me
to go to the window.'

'Go on,' said Julian. He was puzzled. No one in the
world but Anne could have known that Dick was in
the barn – and it certainly wasn't Anne out there in
the night!

'Well, I went to the window,' said Dick, 'and I saw,
rather dimly, of course, a wild-eyed looking fellow.
He couldn't see me in the darkness of the barn. I just
mumbled, "I'm here," hoping he would think I was
whoever he wanted.'

'What did he say next?' asked George.

'He said something that sounded stuff and non-
sense,' said Dick. 'He said it twice. It was "Two-
Trees. Gloomy Water. Saucy Jane." And he said
"Maggie knows." Just like that!'

There was a silence. Then George laughed. 'Two-
Trees! Gloomy Water! Saucy Jane – and Maggie
knows about it! Well, it *must* have been a dream,
Dick! You know it must. What do you think, Julian?'

'Well – it does sound a bit nonsensical to have someone come in the middle of the night and call Dick by
name and give him a strange message that doesn't
mean a thing to him!' said Julian. 'It sounds more
dream-like than real. I'd say it was a dream too.'

Dick began to think they were right – and then a sudden thought struck him. He sat up straight. 'Wait a bit!' he said. 'I've remembered something! The man slipped a bit of paper through the broken pane of the window, and I picked it up!'

'Ah – that's different,' said Julian. 'Now – if you can't find that paper, it's all a dream and you dreamt the paper too – but if you *can* find it, well the whole thing is true. Very peculiar indeed – but true.'

Dick searched quickly in his pockets. He felt paper in one of them, and drew it out. It was a dirty, crumpled piece, with a few words on it and a few lines. He held it out to the others in silence, his eyes shining.

'Is this the paper?' asked Julian. 'My word – so you didn't dream it after all, then!'

He took the paper. Four heads bent over it to examine it. No, five – because Timmy wanted to see what they were all so interested in. He thrust his hairy head between Julian's and Dick's.

'I can't make any sense of this paper,' said Julian. 'It's a plan of some kind, I think – but what of, or where, it's impossible to know.'

'The fellow said that Maggie had one of these bits of paper too,' said Dick, remembering.

'Who in the wide world *is* Maggie?' said George, 'And why should Maggie know?'

'Any more to tell?' asked Julian, intensely interested now.

'Well – the son of the deaf old woman came into the barn later on,' said Dick. 'And he sat and waited and waited, and muttered and muttered – and then when I woke up he wasn't there. So I thought I must have dreamt him too. He didn't see me, of course.'

Julian pursed up his lips and frowned. Then Anne spoke excitedly.

'Dick! Ju! I think I know why the second man came into the barn. It was the *second* man that the wild-eyed man wanted to give the message to, and the bit of paper – not to Dick. He didn't want *Dick*. But he had seen him creep into the barn, and I suppose he thought Dick was the man he really wanted and that he was in the barn waiting for him!'

'That's all very well – but how did he know my name?' asked Dick.

'He didn't know it! He didn't know it was you at all!' said Anne, excitedly. 'The other man's name must have been Dick too! Don't you *see*? They must have planned to meet there, the wild-eyed man and the old woman's son – and the first man saw Dick go in, so he waited a bit and then went and tapped on the window! And when he called "Dick! Dick!" of course Dick thought it was he that he wanted, and he took the message and everything! And then the other man, the real Dick came along – and was too late to meet the first one. *Our* Dick had met him and got the message!'

Anne was quite breathless after this long speech. She sat and stared at the others eagerly. Didn't they think she was right?

They did, of course. Julian clapped her on the back.

'Well worked out, Anne! Of course that's what happened.'

Dick suddenly remembered the boy they had met on the way down from the old woman's cottage to Beacons Village – the whistling boy. What had he said about the old woman and her son?

'Anne – what did that whistling boy say? Wait a bit – he said that was Mrs. Taggart's place – and he said we'd better not go there or her son would drive us off. And he said – yes, I remember now – he said "Dirty Dick we call him – he's a terror!" Dirty *Dick*! His name *must* be Dick then! Why didn't I think of it before?'

'That proves that Anne is right,' said Julian, pleased. Anne looked pleased too. It wasn't often that she thought of something clever before the others did!

They all sat thinking. 'Would this have anything to do with the escaped prisoner?' said George at last.

'It might,' said Julian. 'He might have been the prisoner himself, that fellow who came with the message. Did he say who the message was from?'

'Yes,' said Dick, trying to remember. 'He said it was from Nailer. I think that was the name – but it was all given in whispers, you know.'

'A message from Nailer,' said Julian. 'Well – perhaps Nailer is in prison – a friend of the man who escaped. And maybe when he knew this fellow was going to make a dash for it, he gave him a message for someone – the man at that old cottage, son of the old woman. They may have had a prearranged plan.'

'How do you mean?' asked Dick, looking puzzled.

'Well – the old woman's son, Dirty Dick, may have known that when the bells rang out, this fellow was making a run for it – and would come to bring him a message. He was to wait in the barn at night if the bells rang, just in case it was Nailer's friend who had escaped.'

'Yes, I see,' said Dick. 'I think you're right. Yes, I'm sure you are. My word, I'm glad I didn't know that fellow at the window was an escaped convict!'

'And *you've* got the message from Nailer!' said Anne. 'What a peculiar thing! Just because we lost our way and went to the wrong place, you get a message from a prisoner given you by one who's escaped! It's a pity we don't know what the message means – or the paper either.'

'Had we better tell the police?' said George. 'I mean – it may be important. It might help them to catch that man.'

'Yes,' said Julian. 'I think we *should* tell the police. Let's have a look at our map. Where's the next village?'

He looked at the map for a minute. 'I think really we might as well go on with what I had planned,' he said. 'I planned we should reach this village here – Reebles, look – in time for lunch, in case we hadn't got sandwiches. We'd have gone there for drinks anyway. So I vote we just carry on with our ramble, and call in at Reebles police station – if there is one – and tell them our bit of news.'

They all got up. Timmy was glad. He didn't
approve of this long sit-down so soon after breakfast.
He bounded ahead in delight.

'His leg's *quite* all right,' said Anne, pleased. 'Well
I hope it teaches him not to go down rabbit holes
again!'

It didn't, of course. He had his head down half a
dozen within the next half-hour, but fortunately he
could get no farther, and he was able to pull himself
out quite easily.

The four saw little wild ponies that day. They came
trotting over a hillock together, small and brown, with
long manes and tails, looking very busy indeed. The
children stopped in delight. The ponies saw them,
tossed their pretty heads, turned one way all together
and galloped off like the wind.

Timmy wanted to go after them, but George held
his collar tightly. No one must chase those dear little
wild ponies!

'Lovely!' said Anne. 'Lovely to meet them as suddenly as that. I hope we meet some more.'

The morning was as warm and sunny as the day
before. Once again the four of them had to take off
their blazers, and Timmy's tongue hung out, wet
and dripping. The heather and wiry grass was soft
underfoot. They followed the stream closely, liking its
brown colour and its soft gurgling voice.

They bathed their hot feet in it as they ate one of
their sandwiches at half past eleven. 'This is bliss!'
said George, lying back on a tuft of heather with her

feet lapped by the water. 'The stream is tickling my feet, and the sun is warming my face – lovely! Oh, get away, Timmy, you idiot! Breathing down my neck like that, and making my face so wet!'

The stream at last joined the path that led to the village of Reebles. They walked along it, beginning to think of dinner. It would be fun to have it in a little inn or perhaps a farm-house, and keep their sandwiches for tea-time.

'But first we must find the police-station,' said Julian. 'We'll get our tale told, and then we'll be ready for our meal!'

Chapter Ten

AN ANGRY POLICEMAN AND A
FINE LUNCH

THERE *was* a police-station at Reebles, a small one
with a house for the policeman attached. As the one
policeman had four villages under his control he felt
himself to be rather an important fellow.

He was in his house having his dinner when the
children walked up to the police-station. They found
nobody there, and walked out again. The policeman
had seen them from his window and he came out,
wiping his mouth. He wasn't very pleased at having to
come out in the middle of a nice meal of sausage and
onions.

'What do you want?' he said, suspiciously. He
didn't like children of any sort. Nasty little things, he
thought them – always full of mischief and cheek. He
didn't know which were worse, the small ones or the
big ones!

Julian spoke to him politely. 'We've come to report
something rather strange, which we thought perhaps
the police ought to know. It might help them to catch
the prisoner who escaped last night.'

'Ha!' said the policeman scornfully. 'You've seen
him too, I suppose? You wouldn't believe how many
people have seen him. 'Cording to them he's been in

every part of the moor at one and the same time, Clever fellow he must be to split himself up like that.'

'Well, one of us saw him last night,' said Julian politely. 'At least, we think it must have been him. He gave a message to my brother here.'

'Ho, he did, did he?' said the policeman, eyeing Dick in a most disbelieving manner. 'So he runs about giving messages to school-boys, does he? And what message did he give you, may I ask?'

The message sounded extremely silly when Dick repeated it to the police. 'Two-Trees. Gloomy Water, Saucy Jane. And Maggie knows.'

'Really?' said the policeman, in a sarcastic voice. 'Maggie knows as well, does she? Well, you tell Maggie to come along here and tell me too. I'd like to meet Maggie – specially if she's a friend of yours.'

'She's not,' said Dick feeling annoyed. 'That was in the message. I don't know who Maggie is! How should I? We thought perhaps the police could unravel the meaning. We couldn't. The fellow gave me this bit of paper too.'

He handed the piece of dirty paper to the policeman, who looked at it with a crooked smile. 'So he gave you this too, did he?' he said. 'Now wasn't that kind of him? And what do you suppose all this is, scribbled on the paper?'

'We don't know,' said Dick. 'But we thought our report might help the police to catch the prisoner, that's all.'

'The prisoner's caught,' said the policeman, with a

smirk on his face. 'You know so much – but you didn't
know that! Yes, he's caught – four hours ago – and
he's safe back in prison now. And let me tell you
youngsters this – I'm not taken in by any silly school-
boy spoofing, see?'

'It's not spoofing,' said Julian, in a very grown-up
manner. 'You should learn to see the difference between the truth and a joke.'

That didn't please the policeman at all. He turned
on Julian at once, his face reddening.

'Now you run away!' he said. 'I'm not having any
cheek from you! Do you want me to take your names
and addresses and report you?'

'If you like,' said Julian, in disgust. 'Have you got

a notebook there? I'll give you all our names, and I myself will make a report to the police in our district when I get back.'

The policeman stared at him. He couldn't help being impressed by Julian's manner, and he calmed down a little.

'You go away, all of you,' he said, his voice not nearly so fierce. 'I shan't report you this time. But don't you go spreading silly stories like that or you'll get into trouble. Serious trouble too.'

'I don't think so,' said Julian. 'Anyway, seeing that you are not going to do anything about our story, may we have back our bit of paper, please?'

The policeman frowned. He made as if he would tear the paper up, but Dick snatched at it. He was too late. The aggravating policeman had torn it into four pieces and thrown it into the road!

'Don't you have laws against scattering litter in your village?' asked Dick, severely, and carefully picked up the four pieces of paper. The policeman glared at Dick as he put the bits into his pocket. Then he made a peculiar snorting noise, turned on his heel and marched back to his sausages and onions.

'And I hope his dinner's gone cold!' said George. 'Horrid fellow! Why should he think we're telling a lot of untruths?'

'It *is* rather a queer story of ours,' said Julian. 'After all – *we* found it a bit difficult to believe when Dick first told it. I don't blame the policeman for disbelieving it – I blame him for his manner. It's a good thing most of our police aren't the same. Nobody would ever report anything.'

'He told us one bit of good news, anyway,' said Anne. 'That escaped prisoner is back in prison again! I'm so relieved to know that.'

'I am too,' said Dick. 'I didn't like the look of him at all. Well, Ju – what do we do now? Forget the whole business? Do *you* think there's anything in that message to follow up? And if so – can we do anything?'

'I don't know,' said Julian. 'We must think a bit. Let's go and see if we can scrounge a meal in some farm-house somewhere. There seem to be plenty around.'

They asked a little girl if there was a farm-house any-where near that would give them dinner. She nodded and pointed.

'See that farm-house up on the hill there? That's my Gran's place. She'll give you dinner, I expect. She used to give dinner in the summer to trippers, and I expect she would give you some too, if you ask her, though it's late in the season.'

'Thanks,' said Julian, and they all went up the lane that curved round the hill-side. Dogs barked loudly as they came near and Timmy's hackles went up at once. He growled.

'Friends, Timmy, friends,' said George. 'Dinner here, Timmy. Dinner, perhaps a nice bone for you. Bone!'

Timmy understood. The fur down his neck lay flat again and he stopped growling. He wagged his tail at the two dogs near the farm-gate who sniffed his doggy-smell suspiciously even when he was some distance away.

A man hailed them. 'What do you kids want? Mind those dogs!'

'We wondered if we could get a meal here!' called back Julian. 'A little girl down in the village said we might.'

'I'll ask my mother,' said the man, and he yelled in an enormous voice to the farm-house nearby. 'Ma! MA! Four kids out here want to know if you can give them a meal.'

A very fat old lady appeared, with twinkling eyes and red cheeks like an apple. She took one glance at the four by the gate, and nodded her head. 'Yes. They look decent children. Tell them to come along in. Better hold their dog's collar though.'

The four walked to the farm-house, George holding Timmy firmly. The other two dogs came up, but as Timmy was hoping for a bone, he was determined to be friendly, and not a single growl came from him, even when the two dogs growled suspiciously. He wagged his tail, and let his tongue hang out.

The other dogs soon wagged theirs, and then it was safe to let Timmy go. He bounded over to them and there was a mad game of 'chase-me-roll-me-over' as George called it.

'Come your ways in,' said the plump old lady. 'Now you'll have to take what we've got. I'm busy today and haven't had time for cooking. You can have a bit of home-made meat-pie, or a slice or two of ham and

tongue, or hard-boiled eggs and salad. Bless you, you
look as pleased as Punch! I'll put the lot on the table
for you and you can help yourselves! Will that do?
There's no vegetables though. You'll have to make do
with pickled cabbage and my own pickled onions and
beetroot in vinegar.'

'It sounds too marvellous for words,' said Julian. 'We
shan't want any sweet after that!'

'There's no pudding today,' said the old lady. 'But
I'll open a bottle or two of our own raspberries and
you can have them with cream if you like. And there's
the cream cheese I made yesterday too.'

'Don't tell us any more!' begged Dick. 'It makes
me feel too hungry. Why is it that people on farms always have the most delicious food? I mean, surely
people in towns can bottle raspberries and pickle onions
and make cream cheese?'

'Well either they can't or they don't,' said George
'My mother does all those things – and even when she
lived in a town she did. Anyway, *I'm* going to when
I'm grown-up. It must be so wonderful to offer
home-made things by the score when people come to
a meal!'

It was extraordinary to think that any children
could possibly eat the meal the four did, after having
had such a huge breakfast. Timmy ate an enormous
dinner too, and then lay down with a sigh. How he
wished he could live at that farm-house! How lucky
those other two dogs were!

A small girl came in shyly as they ate. 'I'm Meg,'

she said. 'I live with my Gran. What are your names?'

They told her. Then Julian had an idea. 'We're walking over your moor,' he said. 'We've been to lots of nice places. But there's one we haven't been to yet. Do you know it? It's called Two-Trees.'

The little girl shook her head. 'Gran would know,' she said. 'Gran! Where's Two-Trees?'

The old lady looked in at the door. 'What's that? Two-Trees? Oh, that was a lovely place once, but it's all in ruins now. It was built beside a queer dark lake, in the middle of the moors. Let's see now – what was it called?'

'Gloomy Water?' said Dick.

'Yes! That's right. Gloomy Water,' said the old lady. 'Are you thinking of going by there? You be careful then, there's marshland around there, just when you least expect it! Now – would you like anything more?'

'No thank you,' said Julian, regretfully, and paid the very modest bill. 'It's the nicest lunch we've ever had. Now we must be off.'

'Off to Two-Trees and Gloomy Water, I hope!' George whispered to Dick. 'That would be really exciting.'

Chapter Eleven

JULIAN'S IDEA

ONCE outside the farm-house Julian looked round at
the others. 'We'll find out how far Two-Trees is and
see if we've got time to pay it a visit,' he said. 'If we
have, we'll go along there and snoop round. If we
haven't we'll go tomorrow.'

'How can we find out how far it is?' said Dick
eagerly. 'Will it be on your map?'

'It may be marked there if the lake is big enough,'
said Julian. They walked down the hill, and took a path
that led once more over the moors. As soon as they were
out of sight and hearing of anyone Julian stopped and
took out his big map. He unfolded it and the four of
them crouched over it as he spread it out on the heather.

'That nice old lady said it was in the middle of the
moors,' said Julian. 'Also we know there's a lake or at
any rate a big pool of some kind.'

His finger traced its way here and there on the map.
Then George gave a cry and dabbed her finger down.

'There, look! It's not really in the middle. See –
Gloomy Water! That must be it. Is Two-Trees
marked as well?'

'No,' said Julian. 'But perhaps it wouldn't be if it's
in ruins. Ruins aren't marked on maps unless they are

important in some way. This can't be important. Well –
that's certainly Gloomy Water marked there. What
do you say? Shall we have a shot at going there this
afternoon? I wonder exactly how far it is.'

'We could ask at the post-office,' said George.
'Probably once upon a time the postman had to take
letters there. They might know. They could tell us the
way to go.'

They went back to the village and found the post-
office. It was part of the village store. The old man who
kept it looked over the top of his glasses at the children.

'Gloomy Water! Now what be you wanting that
for? A real miserable place it is, for all it was so fine
years ago.'

'What happened to it?' asked Dick.

'It was burnt,' said the old man. 'The owner was
away, and only a couple of servants were there. It
flared up one night, no one knows how or why – and
was burnt almost to a shell. Couldn't get a fire-engine
out there, you see. There was only a cart-track to the
place.'

'And wasn't it ever built up again?' asked Julian.
The old man shook his head.

'No. It wasn't worth it. The owner just let it fall to
rack and ruin. The jackdaws and the owls nest there
now, and the wild animals snuggle in the ruins. It's a
queer place. I once went out to see it, hearing tales of
lights being seen there. But there was nothing to see but
the shell of the place, and the dark blue water. Ah,
Gloomy Water's a good name for that lake!'

'Could you tell us the way? And how long would it take us to get there?' asked Julian.

'What for do you want to go and gaze at a poor old ruin?' said the old man. 'Or do you want to bathe in the lake? Well, don't you do so – it's freezing cold!'

'We just thought we'd go and see Gloomy Water,' said Julian. 'Such a strange name. Which is the way, did you say?'

'I didn't say,' said the old fellow. 'But I will if so be you're set on it. Where's your map? Is that one in your hand?'

Julian spread it out. The old fellow took a pen from his waistcoat pocket and began to trace a path over the moor. He put crosses here and there.

'See them crosses? They mark marshland. Don't go treading there, or you'll be up to your knees in muddy water! You follow these paths I've inked in for you and you'll be all right. Keep your eyes open for deer — there's plenty about those parts, and pretty things they are too.'

'Thank you very much,' said Julian, folding up the map. 'How long would it take us to get there from here?'

'Matter of two hours or more,' said the old man. 'Don't you try to go this afternoon. You'll find yourselves in darkness coming back, and with them dangerous marshy bits you're in danger all the time!'

'Right,' said Julian. 'Thanks very much. Er — we're thinking of doing a bit of camping, as the weather is so beautiful. I suppose you couldn't hire us a ground-sheet or two and a few rugs?'

The other three stared at him in astonishment. Camping out? Where? Why? What was Julian thinking of all of a sudden?

Julian winked at them. The old man was ferreting about in a cupboard. He pulled out two large rubber ground-sheets and four old rugs. 'Thought I had them somewhere!' he said. 'Well, better you camping out in

October than me! Be careful you don't ca.
deaths of cold!'

'Oh thanks – just what we want,' said Ju
pleased. 'Roll them up, you others. I'll settle up .
them.'

Dick, Anne and George folded up the ground-sheets
and the rugs in astonishment. Surely – surely Julian
wasn't thinking of camping out by Gloomy Water?
He must think the message that Dick had been given
was very important!

'Julian!' said Dick, as soon as they got outside.
'What's up? What's all this for?'

Julian looked a little sheepish. 'Well – something
suddenly came over me in the store,' he said. 'I suddenly felt we ought to go to Gloomy Water and snoop
round. I felt excited somehow. And as we've got so
little time this week-end I thought if we took things and
camped out in the ruin we might make more of our few
days.'

'What an idea!' said George. 'Not go on with our
hiking, do you mean?'

'Well,' said Julian. 'If we find nothing, we *can* go
on with our hike, of course. But if there's anything
interesting, it's up to us to unearth it. I'm quite sure
there's something up at Two-Trees.'

'We might meet Maggie there!' said Anne, with a
giggle.

'We might!' said Julian. 'I feel quite free to go and
investigate on our own seeing that we've made our
report to the police, and it's been turned down with

scorn. *Somebody* ought to follow up that message – besides Maggie !'

'Dear Maggie,' said Dick. 'I wonder who in the wide world she is !'

'Somebody worth watching if she's the friend of convicts,' said Julian, more soberly. 'Look, this is what I thought we'd do – buy some extra food, and go along to Gloomy Water this afternoon, arriving there before dark. We'll find a good place to shelter in – there must be some good spot in the old ruin – and get heather or bracken for beds. Then tomorrow we can be up bright and early to have a look round.'

'It sounds smashing,' said Dick, pleased. 'Sort of thing we like. What do you say, Tim ?'

'Woof,' said Tim, solemnly, bumping his tail to and fro across Dick's legs.

'And if we find there's absolutely nothing of interest, well, we can come back here with the things we've borrowed, and go on with our hike,' said Julian. 'But we'll have to sleep the night there because it will be dark by the time we've had a look round.'

They bought some loaves of bread, some butter and potted meat, and a big fruit cake. Also some more chocolate and some biscuits. Julian bought a bottle of orangeade as well.

'There's sure to be a well,' he said. 'Or a spring of some sort. We can dilute the orangeade and drink it when we're thirsty. Now I think we're ready. Come on !'

They couldn't go as fast as usual because they were

carrying so many things. Timmy was the only one that ran as fast as ever – but then Timmy carried nothing but himself!

It was a really lovely walk over the moorlands. They climbed fairly high and had wonderful views all over the autumn country-side. They saw wild ponies again, in the distance this time, and a little herd of dappled deer, that sped away immediately.

Julian was very careful to take the right paths – the ones traced so carefully on the map by the old man in the post-office. 'I expect he knew the way well because he was once a postman and had to take letters to Two-Trees!' said Dick, bending over the map. 'We're getting on, Ju – halfway there!'

The sun began to sink low. The children hurried as much as they could because once the sun had gone darkness would soon come. Fortunately the sky was very clear, so twilight would be later than it had been the night before.

'It looks as if the moorland near here gives way soon to a little bit of wooded country, according to the map,' said Julian. 'We'll look out for clumps of trees.'

After another little stretch of moorland Julian pointed to the right. 'Look!' he said. 'Trees! Quite a lot – a proper little wood.'

'And isn't that water over there?' said Anne. They stood still and gazed hard. Was it Gloomy Water? It might be. It looked such a dark blue. They hurried on eagerly. It didn't look very far now. Timmy ran ahead, his long tail waving in the air.

They went down a little winding path and joined a cart-track that was very much overgrown – so overgrown that it hardly looked like a track. 'This must lead to Two-Trees,' said Julian. 'I wish the sun wasn't going down so quickly. We'll hardly have any time to look round!'

They entered a wood. The track wound through it. The trees must have been cleared at some time to make a road through the wood. And then, quite suddenly, they came on what had once been the lovely house of Two-Trees.

It was a desolate ruin, blackened and scorched with fire. The windows had no glass, the roof had gone, except for a few rafters here and there. Two birds flew up with a loud cry as the children went near.

'Two Maggies!' said Anne, with a laugh. They were black and white magpies, their long tails stretched out behind them. 'I wonder if they know the message too.'

The house stood on the edge of the lake. Gloomy Water was indeed a good name for it. It lay there, smooth and dark, a curious deep blue. No little waves lapped the edge. It was as still as if it were frozen.

'I don't like it,' said Anne. 'I don't like this place at all! I wish we hadn't come!'

Chapter Twelve

A HIDING PLACE AT TWO-TREES

NOBODY particularly liked the place. They all stared round and Julian pointed silently to something. At each end of the house was the great burnt trunk of a big tree.

'Those must be the two trees that gave the place its name,' said Julian. 'How horrid they look now, so stiff and black. Two-Trees and Gloomy Water – all so lonely and desolate now.'

The sun disappeared and a little chill came on the air. Julian suddenly became very busy. 'Come on – we must see if there's anywhere to shelter at all in this old ruin!'

They went to the silent house. The upper floors were all burnt out. The ground floor was pretty bad too, but Julian thought it might be possible to find a sheltered corner.

'This might do,' he said, coming out of a blackened room and beckoning the others to him. 'There is even a mouldy carpet still on the floor! And there's a big table. We could sleep under it if it rained – which I don't think it will do!'

'What a horrid room!' said Anne, looking round. 'I don't like its smell, either. I don't want to sleep here.'

'Well, find somewhere else then, but be quick about it,' said Julian. 'It will soon be dark. I'm going to collect heather and bracken straight away, before it's too dark. Coming, Dick and George?'

The three of them went off and came back with vast armfuls of heather and brown bracken. Anne met them, looking excited.

'I've found somewhere. Somewhere much better than this horrid room. Come and look.'

She took them to what once had been the kitchen. A door lay flat on the floor at the end of the room, and a stone stairway led downwards.

'That leads down to the cellars,' said Anne. 'I came in here and saw that door. It was locked and I couldn't open it. Well, I tugged and tugged and the whole door came off its rusty old hinges and tumbled down almost on top of me! And I saw there were cellars down there!'

She stared at Julian beseechingly. 'They'll be dry. They won't be burnt and black like everywhere else. We'll be well-sheltered. Can't we sleep down there? I don't like the feel of these horrid burnt rooms.'

'It's an idea,' said Julian. He switched on his torch and let the beam light up the cellar below. It seemed spacious and smelt all right.

He went down the steps, Timmy just in front. He called up in surprise.

'There's a proper room down here, as well as cellars all round. Maybe it was a kind of sitting-room for the staff. It's wired for electricity too – they must have had their own electricity generator. Yes – we'll certainly come down here.'

It was a queer little room. Moth-eaten carpets were on the floor, and the furnishings were moth-eaten too and covered with dust. Spiders had been at work and George slashed fiercely at the long cobwebs that hung down and startled her by touching her face.

'There are still candles in the candle-sticks on this shelf!' said Dick, surprised. 'We can light them and have a bit of brightness when it's dark. This isn't bad at all. I must say I agree with Anne. There's something hateful about those burnt-out rooms.'

They piled heather and bracken into the cellar room on the floor. The furniture was so old and moth-eaten that it gave beneath their weight, and was useless for sitting on. The table was all right though. They soon set out their food on it after George had wiped it free of dust. She caused them all to have fits of choking because she was so vigorous in her dusting! They were driven up into the kitchen till the dust had settled.

It was dark outside now. The moon was not yet up. The wind rustled the dry leaves left on the trees around, but there was no lap-lap of water. The lake was as still as glass.

There was a cupboard in the cellar room. Julian opened it to see what was there. 'More candles – good!' he said, bringing out a bundle. 'And plates and cups. Did anyone see a well outside? If so we could dilute some orangeade and have a drink with our supper.'

No one had noticed a well – but Anne suddenly remembered something queer she had seen in a corner of the kitchen, near the sink.

'I believe I saw a pump up there!' she said. 'Go and see, Ju. If so, it might still work.'

He went up the cellar-steps with a candle. Yes — Anne was right. That *was* an old pump over there in the corner. It probably pumped water into a tank and came out of the kitchen taps.

He turned on a big tap which was over the large sink. Then he took the handle of the pump and worked it vigorously up and down. Splash! Splash! Water came flooding through the big tap and splashed into the sink! That was good.

Julian pumped and pumped, feeling that he had better get rid of any water running into the tank for the first time for years. The tank might be dirty or rusty — he must wash it round with a good deal of pumped water first.

The water seemed to be clean and clear, and was certainly as cold as ice! Julian held a cup from the cellar cupboard under the tap, and then tasted the water. It was delicious.

'Good for you, Anne!' he called, going down the cellar-steps with a cupful of water. 'Dick, you find some more cups — or a jug or something in that cupboard, and we'll wash them out and fill them with water for our orangeade.'

The cellar room looked very cheerful as Julian came down the steps. George and Anne had lighted six more candles, and stuck them about here and there. The light they gave was very pleasant, and they also warmed the room a little.

'Well, I suppose as usual, everyone wants a meal?' said Julian. 'Good thing we bought that bread and potted meat and stuff. I can't say I'm as hungry as I was at breakfast, but I'm getting that way.'

The four squatted round on their beds of heather and bracken. They had put down their ground-sheets first in case the floor was damp, though it didn't seem to be. Over bread and butter and potted meat they discussed their plans. They would sleep there for the night and then have all the next day to examine Two-Trees and the lake.

'What exactly are we looking for?' asked Anne. 'Do you suppose there's some secret here, Julian?'

'Yes,' said Julian. 'And I think I know what it is!'

'What?' asked George and Anne, surprised. Dick thought he knew. Julian explained.

'Well, we know that a prisoner called Nailer sent an important message by his escaped friend to two people – one he wanted to send to Dirty Dick – but he didn't get it – and the other to Maggie, whoever she is. Now what secret does he want to tell them?'

'I think I can guess,' said Dick. 'But go on.'

'Now suppose that Nailer has done some big robberies,' said Julian. 'I don't know what. Jewellery robberies probably, because they are the commonest with big criminals. All right – he does a big robbery – he hides the stuff till he hopes the hue and cry will be over – but he's caught and put into prison for a number of years. But he doesn't tell where the stuff is hidden! He daren't even write a letter to tell his friends outside

the prison where it is. All his letters are read before they
leave the prison. So what is he to do?'

'Wait till someone escapes and then give him a message,' said Dick. 'And that's just what happened, isn't
it, Julian? That round-headed man I saw was the escaped prisoner, and he was sent to tell Dirty Dick and
Maggie where the stolen goods were hidden – so that
they could get them before anyone else did!'

'Yes. I'm sure that's it,' said Julian. 'His friend, the
escaped prisoner, probably wouldn't understand the
message at all – but Dirty Dick and Maggie would,
because they knew all about the robbery. And now
Maggie will certainly try to find out where the stuff is.'

'Well, we must find it first!' said George, her eyes
gleaming with excitement. 'We're here first, anyway.
And tomorrow, as early as possible we'll begin to snoop
round. What was the next clue in the message, Dick?
After Two-Trees and Gloomy Water.'

'Saucy Jane,' said Dick.

'Sounds a silly sort of clue,' said Anne. 'Do you suppose Maggie and Jane are *both* in the secret?'

'Saucy Jane sounds more like a boat to me,' said
Dick.

'Of *course*!' said George. 'A boat! Why not?
There's a lake here, and I imagine that people don't
build a house beside a lake unless they want to go boat-
ing and bathing and fishing. I bet we shall find a boat
called Saucy Jane tomorrow – and the stolen goods
will be inside it.'

'Too easy!' said Dick. 'And not a very clever place

either. Anyone could come across goods hidden in a boat. No – Saucy Jane is a clue, but we shan't find the stolen goods in her. And remember, there's that bit of paper as well. It must have something to do with the hiding-place too, I should think.'

'Where is it?' asked Julian. 'That wretched policeman! He tore it up. Have you still got the pieces, Dick?'

'Of course,' said Dick. He fished in his pocket and brought them out. 'Four little pieces! Anyone got some gummed paper?'

Nobody had – but George produced a small roll of Elastoplast. Strips were cut and stuck behind the four portions of paper. Now it was whole again. They all examined it carefully.

'Look – four lines drawn, meeting in the centre,' said Julian. 'At the outer end of each line there's a word, so faintly written I can hardly read one of them. What's this one? "Tock Hill." And this next one is "Steeple". Whatever are the others?'

They made them out at last. ' "Chimney," ' said Anne. 'That's the third.'

'And "Tall Stone" is the fourth,' said George. 'Whatever do they all mean? We shall never, never find out!'

'We'll sleep on it,' said Julian, cheerfully. 'It's wonderful what good ideas come in the night. It will be a very interesting little problem to solve tomorrow!'

Chapter Thirteen

A NIGHT IN THE CELLAR

THE piece of paper was carefully folded and this time
Julian took it for safe keeping. 'I can't imagine what
it means, but it's clearly important,' he said. 'We may
quite suddenly come on something – or think of something – that will give us a clue to what the words and
the lines mean on the paper.'

'We mustn't forget that dear Maggie has a copy of
the paper too,' said Dick. 'She probably knows better
than we do what it all means !'

'If she does, she will pay a visit to Two-Trees too,'
said Anne 'We ought to keep a look-out for her.
Should we have to hide if we saw her ?'

Julian considered this. 'No,' he said, 'I certainly
don't think we should hide. Maggie can't *possibly* guess
that we have had the message from Nailer, and the
paper too. We had better just say we are on a hike and
found this place and thought we would shelter here. All
perfectly true.'

'And we can keep an eye on her, and see what she
does if she comes !' said Dick, with a grin. 'Won't she
be annoyed !'

'She wouldn't come alone,' said Julian, thoughtfully.

294 Five on a hike together

'I should think it quite likely that she would come with
Dirty Dick! He didn't get the message, but she did –
and probably part of her message was the statement
that Dirty Dick would know everything too. So she
would get in touch with him.'

'Yes – and be surprised that he hadn't got the message or the paper,' said George. 'Still, they'd think that
the escaped fellow hadn't been able to get to Dirty
Dick.'

'All very complicated,' said Anne, yawning. 'I can't
follow any more arguments and explanations – I'm half
asleep. How long are you going to be before you settle
down?'

Dick yawned too. 'I'm coming now,' he said. 'My
bed of bracken and heather looks inviting. It's not at all
cold in here, is it?'

'The only thing I don't like is the thought of those
cellars beyond this little underground room,' said
Anne. 'I keep thinking that Maggie and her friends
might be there, waiting to pounce on us when we are
asleep.'

'You're silly,' said George, scornfully. 'Really silly!
Do you honestly suppose that Timmy would lie here
quietly if there was anyone in those cellars? You know
jolly well he would be barking his head off!'

'Yes. I know all that,' said Anne, snuggling down in
her heathery bed. 'It's just my imagination. You
haven't got any, George, so you don't bother about im-
aginary fears. I'm not really scared while Timmy is
here. But I do think it's funny the way we always

plunge into something peculiar when we're together.'

'Adventures always do come to some people,' said Dick. 'You've only got to read the lives of explorers and see how they simply *walk* into adventures all the time.'

'Yes, but I'm not an explorer,' said Anne. 'I'm an ordinary person, and I'd be just as pleased if things *didn't* keep happening to me.'

The others laughed. 'I don't expect anything much will happen this time,' said Julian, comfortingly. 'We go back to school on Tuesday and that's not far off. Not much time for anything to happen!'

He was wrong of course. Things can happen one after the other in a few minutes! Still, Anne cuddled down feeling happier. This was better than last night when she was all alone in that horrid little loft. Now she had all the others with her, Timmy too.

Anne and George had one big bed between them. They drew their two rugs over themselves, and put their blazers on top too. Nobody had undressed because Julian had said that they might be too cold in just their night things.

Timmy as usual put himself on George's feet. She moved them because he was heavy. He wormed his way up the bed and found a very comfortable place between the knees of the two girls. He gave a heavy sigh.

'That means he's planning to go to sleep!' said George. 'Are you quite comfortable, Anne?'

'Yes,' said Anne, sleepily. 'I like Timmy there. I feel safe!'

Julian was blowing out the candles. He left just one
burning. Then he got into his bed of bracken and
heather beside Dick. He felt tired too.

The four slept like logs. Nobody moved except Timmy, who got up once or twice in the night and sniffed
round inquiringly. He had heard a noise in the cellars.
He stood at the closed door that led to the cellars and
listened, his head on one side.

He sniffed at the crack. Then he went back to bed,
satisfied. It was only a toad! Timmy knew the smell
of toads. If toads liked to crawl about in the night, they
were welcome to!

The second time he awoke he thought he heard
something up in the kitchen above. He padded up the
steps, his paws making a click-click-click as he went.
He stood in the kitchen silently, his eyes gleaming like
green lamps, as the moon shone on him.

An animal with a long bushy tail began to slink away
outside the house. It was a fine fox. It had smelt unusual smells near the old ruin – the scent of people and
of a dog, and it had come to find out what was
happening.

It had slunk into the kitchen and then smelt the
strong scent of Timmy in the room below. As quietly as
a cat it had slunk out again – but Timmy had
awakened!

Now the dog stood watching and waiting – but the
fox had gone! Timmy sniffed its scent and padded to
the door. He debated whether to bark and go after the
fox.

The scent grew very faint, and Timmy decided not to make a fuss. He padded back to the steps that led down to the cellar room, and curled up on George's feet again. He was very heavy, but George was too tired to wake up and push him off. Timmy lay with one ear cocked for a while, and then went to sleep again, with his ear still cocked. He was a good sentinel!

It was dark in the cellar when the one candle went out. There was no daylight or sunshine to wake the children down in that dim little room, and they slept late.

Julian woke up first. He found his bed suddenly very hard, and he turned over to find a comfortable place. The heather and bracken had been flattened with his weight, and the floor below was very hard indeed! The movement woke him up, and he lay blinking in the darkness. Where was he?

He remembered at once and sat up. Dick woke too and yawned. 'Dick! It's half-past eight!!' said Julian, looking at the luminous hands of his wrist-watch. 'We've slept for hours and hours!'

They rolled out of their heathery bed. Timmy leapt off George's feet and came over to them, his tail wagging gladly. He had been half-awake for a long time and was very glad to see Julian and Dick awake too, because he was thirsty.

The girls awoke – and soon there was a great deal of noise and activity going on. Anne and George washed at the big stone sink, the cold water making them squeal. Timmy lapped up a big bowlful of water gladly. The boys debated whether or not to have a splash in the lake. They felt very dirty.

Dick shivered at the thought. 'Still, I think we ought to,' he said. 'Come on, Ju!'

The two boys went down to the lake-side and leapt in. It was icy-cold! They struck out strongly and came back glowing and shouting.

By the time they were back the girls had got break-fast in the cellar room. It was darker than the kitchen, but all of them disliked the look of the burnt, scorched rooms above. The bread and butter, potted meat, cake and chocolate went down well.

In the middle of the meal a sound came echoing into the old house – bells! Anne stopped eating, and her heart beat fast.

But they were not the clanging warning bells she had heard before!

'Church bells,' said Julian at once, seeing Anne's sudden look of fright. 'Lovely sound I always think!'

'Oh *yes*,' said Anne, thankfully. 'So it is. It's Sunday and people are going to church. I'd like to go too, on this lovely sunny October day.'

'We might walk across the moor to the nearest village if you like,' said Dick, looking at his watch. 'But we should be very late.'

It was decided that it was much too late. They pushed their plates aside and planned what to do that day.

'The first thing, of course, is to see if there's a boat-house and find out if there's a boat called *Saucy Jane*,' said Julian. 'Then we'd better try and puzzle out what that plan means. We could wander here and there and see if we can find Tall Stone – and I'll look at the map to see if Tock Hill is marked. That was on the plan too, wasn't it?'

'You boys go and get some more heather and bracken while we clear away and wash up,' said Anne. 'That is if you mean us to camp here another night.'

'Yes. I think we will,' said Julian. 'I think we may find things rather interesting here this week-end!'

Julian went out with Dick and they brought in a great deal more bedding Everyone had complained that the hard floor came through the amount of heather and bracken they had used the night before, and poor George was quite stiff.

The girls took the dirty things up to the big sink to wash them. There was nothing to dry them with but that didn't matter. They laid them on the old worn draining board to dry.

They wiped their hands on their hankies and then felt ready for exploring round outside. The boys were ready too.

With Timmy bounding here and there they went down to the lake. A path had once led down to it, with a low wall on each side. But now the wall was broken, moss had crept everywhere, and the path was choked with tufts of heather and even with small bushes of gorse.

The lake was as still and dark as ever. Some moorhens chugged across it quickly, disappearing under the water when they saw the children.

'Now, what about that boat-house?' said Dick at last. 'Is there one – or not?'

Chapter Fourteen

WHERE IS THE 'SAUCY JANE'?

THEY walked beside the lake-side as best they could. It was difficult because bushes and trees grew right down to the edge. It seemed as if there was no boat-house at all.

And then George came to a little backwater, leading off the lake. 'Look!' she called. 'Here's a sort of river running from the lake.'

'It's not a river. It's only a little backwater,' said Dick. 'Now we *may* find a boat-house somewhere here.'

They followed the backwater a little way, and then Julian gave an exclamation. 'There it is! But it's so covered up with ivy and brambles that you can hardly see it!'

They all looked where he pointed. They saw a long low building built right across the backwater, where it narrowed and came to an end. It was almost impossible to tell that it was a building, it was so overgrown.

'That's it!' said Dick, pleased. 'Now for the *Saucy Jane*!'

They scrambled through bushes and brambles to get to the entrance of the building. It had to be entered by the front, which was over the water and completely open. A broad ledge ran right round the boat-house inside, and the steps that went up to it from the bank outside were all broken away, completely rotted.

'Have to tread warily here,' said Julian. 'Let me go first.'

He tried the old wooden steps, but they gave way beneath him at once. 'Hopeless!' he said. 'Let's see if there's any other way into the boat-house.'

There wasn't – but at one side some of the wooden boards that made the wall of the boat-house were so rotten that they could be pulled away to make an opening. The boys pulled them down and then Julian squeezed through the opening into the dark, musty boat-house.

He found himself on the broad ledge that went round the great shed. Below him was the dark, quiet water with not even a ripple on it. He called to the others.

'Come along in! There's a wooden ledge to stand on here, and it's hardly rotted at all. It must be made of better wood.'

They all went through the opening and stood on the ledge, peering down. Their eyes had to get used to the darkness at first, because the only light came through the big entrance at the farther end – and that was obscured by big trails of ivy and other creepers hanging down from roof to water.

'There *are* boats here!' said Dick, excited. 'Tied up to posts. Look – there's one just below us. Let's hope one of them is the *Saucy Jane* !'

There were three boats. Two of them were half full of water, and their bows were sunk right down. 'Must

have got holes in them,' said Julian, peering about. He had got out his torch and was shining it all round the old boat-house.

Oars were strung along the walls. Dirty, pulpy masses of something lay on the shelves too – rotted cushions probably. A boat-hook stood in one corner. Ropes were in coils on a shelf. It was a dreary desolate sight, and Anne didn't like the queer echoes of their voices in the damp-smelling, lonely boat-house.

'Let's see if any of the boats are called *Saucy Jane*,' said Dick. He flashed his torch on to the nearest one. The name was almost gone.

'What is it?' said Dick, trying to decipher the faded letters. '*Merry* something.'

'*Meg*!' said Anne. '*Merry Meg*. Well, she may be a sister of *Saucy Jane*. What's the next boat's name?'

The torch shone steadily on to it. The name there was easier to read. They all read it at once.

'*Cheeky Charlie*!'

'Brother to *Merry Meg*!' said Dick. 'Well, all I can say is that these poor old boats look anything but merry or cheeky.'

'I'm sure the last one must be *Saucy Jane*!' said Anne, excited. 'I do hope it is!'

They went along the broad ledge and tried to read the name on the half-sunk boat there. 'It begins with C,' said George, disappointed. 'I'm sure it's C.'

Julian took out his handkerchief and dipped it in the water. He rubbed at the name to try and clean it and make it clearer.

It could be read then – but it wasn't *Saucy Jane*!

'*Careful Carrie*!' read the four, mournfully. 'Blow!'

'*Merry Meg, Cheerful Charlie, Careful Carrie,*' said Julian. 'Well, it's quite obvious that *Saucy Jane* belongs to the family of boats here – but where oh where is she?'

'Sunk out of sight?' suggested Dick.

'Don't think so,' said Julian. 'The water is pretty shallow in this boat-house – it's right at the very end of the little backwater, you see. I think we should be able to spot a boat sunk to the bottom. We can see the sandy bottom of the backwater quite clearly by the light of our torches.'

Just to make quite sure they walked carefully all round the broad wooden ledge and flashed their torches on the water that filled the boat-house. There was no completely sunken boat there at all.

'Well, that's that,' said Dick. 'The *Saucy Jane* is gone. Where? Why? And when?'

They flashed their torches round the walls of the boat-house once more. George's eye was caught by a large flat wooden thing standing upright on the ledge at one side of the house.

'What's that?' she said. 'Oh – a raft, isn't it? That's what those paddles are for, then, that I saw on the shelf above'

They went and examined the raft. 'Yes – and in quite good condition too,' said Julian. 'It would be rather fun to see if it would carry us on the water.'

'Ooooh *yes*!' said Anne, thrilled. 'That would be

super. I always like rafts. I'd rather try that raft than any of those boats.'

'Well, there's only one boat that is possible to use,' said Julian. 'The others are obviously no good – they must have big holes in to sink down like that.'

'Hadn't we better look into them carefully just to make sure there's no loot hidden there?' said Dick.

'If you like,' said Julian. 'But *I* think it's *Saucy Jane* that's got the loot – otherwise why mention it by name in that message?'

Dick felt that Julian was right. All the same he went to examine the three boats most methodically. But except for rotted and burst cushions and coils of rope there was nothing to be seen in the boats at all.

'Well – where's the *Saucy Jane*?' said Dick, puzzled. 'All the family are here but her. Can she be hidden anywhere on the banks of the lake?'

'*That's* an idea!' said Julian, who was trying to shift the big raft. 'That's a really good idea! I think we ought to explore all round the lake and see if we can find the *Saucy Jane* hidden anywhere.'

'Let's leave the raft for a bit then,' said George, feeling thrilled at the thought of possibly finding the *Saucy Jane* tucked away somewhere, all the loot hidden in her. 'Let's go now!'

They made their way round the wooden ledge to the opening they had made in the side of the boat-house, and jumped down. Timmy leapt down gladly. He hadn't liked the dark boat-house at all. He ran into the warm sunshine, wagging his tail.

'Now which side of the lake shall we go first?' said Anne. 'The left or the right?'

They went down to the edge of the silent water and looked to left and right. They both seemed to be equally thick with bushes!

'It's going to be difficult to keep close to the edge of the water,' said Julian. 'Anyway, we'll try. The left side looks a bit easier. Come on!'

It was fairly easy at first to keep close to the water, and examine any tiny creek or look under over-hanging bushes. But after about a quarter of a mile the undergrowth became so very thick and grew so close to the water's edge that it was quite impossible to force their way through it without completely ruining their clothes.

'I give up!' said Julian at last. 'I shall have no jersey left in a minute! These spiteful brambles! My hands are ripped to bits.'

'Yes – they *are* spiteful!' said Anne. 'I felt that too!'

Timmy was the only one really enjoying himself. He couldn't *imagine* why the four were scrambling through such thick undergrowth, but as it was just what he liked he was very pleased. He was disappointed when they decided to give up and go back.

'Shall we try the right hand side of the lake, do you think?' said Julian, as they went back, rather disheartened.

'No. Don't let's,' said Anne. 'It looks even worse than this side. It's only waste of time. I'd rather go out on the raft!'

'Well – that would surely be a better way of exploring the banks of the lake than scrambling through prickly bushes, wouldn't it?' said George. 'We'd only need to paddle along slowly and squint into all the little creeks and under over-hanging trees – it would be easy!'

'Of course,' said Dick. 'We were silly not to think of it before. It would be a lovely way of spending the afternoon, anyway.'

They came through the trees and saw the ruined house in the distance. Timmy suddenly stopped. He gave a low growl, and all the others stopped too.

'What's up, Timmy?' said George in a low voice. 'What is it?'

Timmy growled again. The others cautiously retreated behind bushes and looked intently towards the house. They could see nothing out of the way. Nobody seemed to be about. Then what was Timmy growling at?

And then a woman came in sight, and with her was a man. They were talking earnestly together.

'Maggie! I bet it's Maggie!' said Julian.

'And the other is Dirty Dick,' said Dick. 'I recognize him – yes – it's Dirty Dick.'

Chapter Fifteen

MAGGIE – AND DIRTY DICK

THEY watched the couple in the distance, and thought
quickly. Julian had been expecting them, so he was not
surprised. Dick was looking at Dirty Dick, recognizing
the broad, short man, with his hunched-up shoulders
and shock of hair. He didn't like the look of him any
more than when he had seen him up at the old cottage!

Anne and George didn't like the look of the woman
either! She was wearing trousers and had a jacket
draped round her shoulders. She was also wearing sun-
glasses, and smoking a cigarette. She walked quickly
and they could hear her voice. It was sharp and
determined.

'So that's Maggie,' thought Julian. 'Well, I don't
like her. She looks as hard as nails – a good companion for Nailer!'

He moved cautiously towards the other three.
George had her hand on Timmy's collar, afraid that he
might show himself.

'Listen,' said Julian. 'You're none of you to turn a
hair! We'll just walk out into the open, talking cheerfully together and let them see us. If they ask us what
we're doing, you all know what to say. Chatter nonsense as much as you like – put them off and make
them think we're a bunch of harmless kids. If there are

any leading questions asked us – leave *me* to answer them. Ready?'

They nodded. Then Julian swung out from the bushes and walked into the open, calling to Dick. 'Here we are again – there's the old house! My word, it looks worse than ever this morning!'

George and Timmy came bounding out together, and Anne followed, her heart beating fast. She wasn't as good as the others at this sort of thing!

The man and the woman stopped abruptly when they saw the children. They said a few words to one another very rapidly. The man scowled.

The children went towards them, chattering all the time as Julian had ordered. The woman called sharply to them.

'Who are you? What are you doing here?'

'Just hiking,' said Julian, stopping. 'It's our half-term.'

'What do you want to come *here* for then?' asked the woman. 'This is private property.'

'Oh no,' said Julian. 'It's only a burnt-out ruin. Anyone can come. We want to explore this queer lake – it looks exciting.'

The man and the woman looked at one another. It was clear that the idea of the children exploring the lake was surprising and annoying to them. The woman spoke again.

'You can't explore this lake. It's dangerous. People are forbidden to bathe in it or use a boat.'

'We weren't told that,' said Julian, looking aston-

ished. 'We were told how to get here, and no one said
the lake was forbidden. You've been told wrongly.'

'We want to watch the moor-hens, you see,' put in
Anne, suddenly seeing a moor-hen on the water. 'We're
fond of nature.'

'And we've been told there are deer near here,' said
George.

'And wild ponies,' said Dick. 'We saw some yesterday. They were really lovely. Have you seen any?'

This sudden burst of chatter seemed to annoy the

man and the woman more than Julian's answers. The man spoke roughly.

'Stop this nonsense. People aren't allowed here. Clear out before we make you !'

'Why are *you* here, then, if people aren't allowed?' asked Julian, and a hard tone came into his voice. 'Don't talk to us like that.'

'You clear off, I say !' cried the man, suddenly shouting loudly as he lost his temper. He took two or three steps towards them, looking very threatening indeed. George loosed her hold on Timmy's collar.

Timmy also took two or three steps forward. His hackles went up and he emitted a most fearsome growl. The man stopped suddenly, and then retreated.

'Take hold of that dog's collar,' he ordered. 'He looks savage.'

'Then he looks what he is,' said George. 'I'm not taking hold of his collar while you're about. Don't think it !'

Timmy took two or three more steps forward, growling loudly, walking stiffly and menacingly. The woman called out at once.

'It's all right, children. My friend here just lost his temper for a moment. Call your dog back.'

'Not while you are about,' said George. 'How long are you staying?'

'What's that to do with you?' growled the man, but he didn't say any more because Timmy at once growled back.

'Let's come and have something to eat,' said Julian,

loudly, to the others. 'After all, we have as much right to be here as these people have. We don't need to take any notice of them – and we shan't be in *their* way!'

The four children marched forward. Timmy was still loose. He barked savagely once or twice as he came close to the unpleasant couple, and they shrank back at once. Timmy was such a big dog and he looked so very powerful! They eyed the children angrily as they went by, and watched them go into the ruined house.

'On guard, Timmy,' said George, as soon as they were in, pointing to the ruined doorway. Timmy understood at once, and stood in the doorway, a menacing figure with hackles up and snarling mouth. The children went down to the cellar room. They looked round to see if anyone had been there while they were away, but nothing seemed to have been moved.

'They probably haven't even noticed the cellars,' said Julian. 'I hope there's plenty of bread left. I'm hungry. I wish to goodness we were going to have a dinner like the one we had yesterday! I say – what an unpleasant pair Maggie and Dick are!'

'Yes. Very,' said Dick. 'I can't bear Maggie. Horrid common voice and hard face. Ugh!'

'I think Dirty Dick is worse,' said Anne. 'He looks like a gorilla or something with his broad hunched-up body. And WHY doesn't he cut his hair?'

'Fancies himself like that, I expect,' said George, cutting a loaf of bread. 'His surname ought to be Golliwog. Or Tarzan. I'm jolly glad we've got Timmy.'

'So am I,' said Anne. 'Good old Timmy. He hated them, didn't he? I bet they won't come near the door-way with Timmy there!'

'I wonder where they are,' said Dick picking up a great hunk of bread and butter and potted meat. 'I'm going to look.'

He came back in half a minute. 'They've gone to the boat-house, I think,' he said. 'I just caught a sight of one of them moving in that direction. Looking for *Saucy Jane*, I expect.'

'Let's sit down and eat and talk over what we'll do next,' said Julian. 'And what we think *they* will do next! That's quite important. They may be able to read the clues on that paper better than we can If we watch what they do it may give us a guide as to what *we* must do.'

'That's true,' said Dick. 'I imagine that the plan Nailer sent must mean something to Dirty Dick and Maggie, just as the message did.' He chewed at his bread, thinking hard, trying once more to fathom the meaning of that mysterious piece of paper.

'I think on the whole we will follow out our original plan for this afternoon,' said Julian, after a little silence. 'We'll get out that raft and go on the lake with it. It's a harmless looking thing to do. We can examine the banks as we go – and if Maggie and Dick are out in a boat too, we can keep an eye on them as well.'

'Yes Good idea,' said George. 'It's a heavenly after-noon anyway. I'd love to paddle about on the lake with that raft. I hope it's good and sound.'

'Sure to be,' said Dick. 'The wood it's made of is meant to last. Pass the cake, George – and *don't* save Timmy any. It's wasted on him.'

'It isn't!' said George. 'You know he loves it.'

'Yes. But I still say it's wasted on him,' said Dick. 'Good thing we got such an enormous cake! Are there any biscuits left?'

'Plenty,' said Anne. 'And chocolate too!'

'Good,' said Dick. 'I only hope our food will last us out. It won't if George has her usual colossal appetite.'

'What about yours?' said George, indignantly, rising every time to Dick's lazy teasing.

'Shut up, you two,' said Julian. 'I'm going to fill the water jug and have some orangeade. Give me something to take to old Tim.'

They spent about half an hour over their lunch. Then they decided to go and tackle the raft in the boat-house, and see if they could possibly launch it on the lake. It would be heavy, they knew.

They left the old house and went off to the boat-house. Julian suddenly caught sight of something out on the lake.

'Look!' he said, 'they've got one of the boats out of the boat-house – the one that wasn't half-sunk, I suppose! Dirty Dick is rowing hard. I BET they're looking for the *Saucy Jane*!'

They all stood still and watched. Dick's heart sank. Would Maggie and Dirty Dick get there first, and find what he and the other three were looking for? Did they know where the *Saucy Jane* was?

'Come on,' said Julian. 'We'd better get going if we want to keep an eye on them. They may be rowing to where the *Saucy Jane* is hidden!'

They climbed in through the wooden side of the boat-house and went to the raft. Julian saw at once that one of the boats had gone – *Merry Meg*. It was the only boat that was fit to take.

The four began to man-handle the big raft. They took it to the edge of the ledge. It had rope-handles on each side which the children held on to.

'Now – ease her gently,' said Julian. 'Gently does it. Down she goes!'

And down she went, landing with a big splash in the water. She bobbed there gently, a strong sound raft, eager to go out on the lake!

'Get the paddles,' said Julian. 'Then we'll be off.'

Chapter Sixteen

OUT ON THE RAFT

THERE were four little paddles. Dick got them, and
gave everyone one each. Timmy looked down solemnly
at the raft. What was it? Surely he was not expected
to ride on that bobbing, floating thing?

Julian was on the raft already, holding it steady for
the others. He helped Anne on and then George stepped down. Dick came last – well, not quite last, because
Timmy was not yet on.

'Come on, Tim!' said George. 'It's all right! It's not
the kind of boat you're used to, but it acts in the same
way. Come *on*, Timmy!'

Timmy jumped down and the raft bobbed violently.
Anne sat down suddenly with a giggle. 'Oh dear –
Timmy is so *sudden*! Keep still, Tim – there isn't
enough room on this raft for you to walk all over it.'

Julian pushed the raft out of the boat-house. It
knocked against the wooden ledge as it went, and then
swung out on to the backwater outside. It floated very
smoothly.

'Here we go!' said Julian, paddling deftly. 'I'll steer,
Dick. None of you need to paddle till I say so. I can
paddle and steer at the moment, till we get on to the
lake itself.'

They were all sitting on the raft except Timmy, who
was standing up. He was very interested in seeing the
water flow past so quickly. *Was* this a boat then? He

was used to boats – but in boats the water was never quite so near. Timmy put out a paw into the water. It was pleasantly cool and tickled him. He lay down with his nose almost in the water.

'You're a funny dog, Timmy!' said Anne. 'You won't get up too suddenly, will you, or you'll knock me overboard.'

Julian paddled down the little backwater and the raft swung out on to the lake itself. The children looked to see if there was any sign of Maggie and Dirty Dick.

'There they are!' said Julian. 'Out in the middle, rowing hard. Shall we follow them? If they know where the *Saucy Jane* is they'll lead us to it.'

'Yes. Follow them,' said Dick. 'Shall *we* paddle now? We'll have to be quick or we may lose them.'

They all paddled hard, and the raft suddenly swung to and fro in a most alarming manner.

'Hey, stop!' shouted Julian. 'You're all paddling against one another. We're going round in circles. Dick and Anne go one side and George the other. That's better. Watch how we're going, all of you, and stop paddling for a moment if the raft swings round too much.'

They soon got into the way of paddling so that the raft went straight ahead. It was fun. They got very hot and wished they could take off their jerseys. The sun was quite warm, and there was no wind at all – it was really a perfect October afternoon.

'They've stopped rowing,' said George, suddenly. 'They're looking at something – do you suppose they have got a bit of paper like the one we have, with the same marks, and are examining it? I *wish* I could see!'

They all stopped paddling and looked towards the boat in which Maggie and Dirty Dick sat. They were certainly examining something very carefully – their heads were close together. But they were too far away for the children to see if they were holding a piece of paper.

'Come on – we'll get as close to them as we can!' said Julian, beginning to paddle again. 'I expect it will make them absolutely mad to see us so close, but we can't help that!'

They paddled hard again, and at last came up to the boat. Timmy barked. Maggie and Dirty Dick at once looked round and saw the raft and the four children. They stared at them savagely.

'Hallo!' cried Dick, waving a paddle. 'We took the raft out. It goes well. Does your boat go all right?'

Maggie went red with rage. 'You'll get into trouble for taking that raft without permission,' she shouted.

'Whose permission did *you* ask when you took that boat?' shouted back Julian. 'Tell us and we'll ask their permission to use this raft!'

George laughed. Maggie scowled, and Dirty Dick looked as if he would like to throw his oars at them.

'Keep away from us!' he shouted. 'We don't want you kids spoiling our afternoon!'

'We like to be friendly!' called Dick, and made George laugh again.

Maggie and Dirty Dick had a hurried and angry

conversation. They glared at the raft and then Maggie gave an order to Dirty Dick. He took up the oars again, and began to row, looking rather mutinous.

'Come on – follow,' said Julian, so the four began to paddle again following after the boat. 'Maybe we'll learn something now.'

But they didn't. Dirty Dick rowed the boat towards the west bank, and the raft followed. Then he swung out into the middle again, and again the raft followed, the children panting in their efforts to keep up.

Dirty Dick rowed right across to the east bank and stayed there till the children came up. Then he rowed off again.

'Having some nice exercise, aren't you?' called the woman in her harsh voice. 'So good for you all!'

The boat swung out to the middle of the lake again. Dick groaned. 'Blow! My arms are so tired I can hardly paddle. What are they doing?'

'I'm afraid they're just leading us on a wild goose chase,' said Julian, ruefully. 'They have evidently made up their minds that they won't look for the *Saucy Jane* while we're about – they're just tiring us out!'

'Well, if *that's* what they're doing I'm not playing!' said Dick, and he put down his paddle and lay flat on his back, his knees drawn up, panting hard.

The others did the same. They were all tired. Timmy licked each one sympathetically and then sat down on George. She pushed him off so violently that he nearly fell into the water.

'Timmy! Right on my middle!' cried George, surprised and indignant. 'You great clumsy dog, you !'

Timmy licked her all over, shocked at being scolded by George. She was too exhausted to push him away.

'What's happened to the boat?' asked Anne at last. 'I'm too tired to sit up and see.'

Julian sat up, groaning. 'Oh my back ! Now where is that wretched boat? Oh, there it is – right away down the lake, making for the landing-place by the house – or for the boat-house probably. They've given up the search for the *Saucy Jane* for the time being anyway.'

'Thank goodness,' said Anne. 'Perhaps we can give it up too – till tomorrow anyhow ! Stop snuffling down my neck, Timmy. What do you want us to do, Julian.'

'I think we'd better get back,' said Julian. 'It's too late now to start searching the banks of the lake – and anyway somehow I think it wouldn't be much use. The two in the boat didn't appear to be going anywhere near the banks – except when they began to play that trick on us to make us tired out !'

'Well, let's get back then,' said George. 'But I simply must have a rest first. Timmy, I shall push you into the water if you keep sitting on my legs.'

There was a sudden splash. George sat up in alarm. Timmy was not on the raft !

He was swimming in the water, looking very pleased with himself.

'There ! He thought he'd rather jump in than be pushed,' said Dick, grinning at George.

'*You* pushed him in !' said George, looking fierce.

'I didn't,' said Dick. 'He just took a header. He's having a jolly good time. I say – what about putting a rope round him and getting him to pull us to shore? It would save an awful lot of paddling.'

George was just about to say what she thought of *that* idea, when she caught Dick's sly grin. She kicked out at him.

'Don't keep baiting me, Dick. I'll push *you* in, in a
minute.'

'Like to try?' asked Dick, at once. 'Come on. I'd like
a wrestle to see who'd go into the water first.'

George, of course, always rose to a challenge. She
never could resist one. She was up in a moment and
fell on Dick, who very nearly went overboard at once.

'Shut up, you two!' said Julian, crossly. 'We haven't got a change of clothing, you know that. And I don't want to take you back with bronchitis or pneumonia. Stop it, George.'

George recognized the tone in his voice and she stopped. She ran her hand through her short curls and gave a sudden grin.

'All right, Teacher!' she said, and sat down meekly. She picked up her paddle.

Julian picked up his. 'We'll get back,' he said. 'The sun's sinking low. It seems to slide down the sky at a most remarkable speed in October.'

They took a very wet Timmy on board and began to paddle back. Anne thought it was a truly lovely evening. She gazed dreamily round as she paddled. The lake was a wonderful dark blue, and the ripples they made turned to silver as they ran away from the raft. Two moor-hens said 'crek-crek' and swam round the raft in curiosity, their heads bobbing like clockwork.

Anne gazed over the tops of the trees that grew at the lake-side. The sky was turning pink. Away in the distance, on a high slope about a mile away she saw something that interested her.

It looked like a high stone. She pointed at it. 'Look, Julian,' she said. 'What's that stone? Is it a boundary mark, or something? It must be very big.'

Julian looked where she was pointing. 'Where?' he said. 'Oh, that. I can't imagine what it is.'

'It looks like a very tall stone,' said Dick, suddenly catching sight of it too.

'A tall stone,' repeated Anne, wondering where she had heard that before. 'A tall . . . oh, of *course* ! It was printed on that plan, wasn't it – on the piece of paper Dick was given. Tall Stone ! Don't you remember?'

'Yes. So it was,' said Dick and he stared at the far-away stone monument with interest. Then as the raft swung onwards, high trees hid the stone. It was gone.

'Tall Stone,' said Julian. 'It may be only a coincidence, of course. It wants a bit of thinking about, though. Funny we should suddenly spot it.'

'Would the loot be buried there?' asked George, doubtfully. Julian shook his head. 'Oh, no,' he said, 'it is probably hidden in some position explained by that mysterious map. Paddle up, everyone ! We really must get back.'

Chapter Seventeen

TIT FOR TAT!

WHEN they arrived at the boat-house there was no sign of Maggie or Dick. But their boat was in the shed, tied up in front of the other two, where it had been before.

'They're back all right,' said Julian 'I wonder where they are. Don't let's drag this clumsy, heavy raft into the boat-house. I don't feel as if I've any strength left in my arms. Let's drag it under a bush and tie it there.'

They thought this a good idea They pulled the raft up to some thick bushes and tied it firmly to a root that was sticking out of the ground.

Then they made their way to the ruined house, keeping a sharp look-out for Maggie and Dick. There was still no sign of them.

They went in, Timmy first He didn't growl so they knew it was safe He led the way to the cellar steps. Then he growled!

'What's up?' said Julian. 'Are they down there, Tim?'

Timmy ran straight down the steps into the cellar room. He growled again, but it was not the fierce growl he always gave when he wanted to warn that enemies or strangers were near. It was an angry, annoyed growl as if something was wrong.

'I expect dear Maggie and Dirty Dick have been down here and found out where our headquarters are!' said Julian, following Timmy down the steps. He switched on his torch.

The beds of heather and bracken were there as they had left them, and their macs and rugs and rucksacks. Nothing seemed to have been disturbed. Julian lighted the candles on the mantelpiece and the dark little underground room came to life at once.

'What's the matter with Timmy?' asked George, coming down into the room. 'He's still growling. Timmy, what's up?'

'I expect he can smell that the others have been down here,' said Dick. 'Look at him sniffing all round. It's quite clear that *someone* has been here.'

'Anyone hungry?' asked Anne. 'I could do with some cake and biscuits.'

'Right,' said Julian, and opened the cupboard where they had put the food they had bought.

There was none there! Except for the crockery and one or two odds and ends that had been in the cupboard before, there was nothing. The bread had gone, the biscuits, the chocolate – everything!

'Blow!' said Julian, angrily. 'Look at that! The beasts! They've taken all our food – every bit. Not even a biscuit left. We were mad not to think they might do that!'

'Clever of them,' said Dick. 'They know we can't stay here long without food. It's a good way of chasing us out. It's too late to go and get any tonight, anyway –

and if we go tomorrow for some, they'll do what they have come to do in their own good time . . . when we're not here.'

Everyone felt distinctly down in the dumps. They were hungry and tired, and a good meal would have made all the difference. Anne sank down on her bed of heather and sighed.

'I wish I'd left some chocolate in my rucksack,' she said. 'But I didn't leave any there at all. And poor Tim – he's hungry too! Look at him sniffing in the

cupboard and looking round at George. Tim, there's
nothing for you. The cupboard is bare!'

'Where are those two wretches gone?' suddenly said
Julian, fiercely. 'I'll tick them off! I'll tell them what
I think of people who come and rifle cupboards and
take away all the food.'

'Woof,' said Timmy, in full agreement.

Julian went angrily up the stairs. He wondered
again where Maggie and Dirty Dick were. He went to
the empty doorway and looked out. Then he saw
where they were.

Two small tents had been put up under some thickly
growing trees! So that's where the two were going to
sleep. He debated whether or not to go and tell them
what he thought of people who stole food. He decided
that he would.

But when he got over to the tents with Timmy,
there was no one there! Rugs were laid inside, and
there was a primus stove and a kettle and other odds
and ends. At the back of one tent was a pile of something, covered by a cloth.

Julian had a good look into each tent, and then
went to see if he could find out where Maggie and
Dirty Dick had gone. He saw them at last, walking
through the trees. They must have gone for an evening stroll, he thought.

They didn't come back to the tents, but sat down by
the lake. Julian gave up the thought of tackling them
and went back to the others. Timmy was left behind,
snuffling about happily.

'They've got tents,' Julian informed the others when he was back in the cellar room again. 'They're obviously staying put till they've got what they came for. They aren't in the tents – they're out by the lake.'

'Where's Timmy?' asked George. 'You shouldn't have left him behind, Ju. They might do something to him.'

'Here he is!' said Julian, as a familiar noise of claws clattering on the ground came to their ears. Timmy came down the stone steps and ran to George.

'He's got something in his mouth!' said George, in surprise. Timmy dropped it into her lap. She gave a yell.

'It's a tin of shortbread! Where did he get it from?'

Julian began to laugh. 'He must have taken it from one of the tents!' he said. 'I saw something covered up with a cloth in one tent – their food, I imagine! Well, well – tit for tat – they took our food and now Timmy is taking theirs!'

'Fair exchange is no robbery,' grinned Dick. 'Serves them right! I say – Tim's gone again!'

He was back in a minute with something large and paper-covered. It was a big cake! The four roared with laughter. 'Timmy! You're a wonder! You really are!'

Timmy was pleased at this praise. Off he went again and brought back a cardboard box in which was a fine pork-pie. The children could hardly believe their eyes.

'It's a miracle!' said Anne. 'Just as I had made up my mind to starve for hours! A pork-pie of all things! Let's have some.'

'Well, I have no second thoughts about it,' said Julian, firmly. 'They took our food and we deserve some of theirs. Good gracious – don't say Tim's gone again.'

He had! He was enjoying himself thoroughly. He arrived this time with a packet of ham, and the children couldn't *imagine* how he had stopped himself from eating some on the way.

'Fancy carrying it in his mouth and not even *tasting* a bit!' said Dick. 'Tim's a better person than I am. I'd just have to have had a lick.'

'I say – we ought to stop him now,' said Julian, as Timmy ran up the steps again, his tail wagging nineteen to the dozen. 'We're getting a bit too much in exchange!'

'Oh, do see what he brings back this time,' begged Anne. 'Then stop him.'

He came back carrying an old flour bag in which something had been packed. Timmy carried it cleverly by the neck so that nothing had fallen out. George undid the bag.

'Home-made scones – and buns,' she said. 'Timmy, you are very very clever, and you shall have a wonderful supper. But you are not to go and take any more things, because we've got enough. See? No more. Lie down and be a good dog and eat your supper.'

Timmy was quite willing. He wolfed ham and scones and a slice of cake, and then he went up into the kitchen, jumped into the sink and lapped the water lying there. He then jumped down and went to the doorway to look out. He barked. Then he growled loudly.

The children rushed up the stone steps at once. Outside, at a safe distance, was Dirty Dick.

'Have you been taking anything of ours?' he shouted.

'No more than you have been taking of ours!' shouted back Julian. 'Fair exchange, you know, and all that.'

'How dare you go into our tents?' raged the man, his shock of hair making him look very peculiar in the twilight.

'We didn't. The dog fetched and carried for us,' said Julian. 'And don't you come any nearer. He's just longing to fly at you! And I warn you, he'll be on guard tonight, so don't try any funny tricks. He's as strong and savage as a lion.'

'Grrrr,' said Timmy, so fiercely that the man started back in fright. He went off without another word, shaking with anger.

Julian and the others went back to finish a very delicious supper. Timmy went with them – but he planted himself at the top of the cellar steps.

'Not a bad place for him to be in tonight,' said Julian. 'I don't trust that couple an inch. We can give him one of our blazers to lie on. I say – this has boiled up into quite an adventure, hasn't it? It seems frightful to think we'll be back at school on Tuesday!'

'We *must* find the loot first!' said Anne. 'We really must. Let's get out that plan again, Ju. Let's make sure that Tall Stone is marked on it.'

They got it out and put it on the table. They bent over it once more.

'Yes – Tall Stone is marked at the end of one of the lines,' said Julian. 'Tock Hill is at the end of the opposite line. Let's get the map and see if there *is* a Tock Hill.'

They got the map, and studied it. Anne suddenly put her finger down on it. 'There it is. On the opposite side of the lake from where we saw the Tall Stone, Tock Hill on one side. Tall Stone on the other. Surely that *means* something.'

'It does, of course,' said Julian. 'It is bearings given to show the whereabouts of the hidden goods. There are four bearings given – Tall Stone. Tock Hill. Chimney. And Steeple.'

'Listen!' said Dick, suddenly. 'LISTEN! *I* know how to read that map. It's easy.'

The others looked at him in surprise and doubt.

'Read it, then,' said Julian. 'Tell us what it all means. I don't believe you can!'

Chapter Eighteen

A VERY EXCITING TIME

'LET's take all the clues we know,' said Dick, looking excited. 'Two Trees. That's here. Gloomy Water. That's where the hidden stuff must be. *Saucy Jane*. It's a boat that contains the stuff, hidden somewhere on Gloomy Water.'

'Go on,' said Julian, as Dick paused to think.

'Maggie is the next clue – well she's here, probably an old friend of Nailer's,' said Dick. 'She knows all the clues too.'

He jabbed his finger at the piece of paper. 'Now for *these* clues. Listen! We saw Tall Stone when we were out on the lake, didn't we? Very well. There must be SOME spot on the lake from where we can see not only Tall Stone, but also Tock Hill, Chimney and Steeple, whatever they are! There must be only one spot from which we can see all those four things at the same time – and *that's* the spot to hunt in for the treasure!'

There was an astonished silence after this. Julian drew a long breath and clapped Dick on the back.

'Of course! What idiots we were not to see it before. The *Saucy Jane* must be somewhere on – or in – the lake at the spot where all four clues are seen at the same time. We've only got to explore and find out!'

'Yes – but don't forget that Maggie and Dirty Dick know what these clues mean too! They'll be there first

if they possibly can!' said Dick. 'And what's more if
they get the goods we can't do anything about it. We're
not the police! They'll be off and away with their find
and disappear completely.'

Everyone began to feel intensely excited. 'I think
we'd better set off early tomorrow morning,' said
Julian. 'As soon as it's light. Otherwise Maggie and
Dick will get in first. I wish to goodness we had an
alarm clock.'

'We'll go on the raft, and we'll paddle about till we
see Tall Stone again – then we'll keep that in sight till
we see Tock Hill, whatever that is,' said Dick. 'And
once we've spotted that we'll keep both Tall Stone *and*
Tock Hill in sight and paddle round to find out where
we can see a steeple – and then a chimney. I should
think that would be the one chimney left on Two
Trees-house! Did you notice there is just one left, sticking up high?'

'Yes, I noticed,' said Anne. 'What a clever way to
hide anything, Dick. Nobody could possibly know what
the clues meant unless they knew something of the
secret. This is *awfully* exciting!'

They talked about it for some time and then Julian
said they really must try and go to sleep or they would
never wake up early enough in the morning.

They settled down in their beds of heather and
bracken. Timmy lay on Julian's blazer on the top step
of the stairs leading down to the cellar room. He
seemed to think it was quite a good idea to sleep there
that night.

They were all tired and they fell asleep very quickly. Nothing disturbed them in the night. The fox came again and looked into the old house, but Timmy didn't stir. He merely gave a small growl and the fox fled, his bushy tail spread behind him.

The morning came and daylight crept in at the burnt-out doorway and windows. Timmy stirred and went to the door. He looked towards the two tents. No one was about there. He went to the cellar steps and clattered down waking Dick and Julian at once.

'What's the time?' said Julian, remembering immediately that he was to wake early. 'Half-past seven. Wake up, everyone! It's daylight. We've heaps to do!'

They washed hurriedly, combed out their hair, cleaned their teeth, and tried to brush down their clothes. Anne got ready some snacks for them – ham, scones and a piece of shortbread each. They all had a drink of water and then they were ready to go.

There was no sign of anyone near the two tents. 'Good,' said Julian. 'We'll be there first!'

They dragged the raft out and got on to it, taking up the paddles. Then off they went, Timmy too, all feeling tremendously excited.

'We'll paddle out to where we think we were last night when Anne caught sight of Tall Stone,' said Julian. So they paddled valiantly, though their arms were stiff with yesterday's paddling and it was really very painful to use the tired muscles all over again!

They paddled out to the middle of the lake and

looked for Tall Stone. It didn't seem anywhere to be
seen! They strained their eyes for it, but for a long time
it was not to be spotted at all. Then Dick gave a cry.
'It's just come into sight. Look, when we passed those
tall trees on the bank yonder, Tall Stone came into
view. It was behind them before that.'

'Good,' said Julian. 'Now I'm going to stop paddling and keep Tall Stone in sight. If it goes out of sight
I'll tell you and you must back-paddle. Dick, can you
possibly paddle and look out for something that could
be Tock Hill on the opposite side? I daren't take my
eyes off Tall Stone in case it disappears.'

'Right,' said Dick, and paddled while he looked
earnestly for Tock Hill.

'Got it!' he said suddenly. 'It must be it! Look,
over there – a funny little hill with a pointed top.
Julian, can you still see Tall Stone?'

'Yes,' said Julian. 'Keep your eyes on Tock Hill.
Now it's up to the girls. George, paddle away and see
if you can spot Steeple.'

'I can see it now, already!' said George, and for one
moment the boys took their eyes off Tall Stone and
Tock Hill and looked where George pointed. They saw
the steeple of a faraway church glinting in the morning
sun.

'Good, good, good,' said Julian. 'Now Anne – look
for Chimney – look down towards the end of the lake
where the house is. Can you see its one chimney?'

'Not quite,' said Anne. 'Paddle just a bit to the left –
the left, I said, George! Yes – yes, I can see the one

chimney. Stop paddling everyone. We're here!'

They stopped paddling but the raft drifted on, and
Anne lost the chimney again! They had to paddle
back a bit until it came into sight. By that time George
had lost her steeple!

At last all four things were in view at once, and the
raft seemed to be still and unmoving on the quiet
waters of the lake.

'I'm going to drop something to mark the place,' said
Julian, still keeping his eyes desperately on Tall Stone.
'George, can you manage to watch Tall Stone and
Steeple at the same time? I simply must look what I'm
doing for the moment.'

'I'll try,' said George, and fixed her eyes first on Tall
Stone, then on Steeple, then on Tall Stone again, hoping and praying that neither would slip out of sight if
the raft moved on the water.

Julian was busy. He had taken his torch and his
pocket-knife out of his pocket and had tied them together with string. 'I haven't enough string, Dick,' he
said. 'You've got some, haven't you?'

Dick had, of course. He put his hand into his pocket,
still keeping his eyes on Tock Hill and passed his string
over to Julian.

Julian tied it to the end of the string that joined together the knife and torch. Then he dropped them into
the water, letting out the string as they went down
with their weight. The string slid through his hands. It
stopped in a short while and Julian knew that the knife
and torch had reached the bed of the lake.

He felt in his pockets again. He knew he had a cork
somewhere that he had carved into a horse's head.
He found it and tied the end of the string firmly round
it. Then he dropped the cork thankfully into the water.
It bobbed there, held by the string, which led right
down to the knife and torch on the lake-bed below.

'It's done!' he said, with a sigh of relief. 'Take your
eyes off everything! I've marked the place now, so we
don't need to glue our eyes on the four bearings!'

He told them how he had tied together his knife and
torch and dropped them on string to the bottom of the
lake, and then had tied a cork to the other end, so that
it would bob and show them the place.

They all looked at it. 'Jolly clever, Ju,' said Dick.
'But once we slide away from this spot, and it would
be an easy thing to do, we'd find it jolly difficult to find
that cork gain! Hadn't we better tie something else to
it?'

'I haven't got anything else that will float,' said
Julian. 'Have you?'

'I have,' said George, and she handed him a little
wooden box. 'I keep the threepenny bits I collect in
that,' she said, putting the money into her pocket. 'You
can have the box. It will be much easier to see than the
cork.'

Julian tied the box to the cork. It was certainly a
good deal easier to see! 'Fine!' he said. 'Now we're
quite all right. We must be right over the loot!'

They all bent over the edge of the raft and looked
down – and they saw a most surprising sight! Below

them, resting on the bottom of the lake, was a boat! It lay there in the shadows of the water, its outline blurred by the ripples the raft made – but quite plainly it was a boat!

'The *Saucy Jane*!' said Julian, peering down, feeling amazed and awed to think that they had read the bearings so correctly that they were actually over the *Saucy Jane* herself! 'The Nailer must have come here with the stolen goods – got out the *Saucy Jane* and rowed her to this spot. He must have taken his bearings very carefully indeed, and then holed the boat so that she sank down with the loot in her. Then I suppose he swam back to shore.'

'Most ingenious,' said Dick. 'Really, he must be a jolly clever fellow. But I say, Julian – how on earth are we going to get the boat up?'

'I can't imagine,' said Julian. 'I simply – can't – imagine! I hadn't even thought of that.'

Timmy suddenly began to growl. The four looked up quickly to see why.

They saw a boat coming over the water towards them – the *Merry Meg*, with Maggie and Dirty Dick in it. And the children felt quite certain that both were reading the bearings on their piece of paper in exactly the same way as they themselves had!

They were so engrossed in watching for Tall Stone, Tock Hill, Chimney and Steeple that they took no notice of the children at all. 'I don't think they guess for one moment that we've read the bearings and marked the place,' said Julian. 'How wild they'll be when they find we are right over the place they're looking for! Watch out for trouble!'

Chapter Nineteen

MAGGIE AND DICK ARE ANNOYED

THE boat in which Maggie and Dirty Dick were rowing went this way and that as the two searched for the
same objects that the children had already spotted The
four watched them, and George put her hand on
Timmy to stop him barking.

The boat came nearer and nearer. Maggie was trying to keep in view two or three of the bearings at once
and her head twisted from side to side continually. The
children grinned at one another. It had been hard
enough for the four of them to keep all the bearings in
view – it must be very difficult for Maggie, especially
as Dirty Dick didn't seem to be helping very much.

They heard Maggie give sharp orders as the boat
swung this way and that. Then it headed for them,
Dirty Dick growled something to Maggie, who had her
back to them, and she turned round sharply, losing the
view of the things she was looking for.

Her face was full of anger when she saw the raft so
near – and in the place where she wanted *her* boat to
go! Afraid of completely losing the view of the things
she was keeping her eyes on, she turned back again
and hastily looked to see if Tock Hill, Tall Stone and

Steeple were still all to be seen together. She said something in a furious voice to Dirty Dick, and he nodded
with a sour face.

The boat came nearer and they heard Maggie say
'I think I can see it now – yes – a bit farther to the right,
please.'

'She's spotted One Chimney now,' whispered Anne.
'I expect they've got all the bearings. Oh dear – the
boat will bump right into us!'

It did! Dirty Dick rowed viciously at them and the
bows of the boat gave them a terrific jolt. Anne would
have fallen into the water if Julian hadn't grabbed at
her.

He yelled at Dirty Dick. 'Look out, you ass! You
nearly had us over! What on earth do you think you're
doing?'

'Get out of the way then,' growled Dirty Dick.
Timmy began to bark savagely, and the boat at once
drew away from the raft.

'There's plenty of room on this lake,' shouted Julian.
'What do you want to come and disturb us for? We
aren't doing any harm.'

'We're going to report you to the police,' called the
woman, her face red with anger. 'Taking a raft that
doesn't belong to you, sleeping in a house where you've
no right to be – and stealing our food.'

'Don't talk nonsense,' cried Julian. 'And don't you
dare to ram us again. If you do I'll send our dog after
you. He's longing to come.'

'Grrrr!' said Timmy, and showed his magnificent

set of gleaming white teeth. Dirty Dick muttered something quickly to Maggie. She turned round again and
called to them.

'Now look here, you kids – be sensible. My friend
and I have come down here for a quiet week-end, and
it isn't nice to find you four everywhere we go. Go back
and keep out of our way and we won't report you at
all. That's a fair bargain – we won't even say anything
about your stealing our food.'

'We're going back when we think we will,' answered
Julian. 'And no threats or bargains will make any
difference to us.'

There was a silence. Then Maggie spoke hurriedly to
Dirty Dick again. He nodded.

'Is this your half-term?' she called. 'When do you
have to go back?'

'Tomorrow,' said Julian. 'You'll be rid of us then.
But we're going to enjoy ourselves on this raft while
we can.'

There was another hurried conference between the
two. Then Dirty Dick rowed round a little, and Maggie began to peer down into the water. She suddenly
looked up, nodded at Dirty Dick, and he rowed away
again towards the end of the lake! Not another word
did the couple say.

'I can see what they've decided to do,' said Julian,
in a pleased voice. 'They think we'll be gone by tomorrow, so they'll wait till the coast is clear and then
they'll come and collect the loot in peace. Did you see
Maggie looking down into the water to spot the boat?

I was afraid she would also spot our mark – the cork and the box ! But she didn't.'

'I don't know why you sound so pleased,' said George. 'We can't get the boat up, you know that – and *I* don't feel pleased that we'll have to leave tomorrow and let that horrid pair collect the loot. I imagine they'll have some clever grown-up way of pulling up the boat from the bed of the lake – which they will do when we've gone tomorrow.'

'You're not very bright today, George,' said Julian, watching the boat being rowed farther and farther away. 'I told them we'd be gone tomorrow, hoping they would clear off and wait – and leave us time to get the loot ourselves. I think we can !'

'How?' said three voices at once, and Timmy looked inquiringly at Julian too.

'Well, we don't need to pull up the *boat*,' said Julian. 'We only want the loot. What's to prevent us from going down and getting it ? I'm quite prepared to strip and dive down to the bottom there and feel about for any sack or bag or box. If I find one I'll come up for air, borrow a bit of rope from the raft and go down again – tie the rope to the sack and you can haul it up to the surface !'

'Oh Julian – it sounds so easy – but is it really ?' said Anne. George and Dick considered the proposal carefully. They were most impressed by Julian's idea.

'Well, it may turn out to be much more difficult than it sounds, but I'm jolly well going to try it,' said Julian, and began to strip off his jersey.

Anne felt the water. It was very very cold to her warm hand. 'Ugh! I'd hate to dive down to the bottom of this horrid cold dark lake,' she said. 'I think you're brave, Ju.'

'Don't talk rubbish!' said Julian.

He was ready to go in now. He dived neatly into the water with hardly a splash. The other three craned over the edge of the raft to watch. They could see him down, deep down in the water, a ghostly figure. He stayed down such a long time that Anne got worried.

'He can't hold his breath all that time!' she said, 'He can't!'

But Julian could. He was one of the star swimmers and divers at his school, and this was easy to him. He came up again at last, and panted hard, trying to make up for holding his breath so long. The others waited patiently. At last his breathing grew more even and he grinned at them.

'Ah – that's better! Well – it's there!' he said, triumphantly.

'*Is* it!' said everyone, thrilled. 'Oh Julian!'

'Yes. I dived right down to the boat – almost got there with the force of my dive – had to swim just a couple of strokes perhaps. And there was the poor old boat, rotting to bits. And in one end is a waterproof bag – almost a sack, it's so big. I ran my hands over it, and it's waterproof all right – so the loot must be packed in there.'

'Did it feel heavy?' asked Dick.

'I gave it a tug and couldn't move it,' said Julian.
'Either it's wedged in somehow or is really heavy. Anyway we can't fetch it out by diving down for it. I'll have
to dive down again, fix a rope to it, then come up – and
we'll give a heave-ho and up she'll come!'

Julian was shivering. Anne picked up the blazer she
had brought and gave it to him to dry himself with.
Dick looked hurriedly over the raft. There were certainly bits and pieces of rope sticking out here and
there, some of it half-rotten; and a short length
was tucked into a space between two planks of the raft.

It was much too short though – and surely the other
bits and pieces would never join to make a long
enough rope?

'The bits of rope we've got won't do, Julian,' said
Dick. Julian was drying himself and looking towards
the end of the lake, where Two-Trees stood. He was
frowning. The others looked too.

The boat had reached the bank there, and had been
pulled up. One of the couple, the children couldn't see
which, was standing up on the bank – and something
was glinting in the sun, something he or she was holding!

'See that glint?' said Julian. 'Well, that's either Maggie or Dirty Dick using field-glasses. They're going to
keep an eye on us while we're here – just to make sure
we don't suddenly spot the boat, I suppose! They don't
guess we've already found it. I bet they were worried
when they saw I'd taken a header into the water just
over the sunken boat!'

'Oh – so that's what the flash is,' said George. 'The glint of field-glasses! Yes – they're watching us. Blow! That will put an end to us trying to haul up the loot, Ju. They'd see it and wait for us!'

'Yes. No good trying for that now,' said Julian. 'Anyway, as Dick says, we've not got enough rope. We'll have to get some from the boat-house.'

'But when do you propose to get the bag out of the sunk boat?' asked Dick. 'They'll keep those field-glasses on us even if we go out again this afternoon.'

'There's only one time to go when they *won't* have their glasses watching us,' said Julian, beginning to dress himself very rapidly, 'and that's tonight. We'll go tonight! My word – what an adventure!'

'Don't let's,' said Anne, in a small voice.

'There'll be a moon,' said George, excited.

'Smashing idea!' said Dick, thumping Julian on the back. 'Let's go back now so that they won't have any suspicions of us, and make our plans for tonight. And we'd better keep an eye on them too in case they row out to this spot themselves this afternoon.'

'They won't,' said Julian. 'They daren't run any risk of us spotting what they're doing. They will be sure to wait till we've gone.'

'And till the loot is gone!' said George with a laugh. 'I say – I do hope those two wretches haven't gone and taken our food again!'

'I hid it down in the cellars beyond our room – and locked the door leading there – and here's the key,' grinned Julian, holding up a large key.

'You never told us!' said George. 'Julian, you're a genius! How do you manage to think of things like that?'

'Oh – just brains!' said Julian, pretending to look modest, and then laughing. 'Come on – if I don't get warm quickly I'll have a most almighty chill!'

Chapter Twenty

IN THE MOONLIGHT

THEY paddled rapidly away. Dick took a last glance back to make sure that the cork and the box were still bobbing on the water to mark the place where the sunken boat lay. Yes – they were still there.

'It'll be maddening if it's cloudy tonight and the moon doesn't come out,' said George, as they paddled. 'We shouldn't be able to see Tock Hill, Tall Stone and the rest – and we might paddle for ages in the dark without spotting our cork-and-box mark.'

'Don't cross your bridges before you come to them,' said Dick.

'I'm not,' said George. 'I was only just *hoping* that wouldn't happen.'

'It won't,' said Julian, looking at the sky. 'The weather's set fine again.'

As soon as Maggie saw the children coming back again, she and Dirty Dick disappeared into their tents. Julian grinned. 'They've heaved a sigh of relief and gone to have a snack,' he said. 'I could do with one myself.'

Everyone felt the same. Paddling was hard work, and the air on the lake was keen – quite enough to give anyone a large appetite!

They pushed the raft into its hiding-place again.

Then they made their way to the old house. They went down into the cellar room. Timmy growled and sniffed about again.

'I bet Maggie and Dirty Dick have been here, snooping round again,' said George. 'Looking for their pork-pie and ham! Good thing you locked it up, Ju!'

Julian unlocked the door into the cellars beyond, and brought out the food. 'A large toad was looking at it with great interest,' he said, as he brought it back. 'Timmy also looked at the toad with interest – but he's wary of toads by now. They taste much too nasty when pounced on!'

They took the meal up into the sunshine and enjoyed it. The orangeade was finished so they drank the cold clear water, pumping some vigorously.

'Do you know it's a quarter to three?' said Julian amazed. 'Where has the time gone? In a couple of hours or so it will be dark. Let me see – the moon will be well up about eleven o'clock. That's the time to go, I think.'

'Please don't let's,' said Anne. Julian put his arm round her.

'Now you know you don't mean that, Anne,' he said. 'You know you'll enjoy it all when the time comes. You couldn't bear to be left out of it! Could you?'

'No. I suppose I couldn't,' said Anne. 'But I *don't* like Maggie and Dirty Dick!'

'Nor do we,' said Julian, cheerfully. 'That's why we're going to beat them at their own game. We're on the side of the right, and it's worth while running into a bit of danger for that. Now let's see – perhaps we'd better just keep an eye on that couple till it's dark – just in *case* they try any funny tricks – and then we'll have a snooze, if we can, so as to be sure to be lively tonight.'

'There they are!' said Anne. As she spoke Maggie and her companion came out of their tents. They had a few words together and then walked off to the moorland.

'Taking their usual stroll, I suppose,' said Dick. 'Let's have a game of cricket. There's a bit of wood over there for a bat, and I've got a ball in my rucksack.'

'Good idea,' said Julian. 'I still feel a bit chilled from my bathe. Brrrrrr! That water was cold I don't feel very thrilled at the thought of diving in tonight!'

'I'll do that,' said Dick, at once. 'My turn this time!'

'No. I know exactly where to spot the loot,' said Julian. 'I'll have to go down. But you can come down too, if you like, and help to tie the rope on to it.'

'Right,' said Dick. 'Now look out – I'm going to bowl!'

They enjoyed their game. The sun sank lower and lower, then it disappeared. A cloud came over the sky and darkness came quickly. George looked up at the sky anxiously.

'It's all right,' said Julian. 'It'll clear. Don't you worry!'

Before they went back into the house Julian and Dick slipped down to the boat-house for the coil of

rope they would want that night. They found it easily
enough and came back, pleased. It was quite good
strong rope, frayed only in one place,

Julian was right about the weather. The sky cleared
again in about an hour, and the stars shone crisply,
Good!

Julian put Timmy on guard at the doorway. Then
he and the others went into the dark cellar-room and
lighted a couple of candles. They all snuggled down
into their beds of heather.

'I shan't be able to snooze,' complained Anne. 'I feel
much too excited'

'Don't snooze then,' said Dick. 'Just have a rest and
wake us up at the right time!'

Anne was the only one who didn't fall into a comfortable doze. She lay awake, thinking of this new
adventure of theirs. Some children always had adventures and some didn't. Anne thought it would be much
nicer to *read* about adventures than to have them. But
then probably the ones who only read about them
simply longed to have the adventures themselves! It
was all very difficult.

Anne woke the others at ten to eleven. She shook
George first, and then the boys. They were all in such
a comfortable sleep that it was hard to wake them.

But soon they were up and about, whispering.
'Where's the rope? Good, here it is. Better put on
blazers *and* macs. It'll be freezing on the lake. Everyone ready? Now – not a sound!'

Timmy had come to the cellar room as soon as he

had heard them stirring. He knew he had to be quiet so he didn't give even one small bark. He was thrilled to find they were going out into the night.

The moon was well up now, and although it was not full, it was very bright. Small clouds swam across the sky, and every now and again the moon went behind one of them and the world became dark. But that was only for a minute or two, then out it came again, as brilliant as ever.

'Any sign of the others?' whispered Dick. Julian stood at the doorway and looked towards the tents. No – all was quiet there. Still, it would be better if he and the others crept round the side of the house and kept in the shadows.

'We don't want to run any risk of them spotting us now,' whispered Julian, giving his orders. 'Keep out of the moonlight, whatever you do. And see that Tim walks to heel, George.'

Keeping well in the shadows the five crept down to the lake-side. The water gleamed in the moonlight, and a bright moon-path ran all down it, lovely to see. The lake looked very dark and brooding. Anne wished it had a voice of some kind – even the little lap-lap-lap of waves at the edge. But there was none.

They pulled out the raft and threw the coil of rope on to it. Then they clambered on, enjoying its smooth bob-bob-bobbing as they paddled out on the water. They were off !

Timmy was thrilled. He kept licking first one of the four, then another. He loved going out in the night,

The moon shone down on the little company and turned every little ripple to silver as the raft bobbed over the water.

'It's a heavenly night,' said Anne, looking round at the silent trees that lined the banks. 'The whole place is so quiet and peaceful.'

An owl immediately hooted very loudly indeed from the trees and Anne jumped violently.

'Now don't start all the owls hooting by talking about how quiet everything is,' teased Julian. 'I agree though that it really is a heavenly evening. How calm and mirror-like this lake is. I wonder if it ever produces a wave of any sort! Do you suppose it stays like this even in a storm?'

'It's a queer sort of lake,' said Dick. 'Look out, Timmy – that's my ear. Don't lick it all away. I say – anyone looking out for our four bearings?'

'Well, we know more or less where we've got to paddle the raft to,' said Julian. 'We'll go in that direction and then see if we're spotting the bearings. I'm sure we're going right at the moment.'

They were. George soon saw Tall Stone, and then Tock Hill came into sight. It wasn't long before Steeple was seen too, shining in the moonlight.

'I bet the Nailer came and hid his loot out here on a moonlit night,' said Julian. 'All the bearings can be seen so very clearly – even Tall Stone. We really must find out sometime what it is. It looks like a great stone pointer of some sort, put up in memory of something or somebody.'

'There's One Chimney now,' said Anne. 'We have got them all in view – we should be near our mark.'

'We are!' said Dick, pointing to a little dark bobbing thing nearby. 'The cork and the box. How extremely clever we are! I really have a great admiration for the Five!'

'Idiot!' said Julian. 'Go on, strip now, Dick – we'll do our job straight away. Brrrrrrr! It's cold!'

Both boys stripped quickly, putting their clothes into a neat pile in the middle of the raft. 'Look after them, Anne,' said Julian. 'Got the rope, Dick? Come on, then, in we go. We can't see the boat now, the waters are so dark – but we know it's just below the cork and the box!'

The boys dived in one after the other. Splash! Splash! They were both beautiful divers. The raft rocked as they plunged in and Timmy nearly went in too.

Julian had dived in first. He opened his eyes under the water and found that he could see the sunken boat just below him. With two strong strokes he reached it, and tugged at the waterproof bag there. Dick was beside him almost at once, the rope in his hands. The boys twisted it tightly round the top part of the bag.

Before they could finish the job they had to rise up to the surface to breathe. Dick couldn't hold his breath under water as long as Julian and he was up first, gasping painfully. Then Julian shot up and the night was full of great, painful breaths, as the boys gasped in the air they longed for.

The girls knew better than to ask anything just then. They waited anxiously till the boys' breathing grew easier. Julian turned and grinned at them.

'Everything's all right!' he said. 'Now – down we go again!'

Chapter Twenty-one

THE SACK AT LAST!

DOWN went the boys again and once more the raft jerked violently. The girls peered anxiously over the edge, waiting for them to return.

Julian and Dick were down at the sunken boat in a matter of a second or two. They finished the task of tying the rope to the waterproof bag. Julian gave it a hard jerk, hoping to free it if it were wedged tightly into the boat. He took the rest of the rope length in his hands in order to take it up to the surface.

Then, bursting for breath again, the two boys shot up to the raft, popping out of the water with loud gasps. They climbed on board.

They took a minute to get their breath and then Dick and Julian took the rope together. The girls watched, their hearts beating fast. Now was the test! Would that waterproof sack come up – or not?

The boys pulled strongly but without jerking. The raft slanted and Anne made a grab at the pile of clothes in the middle. Dick fell off into the water again.

He climbed back, spluttering. 'Have to pull more smoothly,' he said. 'I felt the sack give a bit, didn't you?'

Julian nodded. He was shivering with cold, but his eyes were shining with excitement. Anne put a macin-

tosh round his shoulders and one round Dick's too.
They never even noticed!

'Now – pull again,' said Julian. 'Steady does it –
steady – steady! It's coming! Gosh, it's really coming.
Pull, Dick, pull!'

As the heavy bag came up on the end of the rope, the
raft slanted again, and the boys pushed themselves back
to the other side of the raft, afraid of upsetting everyone into the water. Timmy began to bark excitedly.

'Be quiet, Timmy,' said George at once. She knew
how easily sound travels over water, and she was afraid
the couple in the tents might hear him.

'It's coming – it's there, look – just below the surface!' said Anne. 'One more pull, boys!'

But it was impossible to pull the heavy bag on board
without upsetting the raft. As it was, the girls got very
wet when the water splashed over the raft as it jerked
and slanted.

'Look – let's paddle back to the shore and let the sack
drag behind us.' said Julian, at last. 'We shall only
upset the raft. Dress again, Dick, and we'll get back to
the old house and open the sack in comfort. I'm so cold
now that I can hardly feel my fingers.'

The boys dressed as quickly as they could. They
were shivering, and were very glad to take up their
paddles and work hard to get the raft back to shore.
They soon felt a welcome warmth stealing through
their bodies, and in ten minutes had stopped shivering.
They felt very pleased with themselves indeed.

They looked back at the bulky object following

them, dragging along just under the surface. What was in that bag? Excitement crept over all of them again, and the paddles struck through the water at top speed as all the four strained to get back as quickly as possible. Timmy felt the excitement too, and wagged his long tail without ceasing as he stood in the middle of the raft, watching the thing that bobbed along behind them.

They came at last to the end of the lake. Making as little noise as possible they dragged the raft under its usual bush. They did not want to leave it out on the bank in case Maggie and Dirty Dick saw that it had been used again, and started wondering.

Dick and Julian dragged the waterproof sack out of the water. They carried it between them as they went cautiously back to the house. It looked a most miserable, grotesque place with its burnt-out roof, doorways and windows – but the children didn't notice its forlorn appearance in the moonlight – they were far too excited!

They walked slowly up the overgrown path between the two broken-down walls, their feet making no sound on the soft mossy ground. They came to the doorway and dragged the bundle into the kitchen.

'Go and light the candles in the cellar room,' said Julian to George. 'I just want to make sure that that couple are not snooping anywhere about.'

George and Anne went to light the candles, flashing their torches before them down the stone steps. Julian and Dick stood at the open doorway, facing the moonlight, listening intently. Not a sound was to be heard, not a shadow moved!

They set Timmy on guard and left him there, dragging the dripping, heavy bundle across the stone floor of the kitchen. They bumped it down the cellar steps – and at last had it before them, ready to be opened!

Julian's fingers fumbled at the knots of the rope. George couldn't bear waiting. She took a pocket-knife and handed it to Julian.

'For goodness' sake, cut the rope!' she said. 'I simply can't wait another moment.'

Julian grinned. He cut the rope – and then he looked to see how to undo the waterproof wrapping.

'I see,' he said. 'It's been folded over and over the goods, and then sewn up to make a kind of bag. It must have kept the loot absolutely waterproof.'

'Buck *up*!' said George. 'I shall tear it open myself in a minute!'

Julian cut the strong stitches that closed the covering. They began to unwrap the bundle. There seemed to be yards and yards of waterproof covering! But at last it was off – and there, in the middle of the mass of waterproof, were scores of little boxes – leather-covered boxes that everyone knew at once were jewel-boxes!

'It *is* jewellery then!' said Anne, and she opened a box. They all exclaimed in wonder.

A magnificent necklace glittered on black velvet. It shone and glinted and sparkled in the candlelight as if it were on fire. Even the two boys gazed without a word. Why – it was fit for a queen!

'It must be that wonderful necklace stolen from the Queen of Fallonia,' said George at last. 'I saw a picture of it in the papers. What diamonds!'

'Oooh – are they *diamonds*!' said Anne, in awe. 'Oh Julian – what a lot of money they must be worth! A hundred pounds, do you think?'

'A hundred thousand pounds more likely, Anne,' said Julian, soberly. 'My word – no wonder the Nailer hid these stolen goods carefully, in such an ingenious place. No wonder Maggie and Dirty Dick were longing to find them. Let's see what else there is.'

Every box contained precious stones of some kind – sapphire bracelets, ruby and diamond rings, a strange and wonderful opal necklace, ear-rings of such enormous diamonds that Anne was quite sure no one would be able to bear the weight of them!

'I would never, never dare to own jewellery like this,' said Anne. 'I should always be afraid of its being stolen. Did it all belong to the Queen of Fallonia?'

'No. Some to a princess who was visiting her,' said Julian. 'These jewels are worth a king's ransom. I just hate the thought of being in charge of them, even for a little while.'

'Well, it's better that we should have them, rather than Maggie or Dirty Dick,' said George. She held a string of diamonds in her hands and let them run through her fingers. How they sparkled! No one could have imagined that they had been at the bottom of a lake for a year or two!

'Now let's see,' said Julian, sitting down on the edge

of the table. 'We're due back at school tomorrow afternoon, Tuesday – or is it Tuesday already? It must be past midnight – gosh, yes, it's almost half past two! Would you believe it?'

'I feel as if I'd believe anything,' said Anne, blinking at the glittering treasure on the table.

'We'd better start off fairly early tomorrow,' went on Julian. 'We've got to get these things to the police ...'

'*Not* to that awful policeman we saw the other day!' said George, in horror.

'Of course not. I think our best course would be to ring up that nice Mr. Gaston and tell him that we've got important news for the police and see which police station he recommends us to go to,' said Julian. 'He might even arrange a car for us, so that we don't need to take this stuff about in buses. I'm not particularly keen on carrying it about with me!'

'Have we got to carry all these boxes?' said George, in dismay.

'No. That would be asking for trouble if anyone spotted them,' said Julian. 'I fear we'll just have to wrap up the jewels in our hankies and stuff them down into the bottom of our rucksacks. We'll leave the boxes here. The police can collect them afterwards if they want to.'

It was all decided. The four divided up the glittering jewellery and wrapped it carefully into four handkerchiefs, one for each of them. They stuffed the hankies into their rucksacks.

'We'd better use them for pillows,' said Dick. 'Then they'll be quite safe.'

'What! These horrid rough bags!' said Anne. 'Why? Timmy's on guard, isn't he? I'll put mine beside me under the rug but I just won't put my head on it.'

Dick laughed. 'All right, Anne. Timmy won't let any robber through, I'm quite sure. Now – we start off first thing in the morning, do we, Julian?'

'Yes. As soon as we wake,' said Julian. 'We can't have much to eat. There's only a few biscuits and a bit of chocolate left.'

'*I* shan't mind,' said Anne. 'I'm so excited that at the moment I don't feel I'll ever eat anything again!'

'You'll change your mind tomorrow,' said Julian with a laugh. 'Now – to bed, everyone.'

They lay down on their heather and bracken, excited and pleased. What a week-end! And all because Dick and Anne had lost their way and Dick slept in the wrong barn!

'Good-night,' said Julian, yawning. 'I feel very very rich – richer than I'll ever be in my life again. Well – I'll enjoy the feeling while I can!'

Chapter Twenty-two

AN EXCITING FINISH

THEY awoke to hear Timmy barking. It was daylight already. Julian leapt up the steps to see what was the matter. He saw Maggie not very far away.

'Why do you keep such a fierce dog?' she called. 'I just came to see if you wanted to take any food with you. We'll give you some if you like.'

'It's *too* kind of you, all of a sudden!' said Julian. How anxious Maggie was to get rid of them! She would even give them food to get rid of them quickly. But Julian didn't want any food from Maggie or Dirty Dick!

'Do you want some, then?' asked the woman. She couldn't make Julian out. He looked a youngster, and yet his manner was anything but childish. She was rather afraid of him.

'No thanks,' said Julian. 'We're just about to go. Got to get back to school today, you know.'

'Well, you'd better hurry then,' said the woman. 'It's going to rain.'

Julian turned on his heel, grinning. It wasn't going to rain. Maggie would say anything to hurry them away! Still, that was just what Julian wanted – to get away as quickly as possible!

In ten minutes' time the four children were ready to

go. Each had rucksack and mac on their back – and each had jewels worth thousands of pounds in their charge! What a very extraordinary thing.

'It will be a lovely walk across the moors,' said Anne, as they went along. 'I feel like singing now everything's turned out all right. The only thing is – nobody at school will believe George or me when we tell them what's happened.'

'We shall probably be set a composition to do – "What did you do on your half-term?"' said George. 'And Miss Peters will read ours and say "Quite well-written, but *rather* far-fetched, don't you think?"'

Everyone laughed. Timmy looked round with his tongue out and what George called 'his *smiling* face'. Then his 'smile' vanished, and he began to bark, facing to the rear of the children.

They looked round, startled. 'Gosh – it's Maggie and Dirty Dick – rushing along like fury!' said Dick. 'What's up? Are they sorry we've gone and want us back again?'

'They're trying to cut us off,' said Julian. 'Look – they've left the path and they're going to take a short cut to come across us. There is marshland all round, so we can't leave our own path. What idiots they are! Unless they know this bit of marsh-moor country they'll get bogged.'

Maggie and Dirty Dick were yelling and shouting in a fury. Dirty Dick shook his fists, and leapt from tuft to tuft like a goat.

'They look as if they have gone quite mad,' said

Anne, suddenly afraid. 'What's the matter with them?'

'I know!' said George. 'They've been into our cellar room – and they've found that waterproof covering and all those empty boxes. They've found out that we've got the goods!'

'Of course!' said Julian. 'We should have thrown all the boxes into the cellars beyond. No wonder they're in a fury. They've lost a fortune to us four!'

'What do they think they can do now, though?' said Dick. 'We've got Timmy. He'll certainly fly at them if they come too near. But Dirty Dick looks mad enough to fight even Timmy. Honestly, I think he's gone off his head.'

'I think he has,' said Julian, startled by the man's mad shouts and behaviour.

He looked at Anne, who had gone white. Julian felt sure that Timmy would go for Dirty Dick and bring him to the ground, and he didn't want Anne to see dog and man fighting savagely. There was no doubt that Dirty Dick was quite out of his mind with rage and disappointment.

Timmy began to bark fiercely. He snarled, and looked very savage. He could see that the man was spoiling for a fight with someone. All right – Timmy didn't mind!

'Let's hurry on,' said Julian. 'But no short cuts for us, mind – we'll keep strictly to the path. Maggie is in difficulties already.'

So she was. She was floundering ankle deep in marshy ground, yelling to Dirty Dick to help her. But he was too intent on cutting right across the children's path.

And then *he* got into difficulties too! He suddenly sank up to his knees! He tried to clamber out and reach a tuft of some sort. He missed his footing and went down again. He gave an anguished yell. 'My ankle! I've broken it! Maggie, come over here!'

But Maggie was having her own difficulties and paid no attention. The children stopped and looked at Dirty Dick. He was sitting on a tuft, nursing his foot, and even from where the children stood they could see that his face was deathly white. He certainly had done something to his ankle.

'Ought we to help him?' said Anne, trembling.

'Good gracious no!' said Julian. 'He may be pretending for all we know – though I don't think so. The chase is over, anyway. And if, as I think, Dirty Dick really has injured his ankle, he won't be able to get far out of that marsh – and nor will Maggie by the look of her – down she goes again, look! It may be that the police will find it very easy to pick up that unpleasant couple when they come along to look for them.'

'Nicely embedded in the marsh,' said Dick. 'Well, personally, I don't feel sorry for either of them. They're bad lots.'

They went on their way again, Timmy gloomy because he hadn't had a fight with Dirty Dick after all. They walked all the way to Reebles. It took them two hours.

'We'll go to the post-office, and telephone from there,' said Julian.

The old man was pleased to see them again. 'Had a nice time?' he said. 'Did you find Two-Trees?'

Julian left him talking to the others while he went to look up Mr. Gaston's telephone number. He found it – and hoping devoutly that Mr. Gaston wouldn't mind giving his help, he rang him up.

Mr. Gaston answered the telephone himself. 'Hallo? Who? Oh, yes, of course I remember you. You want a bit of help? Well, what can I do for you?'

Julian told him. Mr. Gaston listened in amazement.

'WHAT! You've found the Fallonia jewels! I can't believe it! In your rucksacks now, you say! Bless us all! You're not spoofing me, are you?'

Julian assured him that he wasn't. Mr. Gaston could hardly believe his ears. 'Right. Right – of course I'll put you in touch with the police. We'd better go to Gathercombe – I know the Inspector there, a fine fellow. Where are you? Oh yes, I know it. Wait there and I'll fetch you in my car – in about half an hour, say.'

He rang off and Julian went to find the others, delighted that he had thought of getting into touch with Mr. Gaston. Some grown-ups were so jolly decent – and they knew exactly what to do. The other three were delighted too, when he told them.

'Well, I must say that although it's nice to have things happening to us, it's a sort of safe, comfortable feeling when we hand over to the grown-ups,' said George. 'Now I only want one thing – breakfast!'

'We'd better have a mixture of breakfast and lunch,' said Julian. 'It's so late.'

'Oh yes – let's have brunch!' said Anne, delighted, 'I love brunch.'

So they had some 'brunch' – sandwiches, buns, biscuits and ginger-beer, which they bought at a little shop down the road. And just as they were finishing, up swept Mr. Gaston in an enormous car!

The four children grinned at him with pleasure. Julian introduced Anne and Dick. Timmy was thrilled to see him again and offered him a polite paw, which Mr. Gaston shook heartily.

'Nice manners your dog's got,' he said, and pressed down the accelerator. Whoooosh! Away they went at top speed, with Timmy sticking his head out of the window as he always did in a car.

They told their extraordinary story as they went. Mr. Gaston was full of admiration for all they had done. 'You're a bunch of plucky kids!' he kept saying. 'My word, I wish you were mine!'

They came to the police station. Mr. Gaston had already warned the inspector they were coming, and he was waiting for them.

'Come along into my private room,' he said. 'Now first of all – where are these jewels? Have you really got them with you? Let's have a look at them before you tell your story.'

The children undid their rucksacks – and out of the hankies inside they poured the shining, glittering jewellery on to the oak table.

The inspector whistled and exchanged a look with Mr. Gaston. He picked up the diamond necklace.

'You've got them!' he said. 'The very jewels! And
to think the police everywhere have been hunting for
them for months and months and months. Where did
you find them, youngsters?'

'It's rather a long story,' said Julian. He began to
tell it, and he told it well, prompted by the others, when
he forgot anything. Mr. Gaston and the inspector
listened with amazement on their faces. When Julian
came to the bit where Dirty Dick and Maggie had been
left floundering in the marshes, the inspector interrupted him.

'Wait! Would they still be there? They would?
Right. Half a minute!'

He pressed a bell and a policeman appeared. 'Tell
Johns to take his three men and the car, and go to the
Green Marshes, near Gloomy Water,' ordered the in-
spector. 'He's to pick up two people floundering there –

man and woman. Our old friends Dirty Dick and
Maggie Martin! Look sharp!'

The policeman disappeared. Anne hugged herself.
Now that awful couple would be put into safe custody
for some time, thank goodness – till she had forgotten
about them! Anne hadn't liked them a bit.

Julian's tale came to an end. The inspector looked
across at the tousle-headed, dirty, untidy group and
smiled. He held out his hand. 'Shake!' he said. 'All
of you! You're the kind of kids we want in this country – plucky, sensible, responsible youngsters who use
your brains and never give up! I'm proud to meet
you!'

They all shook hands with him solemnly. Timmy
held up his paw too, and the inspector grinned and
shook that too.

'And now – what's your programme?' asked Mr.
Gaston, getting up.

'Well – we're all supposed to be back at school by
three o'clock,' said Julian. 'But I don't think we can
arrive looking like this. We'd get into awful rows! Is
there a hotel where we can have a bath and clean ourselves up a bit?'

'You can do that here,' said the inspector. 'And if
you like I'll run you back to your schools in the police
car. We can't do too much for people who produce the
Fallonia jewels out of rucksacks, you know. Bless us
all – I can't believe it!'

Mr. Gaston said good-bye and went, saying that he
was very proud to have made friends with them. 'And

don't you get stuck down any more rabbit-holes!' he
said to Timmy, who wuffed happily at him.

They bathed and washed every inch of themselves.
They found their clothes neatly folded and brushed,
and felt grateful. They brushed their hairs and
arrived looking very clean and tidy in the inspector's
private room. He had a man there, inspecting the
jewels and labelling them before he put them away
into boxes.

'You'll be interested to know that we have picked up
your couple,' he told them. 'The man had a broken
ankle and couldn't stir a step. The woman was thigh
deep in the marsh when we found her. They quite
welcomed the police, they were so fed up with everything!'

'Oh *good*!' said the four, and Anne beamed with
relief. That settled Maggie and Dirty Dick then!

'And these *are* the Fallonia jewels,' said the inspector. 'Not that I had any doubt of it. They are now
being checked and labelled. I've no doubt the Queen
of Fallonia and her titled friend will be extremely
pleased to hear of your little exploit.'

A clock struck half past two. Julian looked at it.
Half an hour only to get back in time. Would they do
it?

'It's all right,' said the inspector, with his wide grin.
'Car's at the door. I'll come and see you off. You'll all
be back at your schools in good time – and if anyone
believes your tale I'll be surprised. Come along!'

He saw them into the car, Timmy too. 'Good-bye,'

he said, and saluted them all smartly. 'I'm proud to have met you – good luck to you, Famous Five!'

Yes, good luck to you, Famous Five – and may you have many more adventures!

A complete list of the FAMOUS FIVE ADVENTURES *by Enid Blyton*

Five On A Treasure Island
Five Go Adventuring Again
Five Run Away Together
Five Go To Smuggler's Top
Five Go Off In A Caravan
Five On Kirrin Island Again
Five Go Off To Camp
Five Get Into Trouble
Five Fall Into Adventure
Five On A Hike Together
Five Have A Wonderful Time
Five Go Down To The Sea
Five Go To Mystery Moor
Five Have Plenty Of Fun
Five On A Secret Trail
Five Go To Billycock Hill
Five Get Into A Fix
Five On Finniston Farm
Five Go To Demon's Rock
Five Have A Mystery To Solve
Five are Together Again

A complete list of the SECRET SEVEN ADVENTURES *by Enid Blyton*

The Secret Seven
Secret Seven Adventure
Well Done, Secret Seven
Secret Seven On The Trail
Go Ahead Secret Seven
Good Work, Secret Seven
Secret Seven Win Through
Three Cheers, Secret Seven
Secret Seven Mystery
Puzzle For The Secret Seven
Secret Seven Fireworks
Good Old Secret Seven
Shock For The Secret Seven
Look Out Secret Seven
Fun For The Secret Seven

THE ENID BLYTON TRUST
FOR CHILDREN

Now that you have finished this book, please think for a moment about those children who are unable to do the exciting things you and your friends do.

Help them by sending a donation, large or small, to THE ENID BLYTON TRUST FOR CHILDREN. The Trust will use all your gifts to help children who are sick or handicapped and need to be made happy and comfortable.

Please send your postal orders or cheques to:

The Enid Blyton Trust for Children
International House
1, St Katharine's Way
London
E1 9UN

Thank you for your help.

Do YOU belong to the FAMOUS FIVE CLUB?

Have YOU got the FAMOUS FIVE BADGE?

There are friends of the FAMOUS FIVE all over the world.

Wear the FAMOUS FIVE badge and you will know each other at once.

If you would like to join the club, send a 25p postal order or postage stamps, but no coins please, with a stamped envelope addressed to yourself, inside an envelope addressed to:

FAMOUS FIVE CLUB
c/o Darrell Waters Ltd
International House
1, St Katharine's Way
London
E1 9UN

You shall have your badge and a membership card as soon as possible, and your gifts will be used to help and comfort children in hospital.

Post·A·Book